LARP Night

ON

Union Station

Book Fourteen of EarthCent Ambassador

LARP Night on Union Station

Foner Books

ISBN 978-1-948691-03-1

Copyright 2018 by E. M. Foner

Northampton, Massachusetts

One

"In conclusion, it is the view of Union Station Embassy that the proposed system of sabbaticals for diplomatic personnel could be greatly improved by the addition of roving replacement teams, allowing for the ambassador and the embassy manager to take their leave simultaneously, thereby ensuring a transition unmarred by personal idiosyncrasies."

Kelly nodded her head in agreement with her own words as the station librarian completed the playback of her weekly report to EarthCent.

"Are you ready for me to send this yet, or shall we go for an eighth draft?" Libby inquired patiently.

"All set. Do you think I was being too obvious about wanting to take my vacation at the same time as Donna?"

"It's not a vacation, it's a sabbatical. The idea is to promote professional development through travel and research."

"Right. Like anybody really does that."

"They will if they want to get paid for the time off. You'll have to submit a request for sabbatical that details your intended goals, plus a report on your progress when you return to work. Donna is already investigating the possibility of shadowing some of the embassy managers of other species on the station in order to report on how their embassies function."

"I didn't see those requirements," the ambassador spluttered. "I thought a sabbatical just meant we would get a long vacation every seven years. The last time I traveled anywhere I got kidnapped by Vergallian revolutionaries, and Joe is happy at home brewing his beer and helping Paul with the ships. I think that going somewhere else for a vacation would be like work for both of us."

"You could remain on Union Station and focus on research."

"I can get credit for reading?"

"Not Victorian novels," Libby warned the ambassador, whose face fell. "The program is modeled on sabbaticals at Earth's academic institutions from the early twentieth century, before all of the abuses began. If you published something related to diplomacy—"

"But I just did," Kelly interrupted. "If Jeeves hadn't written his stupid *EarthCent for Humans*, my book would be the bestseller in the Galactic Free Press 'EarthCent Diplomacy' category."

"You can't take credit on sabbatical for work you did prior to going on leave. It has to be new research or the continuation of an ongoing project."

"I've been the Minister of Intelligence forever. Can I get credit for that?"

"You'll think of something. Daniel is about to stop by."

Kelly got up from her desk to greet her associate ambassador and waved open the doors.

"Any news from Flower?" she asked.

"I just got off a holoconference with Woojin. He says 'Hi' from Lynx and Em."

"I never realized how many alien functions and ceremonies Lynx was attending in my place until after she left.

Hey, you wouldn't be interested in a Dollnick royal ascension..."

"No," Daniel cut her off. "But play your sabbatical card right and Lynx might be back at the same time you return. She and Woojin only committed to one year with Flower, though I'm guessing they'll extend it until Em is ready for Libby's school."

"Sounds like they're doing well, then."

"Flower just left Earth for her first destination, but they had several months in orbit to get their act together while bringing people and equipment up on the elevator. All of my sovereign human communities are really looking forward to the first visit, especially since we were able to procure pretty much everything they requested. Eccentric Enterprises is going to have a job balancing their books when it's all said and done."

"So you won't be requesting leave yourself anytime soon?"

"No, knock yourself out. I heard they're going to use a lottery system to start handing out sabbaticals so that all of the experienced ambassadors don't go out at the same time. Apparently Hildy Gruen got a hold of an old lottery machine that spits out numbered ping pong balls."

"I just sent in my feedback on the proposal, though I guess I should have read it a little more carefully," Kelly admitted. "I suggested they provide replacement teams that include both an embassy manager and an ambassador."

"So you can go out at the same time as Donna."

"Not just that. All right, maybe, but it makes sense when you think about it. Besides, I need her to help with Dorothy's wedding planning."

"From what my wife tells me, the dress is in its final stages. Jeeves has been grumbling about all of the time your daughter has put into it, but Shaina says that bridal stuff could turn into a big seller for SBJ Fashions."

"Did your wife really use the term 'bridal stuff?'"

"Probably not."

A large Cayl hound trotted into Kelly's office and sat down on her haunches in front of Daniel. There the dog tilted her head and favored the associate ambassador with a quizzical look.

"Hello, Queenie," the ambassador greeted her. "Are Shaina and the kids with you?"

The dog shook her head in the negative, keeping her eyes on Daniel the whole time.

"Do you have any treats?" he asked Kelly out of the side of his mouth.

"All out. Looks like it's time for you to go home."

The ambassador couldn't help smiling as Daniel was escorted out of her office by Queenie, the former trying to negotiate a deal with the latter that would allow him to stop in his own office to pick up some work to bring home. The Cayl hound was having none of it.

"I guess that's it for me too, Libby," Kelly said, retrieving her purse from the desk's otherwise unused deep file drawer. "I'm going to head down to the Little Apple to talk to Ian about catering the wedding before he gets caught up in the dinner rush."

"Chastity just pinged to ask if you were still here," the Stryx librarian responded. "She's sending a reporter to get your comments about the start of Flower's mission. The paper has a beautiful picture of the ship with Earth in the background and they need some text to go with it."

"I guess I can wait up if the reporter doesn't mind walking with me." Kelly paused and glanced at the ceiling. "You never told me what you think about the way we're handling your gift of a Dollnick colony ship."

"Gryph and the other first-generation Stryx are financing the mission, so I'm just the paymaster, and Flower accepted service under a temporary leasing agreement. She isn't a gift."

"You know what I mean."

"I think that some of the ideas that came out of the Open University competition are quite positive, and EarthCent has done an excellent job obtaining cooperation from several other tunnel network members."

"You could have knocked me over with a feather when Ambassador Aainda offered to donate some surplus military hardware for the new police force. It seems like just yesterday they were trying to undermine us at every turn."

"It's a pity the Vergallian ambassadors serve such short tours of duty," Libby concurred. "Most of the species treat an ambassadorial appointment as a career in itself. Both Srythlan and the Grenouthian ambassador have been assigned to Union Station for over three centuries."

"I've noticed that with the exception of Ambassador Beyer, who you promoted to president after his predecessor ran off, the rest of us EarthCent ambassadors seem to be aging in our posts as well."

"Yes. The advanced species all place a high value on personal relationships, and we already get enough complaints in private about your limited lifespans. I don't imagine that your sabbatical replacement will get much done, but as long as you remain on the station, the other ambassadors will know where to find you."

"Doesn't sound like much of a vacation, I mean, sabbatical," Kelly grumbled.

The doors to the embassy slid open and a tall young man entered.

"Bob Steelforth. Galactic Free Press."

"You don't have to introduce yourself every time we meet, Bob," the ambassador told the reporter for perhaps the hundredth time. "You sat next to me at the graduation picnic last weekend."

"I'm a by-the-book guy," Bob said. "The first thing out of every reporter's mouth should be his name and his news service. It wouldn't be fair to you otherwise." —

"Whatever you feel is best, Bob. I'm on my way to the Little Apple to check about catering arrangements for Dorothy's wedding, but you're welcome to come along and ask questions."

"Great. I've always wondered how much it would cost."

"Wedding catering?"

"Yeah, for if I can ever convince Judith to tie the knot. She says it's too old-fashioned, but I can't help believing that it means something more than a checkbox for estate planning."

"What?"

"Estate planning, for when we die," the serious young reporter said as he followed Kelly into the corridor. "You know that in the absence of a will, any assets on a Stryx station go to the spouse. I have some family scattered around here and there, but if anything happens to me, I want Judith to get my stuff. It's really our stuff anyway, except for the life insurance pool money that comes with my job at the paper, and I already made her the beneficiary if I win."

"Why not take the money yourself and then give it to her?"

"You win by dying," Bob explained. "The younger you are, the bigger the share of the pool goes to your beneficiary, but if you're still alive when you reach retirement age, you're out of luck."

"Little Apple," Kelly told the lift tube. "That's really sweet of you, Bob. Joe and I should probably put some more thought into estate planning, but other than asking Libby to take care of the kids if something happens to us, we haven't done anything formal."

"You asked the Stryx librarian to adopt your children?"

"They're too old for adoption. When they were small we had an agreement with Paul and Aisha to take them, but our children went to Libby's school and she probably knows more about them than we do. Did I say probably? Definitely."

Bob followed Kelly out into the Little Apple, staying close by her elbow in the Friday afternoon crowds.

"Can you give me a quote about Flower's maiden voyage?" he asked her. "I sort of went off topic in the lift tube."

"I think that Flower's mission represents a wonderful new chapter for EarthCent, I mean, Eccentric Enterprises, and I have complete confidence in Captain Pyun and his crew."

"How about Flower herself?" the reporter followed up. "Do you think she'll obey orders?"

Kelly grimaced. "One doesn't talk about a twenty-thousand-year-old sentient ship obeying anybody. My reports say that she's proven herself to be a very reasonable AI and that our people value her input as a trusted advisor."

"But will she go where they tell her?"

"I'm sure that Flower will travel to the mutually agreed upon destinations without incident. Am I right in thinking that somebody has told you to expect otherwise?"

"The Thark off-world betting parlor has been giving odds. The Dollnicks placed bets on a whole list of negative outcomes, so punters can take the opposite side really cheap. I've never been much of a gambler, but Judith is always saying that I'm too stodgy, so I thought if I could win big, she might finally take me seriously as husband material."

"How long have the two of you been living together?"

"Too long," Bob said. "I mean, too long without taking it to the next level. I just don't get women."

"Judith may be a bit of a special case," Kelly told him as they entered Pub Haggis. Then she put her hand on the reporter's arm and added, "I meant that in a good way. She's a bit headstrong is all, and while I'm not a gambling person myself, I think you're safe betting on Flower."

"Ambassador," the heavyset restaurateur greeted Kelly. "Don't tell me you've replaced Joe with this youngster."

"Bob Steelforth. Galactic Free Press," the young man repeated.

"I know, Bob. We've met dozens of times," Ian said. "Are you here to report on the catering business?"

"That would be our food and lifestyle correspondent. I'm just curious about how it works so I'll be prepared when it's my turn."

"Smart man. Did you put together the numbers I asked for, Kelly?"

"About that," the ambassador said, looking embarrassed. "I know that the invitation list was around three hundred at last count, but we won't have an exact number until people RSVP."

"Most people who are coming respond right away," Ian told her confidently. "How many have you heard back from so far?"

"Well, none. I haven't exactly sent the invitations yet."

"How many weeks away is the wedding?"

"That's part of it too. The dress is almost ready, but Kevin's family is coming from the other side of the galaxy. He's still working out a good time with them since his sister will be performing the ceremony. And you know that some of the guests are out with Flower, so I ordered the invitations with the date blank. Dring is a terrific calligrapher and he offered to finish them all when we know."

"All right, the exact date isn't important when it's this far out, but I do need a rough idea of the number of guests and what they'll be eating if you want an estimate."

"So, five hundred?"

"Didn't you just say three hundred?" Bob pointed out.

"That was invitations, not guests. Most of Dorothy's friends are single, but I invited a lot of couples, and we're expecting around two hundred aliens. Don't forget that I've been attending weddings as the ambassador for over twenty years so I have a lot of make-up invitations."

"Two hundred aliens would make it sixty/forty," Ian said, taking a pencil from behind his ear and making a note on a paper pad. "I subcontract the alien food to Gem caterers, there's no point in trying to compete with them. We're talking two or three months from now?"

"Something like that," Kelly replied vaguely. "Until we know the exact dates Kevin's sister is available we can't rent the hall. I know I'm not being very helpful, but I just wanted to get an idea of the cost."

"The food bill is the easiest part," Ian reassured her. "Figure ten creds a head for the humans and fifteen for the aliens. If you were doing it in Mac's Bones, that would be it, but as soon as you rent a hall, they try to push you into package deals where you have to buy the flowers and the booze from them as well. I just had a cancellation from the parents of a young woman who booked a ballroom at the Camelot. They just found out that they're stuck with the hotel catering, and there's even a house band if they want live music. No outsiders allowed."

"I'll scratch the Camelot from our list," Kelly said, and Bob nodded in agreement. "I'm kind of hoping the date works out so we can use the Empire Convention Center, because Donna has a lot of experience negotiating with them, and the embassy has booked some pretty big events there."

"Empire is the best," Ian said. "You rent bare walls and a deck for a fixed length of time and everything else is a-la-carte. You'll want them to handle your bar if you book there, at least for the alien guests. What did you have printed on the invitations if you don't have a time or a place?"

"It just says that we invite them to celebrate the wedding of our daughter. The location is definitely Union Station, so the inside of the card instructs everybody to ask a lift tube to take them to Dorothy's wedding."

"I like it. You could actually put off renting a hall to the last minute to get the best price. If all else fails, it would be easy enough to set up in Mac's Bones."

"No," Kelly said forcefully. "That's the one thing Dorothy and I agree on. I'd rather she get married on a park deck than in between a used-spaceship repair shop and an intelligence agency boot camp."

"Do you think we could have our wedding at the training camp?" Bob asked. "I mean, if Judith ever says yes. I just can't see her agreeing to spend real money on a hall, and she's never mentioned anything about parents."

"That seems a bit strange, but we'd be happy to host your wedding. If I know Joe, he'll be willing to run the bar-b-que and insist on throwing in a free keg of beer."

"Thanks for reminding me," Ian said. "Tell Joe I'm on my last barrel and it's getting low, so I'd appreciate a delivery."

"Will do. And you'll be getting your invitation in the mail just as soon as they're ready."

"We have mail? I've never gotten any."

"Me either," Bob said.

"I'm still working on that part. The woman at the invitation shop has a delivery service, but it's pretty expensive, and we'd have to bring them back after Dring does his thing. I was thinking of leaving them all at the InstaSitter office and seeing if they could give them to sitters with nearby assignments to drop off."

"I don't think the sitters go to the office, except for job interviews or problems," the reporter pointed out.

"Maybe the maintenance bots," Ian suggested.

"When I brought it up with Libby, she asked if that's what I wanted for Dorothy's wedding present, so I had to back off."

"You could probably just hire an InstaSitter for the evening to go around delivering them," Bob said. "You know they don't mind people occasionally using the kids as casual help."

"Three hundred invitations? It would take…" Kelly bogged down trying to do the math.

"I figure we can deliver take-out anywhere on the station at ten minutes for the round trip," Ian volunteered. "You could cut that in half since the runner won't have to return after every delivery, and if you plan the route smart, I wouldn't be surprised if a bright teenager could manage thirty deliveries an hour. With navigation help from the station librarian, I'll bet even a younger kid could get through the stack pretty quick."

"You're right," Kelly said. "I'll hire Aisha's daughter and her friends to take care of all of the deliveries on the station."

Two

Samuel frowned at the contents of the intake bin under the counter holding the most recent items brought in by the maintenance bots. After two years of working in the lost-and-found, the teenager prided himself on his ability to recognize most of the finds without having to resort to asking the cataloging system, but there was something strange about this lot.

"Is anybody here?" a voice demanded from the other side of the counter.

"Can I help you?" Samuel asked, popping to his feet. When he saw the bulky alien dressed in some type of leather battle harness studded with fist-sized silver skulls, he almost wished he had stayed under the counter.

"I have lost the Magic Eye of Jyndal," the Verlock woman grated out. "I am a disgrace to the guild of mages."

"When did you first notice it was missing?"

The Verlock held up one finger.

"One Klunk?" Samuel guessed, naming the basic Verlock calendar unit, which happened to correspond with the length of time newly arrived items were stored under the counter before being cataloged.

The alien shook her head in negation.

"A cycle?" he asked, shifting to the Stryx calendar.

The Verlock looked frustrated and made a pushing down motion with both hands.

"Lower? Is there some reason you can't just tell me?"

"Shameful to speak of the loss."

"All right. A day, then?"

The Verlock repeated her sign-language feedback.

"An hour?"

She nodded in the affirmative.

"Well, if it's here it would be in the most recent bin," Samuel said. He crouched back down, pulled out the heavy bin, and heaved it onto the counter. "What does it look like?"

"Forbidden to describe to uninitiated," the Verlock replied at glacial speed. "May I look?"

"We can't allow non-employees to handle the items for liability reasons," Samuel gave the stock answer. "I started my shift just before you came in, and I looked through this bin, but I didn't see anything resembling an eye."

"Enchanted," the Verlock said, and plucked a metal rod with a string of beads wrapped around it from her harness. "May I?"

"As long as you don't touch anything."

"Gurrrrumph," she intoned, waving the rod over the bin. "Look again."

Samuel moved aside a strange battle axe and an elaborate variation on the crossbow that sported a magazine of suction-cup-tipped bolts, and then he froze. A glowing red eye encased in a clear crystal pendant stared up at him malevolently.

"I think I found it. It's on a necklace?"

"Yes," the Verlock said, with as much excitement as Samuel had ever heard from a member of that species. "What is the fee?"

"There's no charge, but it hasn't been officially checked in yet so I have to make a record," the teen said, steeling himself to pick it up by the chain. He walked down the long counter holding the artifact as far as possible from his body and then deposited it on the cataloging turntable.

"Magic Eye of Jyndal," the system identified the object without hesitation. "Increases spell-casting efficacy by three-hundred percent and can be used by master mages for short-distance teleportation."

"It's being reclaimed by the owner," Samuel told the cataloging system and handed it over to the Verlock.

"Thank you," she rumbled, and placed a five-cred tip on the counter before shuffling for the nearest exit.

Samuel pocketed the coin and hesitated for a moment near the turntable, a question on his lips. Then he shrugged and headed back down the counter to put the bin away, but the tallest Drazen he had ever seen entered the lost-and-found before he got there.

"Can I help you?"

"I've lost a circlet of power," the alien said, his tentacle twitching nervously. "It provides a fifty percent boost to my health and strength, and more importantly, it allows me to communicate telepathically with boon companions who also wear the same type of circlet."

"Could you describe it?"

"I thought I just did."

"I mean, what does it look like?"

"Oh. It's an iron hoop inscribed with runes that glow when I'm using it. Kind of like a crown without ornaments."

"An iron circlet. Is this something you just lost?"

"A little over an hour ago."

"If we have it, I'll find it in here," Samuel said, and began sifting through the contents of the bin that was still on the counter. "This wouldn't have anything to do with the Verlock mage who was just in here, would it?"

"Ryenth the Evil?" the Drazen demanded. "She must have lost the Magic Eye of Jyndal because I felt her spells lose their force near the end of the battle. Did you have it? You didn't return it to her, did you?"

"She picked it up just before you came in," the teen said, and then spotted a dull grey circlet that would have been impossible to discern in a box of scrap metal. "Is this it?" he asked, holding it up between his thumb and fore-finger.

"Don't put it on!" the alien shouted. "Whosoever dons the circlet becomes its new master."

"I'm not letting this thing anywhere near my head," Samuel retorted. "Just give me a minute to check it out with the cataloging system and it's yours."

"Sorry, I'm a bit stressed. I thought we had everything planned to perfection, but our assault group was ambushed, and a Horten troll with a club knocked the circlet off my head in the melee. I was lucky to escape with my life after that."

"Cursed circlet of power," the cataloging system announced. "Provides a fifty percent boost to health and strength, but draws off ninety percent from the wearer's luck, and its location can be tracked by any mage in possession of a magic eye."

The Drazen leapt backwards as if he'd been struck. "What? I paid a hundred gold coins for that circlet!"

"Here," Samuel said, picking it off the turntable and extending it towards the alien.

"Are you insane? That circlet is why our quest ended in disaster. No plans can stand a ninety percent hit to luck, and Ryenth the Evil would have seen us coming from ten dungeons away. Keep it," the Drazen concluded, and spun on his heel to exit.

"I don't know what you're talking about, but couldn't you return it to the seller?" Samuel called after him to no avail. He sighed and replaced the iron hoop on the turntable. "I've never had a customer refuse to accept a lost item before, Libby. What do I do with it?"

"If it wasn't for the curse, I'd suggest you wear it yourself," the station librarian responded. "There's no point letting it age down the counter for processing when the owner has already refused to take it back."

"What curse?" a young woman's voice inquired, and Samuel turned to see that his girlfriend had dropped into the lost-and-found for a visit.

"Hey, Viv. I don't know what's going on today. First I got some half-naked Verlock woman looking for a magic eye, and then a giant Drazen came in for this iron hoop, but he took off when the cataloging system told him it was cursed."

"I didn't realize that you could have a magical item and not know it was cursed. I should have checked with Jonah first." The girl shook her head in disgust and fished a package out of her daypack. "Happy Birthday. Check it out with the cataloging system before you put it on."

"Why is everybody suddenly talking about magic and curses? Does this have something to do with the bin of weird stuff the bots brought in just before the start of my shift?"

"I wouldn't know anything about that. You told me to pick an elective we can take together at the Open University so I signed us up for LARPing. And since your eighteenth birthday is next week, I thought I'd kill two birds with one stone and get your present out of the way at the same time."

"What's LARPing?"

"An acronym. Somebody told me it stands for Live Action Role Playing, though that's just an approximation since the Open University is unlikely to follow human rules. Role-playing is getting so popular that the university bookstore opened a special section for magical objects. It never occurred to me that they might be selling cursed goods," she added darkly.

"Sounds pretty cool," Samuel said, eagerly unwrapping his present. "Uh, what is it?"

"A magical garter. It's supposed to protect you from any back-stabbing or weapons wielded from concealment. I figure you're a good enough fencer to handle frontal assaults."

"It looks like something from the girly underwear line Dorothy is trying to talk Jeeves into manufacturing."

"Lingerie. The clerk at the university bookstore swore that the garter is one of a kind."

"Thanks, but I can't wear this," the teen said, and tried to return the gift to the girl, who waved it away. "The other players will all laugh at me."

"You wear it next to your skin where nobody can see it," Vivian said. "Here, at least ask the cataloging system about it."

Samuel shook his head, but he removed the cursed circlet from the turntable and replaced it with the garter.

"Magical garter. Protects female wearers from weapons wielded from concealment," the artificial voice intoned.

"What? The packaging didn't say anything about it only working for females," Vivian cried angrily.

"It's the thought that counts," Samuel told her, relieved by his narrow escape. "Imagine if I had worn the thing and gotten laughed at for nothing. At least it's not cursed. You should wear it."

"I really wanted to give you something that would protect you," the girl said, rummaging through her bag. "I
bought this for myself, but you can have it and I'll wear the
garter. There's no return on magical items."

"How can the university bookstore not accept returns?"

"Well, you don't have to pay with real money, for one
thing. Every player gets a little pile of virtual gold when
they sign up for LARPing, and I spent all of mine today. I
figure you can buy us supplies with yours when we find
out what kind of world we'll be in. Ah, here it is."

"Another ring? You promised you'd let me do the proposal when the time comes."

"It's not an engagement ring, guys don't get one. It's a
ring of stealth."

"Like invisibility?"

"Not exactly. It increases your ability to sneak up on
people, scout, things like that. Ask the cataloging system
about it."

Samuel placed the ring set with a large colorful gem-
stone on the turntable and imparted a gentle spin.

"Ring of stealth and deception," the voice reported.
"Turns shadows into concealing darkness and cloaks its
users in the holographic form of their choice. A rare
object."

"I didn't know it was so special," Vivian said. "It cost
less than the garter. I guess all of the magical items come
with surprises and that's how somebody ended up with a
cursed circlet."

"I'm good with the ring." Samuel slipped it onto his
pinky. "It's a bit garish, though, so I'm only going to put it
on when we're role-playing."

"I wonder if the curse can be removed from that circlet," Vivian said, indicating the iron ring. "Libby?"

"I'm afraid that would be considered competitive information. However, I can say that it has no power one way or the other as long as you don't wear it on your head."

"So we can bring it LARPing and look for an answer there."

"How come you already know so much about this stuff?" Samuel demanded.

"Tinka has been working on forming a LARPing league as a perk for InstaSitters, and she drafted my brother to be one of the guinea pigs for beta testing. Jonah's really getting into it, but he's also the only guy playing with a dozen teenage girls, so that's no surprise."

"And it's all fighting with toy weapons and magical objects? There's a crossbow in that bin that fires darts with suction-cup tips, and a weird axe that gets droopy when I touch the blade."

"From what Jonah says, some of the games are like immersive theatrical experiences, while others involve quests for magical objects or combat missions. The crossbow sounds dangerous, but the axe is definitely a noodle weapon."

"Noodle weapon?"

"They're really high-tech. Jonah said they were developed by the Grenouthians for stage fighting. Noodle weapons are rigid in the air or when they contact other noodle technology, including shields and armor, but if they touch clothing or skin, they go all noodly. The bunnies use them in their action immersives to prevent accidental injuries to the actors."

"Why don't all the Drazen and Horten reenactors use them?" Samuel demanded. "And I know the Vergallians use real weapons in their immersives because sometimes they slice through clothing and even draw blood."

"The Drazens and Hortens are too proud to use safe weapons and the Vergallians are just idiots. Hey, did you say there's a whole bunch of noodle weapons and magical objects that came in today?"

"Apparently there was some kind of battle just an hour ago."

"So it will still be in the security footage," the girl said, her eyes shining.

"I don't know, Vivian," Samuel objected. "We're not supposed to use the cataloging system for our own entertainment."

"Come on, everybody does it. Libby? Can you show us how the cursed circlet was lost?"

"The cataloging system only responds to requests from lost-and-found employees," the station librarian replied.

Vivian leaned over the counter and poked Samuel.

"Oh, all right." He replaced the circlet on the turntable and asked, "Is there security footage of how the circlet was lost?"

A hologram appeared above the turntable, though at first it was difficult to see what was going on because the scene was taking place in a poorly lit cavern of some sort. Then a flash of light illuminated a Dollnick encased in armor and carrying a large two-armed shield, along with a broadsword and an axe.

"Retreat!" the Dolly bellowed. "It's a trap."

The Verlock mage who had just visited the lost-and-found suddenly appeared standing on a stone ledge, the glowing eye upon her chest, and she wielded her wand like a symphony conductor's baton, spitting out words of power at a speed that surprised the humans. A cloud of arrows filled the air as traps were activated, and the small band of adventurers attempted to fall back in good order.

"You shouldn't have returned her magic eye," Vivian observed as the mage skewered a fleeing Frunge with a bolt of lightning.

"Lost-and-found policy," Samuel said. "We aren't here to make ethical calls. Besides, it's just a game."

A giant figure dragging an enormous club loomed up to block the band's exit from the cavern. The new player's skin color was changing back and forth between bright red and black.

"Horten troll!" a Vergallian woman cried, breaking her quarterstaff over its hard head to no effect.

A human who had run forward to help the Dollnick gave a weird battle cry, and stretching way back over his head with both hands, cast his double-headed axe at the Verlock mage. The blade barely grazed her shoulder as she ducked in slow motion, but it cut through the chain of her necklace, and the Magic Eye of Jyndal dropped from her chest and disappeared in a puff of smoke.

A Drazen wearing a circlet on his head that blazed with illuminated runes launched himself at the troll barring the retreat, swinging a giant broadsword. Rather than parrying the blow, the creature allowed the blade to clang off his rocky skin while swiping at the attacker with his club. The enchanted circlet flew from the Drazen's head with the impact and disappeared in a smoky flash, at which point the hologram was extinguished.

"Wow, that looks like fun," Samuel said. "We get university credit for playing?"

"I think what we just saw was more of a dungeon crawl. The Open University LARPs are supposed to be educational."

"But we just learned how to fight a Verlock mage." He grinned across the counter at the girl, and something suddenly hit him. "Hey, are you wearing new heels? I don't remember you being this tall."

"No. I've been gaining on you for almost a year now that you've finally stopped growing so fast. My dad is taller than yours, and our moms are around the same height, so I should make up a little more ground before I'm done."

"Hello?" a man called from the far end of the counter.

"Be right with you," Samuel said, and added in an undertone for Vivian, "It's the axe guy."

"He's huge," she whispered back, keeping pace with Samuel on the other side of the counter. "Like a professional athlete or something."

"Can I help you?" Samuel asked.

"I seem to have misplaced my noodle axe and I've been informed that the lost-and-found is the destination for all dropped items on this station."

"I have it right here but I'll have to check it out," the teen informed him. "So you're not a local?"

"I'm with a band of adventurers. We came here to battle an evil Verlock mage but she turned the tables on us. This tunnel network league play is turning out to be tougher than I anticipated."

Samuel placed the noodle axe on the turntable and gave it a nudge.

"Noodle axe, professional quality," the cataloging system announced.

"It's being claimed by its owner."

"Theodric the Slayer," the man informed them. "It's my professional name."

"I'm Samuel and this is Vivian. We just signed up for our university league," he told the role-player. "There's something I don't get about all of this. How do you measure the effect of pretend magic?"

"There's no pretend about it," Theodric informed them. "The Verlock mages can do some crazy stuff, but the rest of the magical effects are handled by the Stryx for the station league. I've played on some alien worlds where the whole adventure takes place on a holo stage of the same type used to shoot immersives, but on the stations, it's a mix of technologies. Union Station just joined the league, but I've been playing on other stations since I made the junior varsity at twelve."

"Weird that I never heard about this role-playing stuff earlier," Samuel said to Vivian after the man departed with his noodle axe. "I mean, I know about the board games. Paul used to try to get me to play with his group, but I'd rather just practice fencing."

"I wouldn't have known about LARPs if not for Jonah. Don't forget we were pretty busy dancing for a lot of years."

"Thanks for signing us up and for the cool ring. Dinner's on me," the ambassador's son offered. "Pizza sound good? I've got another three hours on my shift, but I'll buy if you fly."

Three

A group of nearly fifty EarthCent Intelligence agents, both analysts and field operatives, gathered in front of the stage used for holo training. Thomas, Chance, and Judith all stood at ease on the raised platform, and a number of aliens from various tunnel network species were seated behind them. At the precise starting time, the senior artificial person launched into his prepared speech.

"I'm sure you're wondering why you were all recalled from your posts to undergo two additional weeks of training," Thomas began. "First, let me assure you that you were chosen because you have excelled in your work and stated your willingness to join the fight against human crime. Eccentric Enterprises is entering the business of supplying police to human populations and EarthCent Intelligence will be providing support. You will see a bump in your base pay to compensate for your additional duties."

The intelligence agents let out a collective sigh of relief at this statement and began smiling and nudging each other.

"Are you going to make us go on those crazy Drazen carnival rides to prove we're tough enough?" one man asked, eyeing the seated aliens nervously.

"No, though you will be working with alien trainers every day," Thomas responded. "The three of us have already undergone the additional training and I promise that you'll find it both fascinating and extremely useful. In short, EarthCent Intelligence has been invited to join ISPOA, the Inter-Species Police Operations Agency. You'll be learning the protocols for making inter-agency requests from each of the participating species, but this isn't a one-sided affair. EarthCent Intelligence has also signed on to provide ISPOA with information about human criminals, including providing the records for all violent felons, certain classes of conmen, and intellectual property thieves."

"Excuse me," a woman in the front row asked. "Does this mean that the aliens will be able to issue warrants for the apprehension of humans?"

"Absolutely," Thomas answered. "Whether we would actually deliver suspects into non-human custody will depend on if we have a mutual extradition treaty with that species, but the main function of ISPOA is information sharing. To put it bluntly, human criminal activity is on the rise, and the other tunnel network members would rather we clean up our own mess when suspects are within our jurisdiction."

"Where is Eccentric Enterprises getting the police from?" another agent asked.

"Building up the local civil authorities is a large part of the colony ship Flower's mission and they've started a police academy on board. The initial personnel are being drawn from ex-mercenaries who have served in police details for alien species, though members of the Sovereign Human Communities Conference have the option of dispatching their own candidates for training aboard the circuit ship."

"How about Earth?" an analyst asked.

Thomas nodded to Judith, who stepped forward to answer the question.

"I've just returned from there, and with financial help from Eccentric Enterprises and alien businesses which are located on Earth, the local authorities have begun rebuilding and modernizing their police forces. Earth actually has its own international agency for police cooperation, something called INTERPOL, though it's been so underfunded for nearly a century that they were down to a handful of data entry clerks and a secretary-general when I visited."

"And we'll be cooperating directly with them?" the analyst followed up.

"EarthCent has applied to ISPOA for a grant to fund an infrastructure upgrade for INTERPOL," Judith answered, the acronyms rolling off her tongue like proper names. "We've been assured that it's just a matter of time before the grant is approved, at which point we'll all be able to share information through the same network."

"Incoming," Chance whispered to Thomas, and quickly left the stage for the all-species restrooms.

The remaining artificial person looked in the direction of the converted ice-harvester and then nudged Judith. "Dorothy alert," he muttered.

"How about patrolling the Sol system?" a man asked. "I recently did my inter-agency training with Drazen Intelligence where I specialized in communications chatter, and my trainer mentioned that the pirates were discussing setting up a base on one of Jupiter's outer moons."

Judith glanced over towards the ice harvester and the approaching girl before replying. "The EarthCent president's office is currently coordinating between the competing interests which have developed bases in the solar system since the space elevator was completed. I'm sure you're all aware that the most powerful political entities on Earth today are the so-called city-states that have formed around major metropolitan areas, and many of them have partnered with private industry to grab a piece of the pie in the solar system."

"Are there any more questions?" Thomas asked. "Good. Most of you have been trained in gathering information on a single tunnel network species, and if we've done the math correctly, each of the ISPOA trainers on the stage behind me will be taking a group of between seven and nine of you. Although the protocols for information sharing are based on a standard template, we've found that each species does things a little differently, so I'll ask you to choose the trainer most closely aligned with your area of expertise."

The aliens rose from their chairs and climbed down from the stage, after which each of them moved off to a pre-designated area of the training grounds with a number of EarthCent Intelligence agents trailing after them like baby ducks. Judith made a futile effort to blend in with the humans following the Dollnick, but the ambassador's daughter homed in on her like a guided missile.

"Hi, Judith. Welcome back."

"Hey, Dorothy. Are you looking for Chance? I think she's in the bathroom."

"I used her the whole time you were away. Besides, you and I have the same build, and she makes everything look so good that it's not helpful. No offence."

"None taken. You know that I'm not into this girly stuff, and it's not really fair for you to stalk us at work like this."

"Come on. I know that you and Chance always go through any inter-agency training before you roll it out to the rank-and-file. I'll bet you have nothing else to do this morning."

"I was going to go shopping, there's no food left in the apartment," Judith replied. She glanced over at Thomas in hopes of salvation, but the artificial person had no help to offer. Head held high, Judith accepted her fate like a good soldier and fell in with the ambassador's daughter.

"This is better than shopping," Dorothy insisted. "It will only take a half an hour and I'll let you raid our refrigerator for whatever you want."

"The last time you said it would be ten minutes and it took the whole afternoon. I ended up with muscle cramps."

"That's because you're not used to wearing heels, which is why you need to practice.

"Why would I practice a skill I have no desire to acquire?" Judith retorted. "This is the last time, Dorothy. I'll even give you the rest of the morning if you need me, but you have to promise not to ask again."

"I swear it," the girl said, putting her hand over her heart. "You're the best. The dress is almost finished, anyway. I just want to make sure it still looks good in movement and you're so athletic."

"Are you planning on doing gymnastics at your wedding?"

"Just dancing," Dorothy replied seriously. She led her reluctant fitting-dummy up the ramp of the ice harvester and into her workroom, which, thanks to all of the white silks and lace, had taken on the appearance of a cloud. "Here, I got you this as a token of my appreciation."

"You didn't have to do that," Judith said, accepting the programmable Union Station gift chit. "Can I use it for groceries?"

"Uh, it's for a place that's better than groceries. Let's get you out of those clothes so you can put on the dress."

"What's better than groceries?"

"It's six private lessons with Marcus, Chastity's husband. I already checked with Bob and he said whatever you want is fine with him."

"You bought us dance lessons?"

"I want you to feel comfortable at the wedding and I know that ballroom dancing has never been your thing," Dorothy explained.

"That's because I don't want it to be my thing!"

"I've seen you fencing with Vivian. Why do you think her footwork is so much better than yours?"

Judith undid the last button on her black fatigues top and let Dorothy pull it off over her shoulders. "I know that she and Samuel danced competitively when they were kids, but six lessons isn't going to make any difference for me."

"Marcus was their trainer, and how do you know that if you haven't tried?"

"It's not fair to Bob," Judith protested, deactivating the magnetic strips that served as laces on her combat boots and stepping free of them.

"I lied when I told you he's okay with it. He loved the idea. He said that if I can get you to go along with it he'll buy me lunch."

Judith's face turned a light shade of pink as she pulled off her pants, but she muttered, "Bob's a goof."

"Here, put this on," Dorothy said, passing the other woman a silky garment.

"I feel like I just degraded my combat readiness by fifty percent," Judith grumbled as the slip settled over her body.

"Now the gown." For the next five minutes, Dorothy issued rapid-fire instructions as she helped the other woman into the dress and its accessories.

"How are you going to dance in this?" the practical-minded EarthCent Intelligence trainer asked. "Even if you don't trip yourself, there must be a thousand creds of silk dragging on the floor behind you for other people to step on."

"Can you keep a secret?"

"About a dress? I think I can manage that."

"Do you remember how to access the shoe interface over your implant to raise the heels?"

"Do I have to?"

"Yes, but that's not what I meant. Go to the same menu and choose the 'peripherals' option."

Judith sighed and navigated through the heads-up display provided by her implant with practiced eye movements. "What am I looking for?"

"Train."

"How is the wedding gown train a shoe peripheral?"

"It's not, but the shoes already had the interface available so we're piggybacking on it for the prototype. Pick a side."

Judith selected the "Gather left" option, and then almost lost her balance from the surprise when all of the trailing silk suddenly appeared artistically suspended below the palm of her left hand.

"How—"

"That's why I added the fingerless wedding gown gloves, though some people call them gauntlets. There's a magnetic monopole sewed into the palm, the same Verlock technology we used in the heels. It's wicked powerful, and it's tuned to only draw the monopoles in the train. I've

31

been working on the exact placements for days to get the draping effect right."

"I have to admit, this is actually pretty cool." Judith took a step or two, holding her left elbow in close to her side and the forearm parallel with the floor. "It doesn't seem to pull on my right leg at all."

"I'm going to apply for a Stryx patent," Dorothy said proudly. "Drilyenth, the Verlock genius who invented our heels did the engineering part, but it was my idea."

"Can I switch hands, or will the train wind around my front?"

"Go ahead, it's all in the programming. I want to launch it with our wedding line, but after that, we may offer it as an add-on kit for existing full-length dresses. Just imagine being able to walk on a park deck without your skirt dragging in the grass."

"I don't own any full-length dresses," Judith replied, selecting the 'Gather right' option from her heads-up display. The bunched train dropped away from her left hand and flowed around her back to the right like magic. "I can't believe how much I'm liking this. Hey, do you think you could add offensive capabilities to your shoes?"

"What?"

"You know, like releasing knock-out gas or firing darts. Who would ever expect command-and-control to be built into ballroom heels?"

"I'm not a weapons designer, Judith, unless your goal is making the other women die from envy. Let's get the dress off and move on to the real work."

"Just once more, I want to watch it," the spy trainer said, twisting her neck to look over her shoulder as the bunched silk fell away from her right hand, spread out on the floor like a liquid, and then leapt back up to her left palm. She couldn't help giggling before letting the train drop again and standing still while Dorothy peeled her like a piece of fruit. "What else do you need me for?"

"Your bridesmaid dress. Did you think you could show up in any old thing?"

"I don't remember—"

"It was the night Bob got promoted to senior correspondent and we all went bowling."

"But I was tipsy!"

"Thomas is my witness. I got you, Chance and Vivian at the same time. Kevin recruited Bob as a groomsman."

"How many bridesmaids do you need?"

"Eight, and I only have six lined up so far, including you. I didn't want to use married women. Mom is inviting lots of aliens from her work, so in addition to my friends, I drafted a couple of Sam and Vivian's classmates to cover more species."

"I'm not going to be the oldest?"

"No, Affie, Flazint and Tinka are all older than you."

"It seems like a lot of bridesmaids, even for you," Judith complained.

"I'm not just making this up," Dorothy said, brandishing a dog-eared copy of *Weddings For Humans*. "Formal weddings with over four hundred guests should have between seven and twelve bridesmaids. I'm practically doing the absolute minimum."

"Does being a bridesmaid mean I have to clean up after the wedding or something?"

"Your job is to make the dress look good. Now let me put my gown away and we'll try yours on."

"Please don't be pink. Please don't be pink," Judith chanted rapidly under her breath.

"It's cream, if that's what you're worried about," Dorothy said over her shoulder as she rummaged through a lace-draped rack of dresses. "Here it is."

"I'll never fit into that," Judith declared, backing away from the proffered wasp-waisted dress.

"Sure you will. Just don't eat breakfast on my wedding day."

"I could not eat breakfast UNTIL your wedding day and I still won't fit into that."

Dorothy frowned and checked the nametag she had sewn into the waist. "Oops, this one is Affie's. I must have given her yours when she stopped by this morning."

"Hello?" a voice called from the entrance to the ice harvester.

"That's her now," the ambassador's daughter said happily. "We're in here."

"Are you trying to tell me that I'm getting fat?" the Vergallian member of the SBJ Fashions design team demanded as she entered the room. "Hello, Judith. Here for your dress fitting?"

"Yeah. It seems that you have it."

"Oops," Affie said, favoring the intelligence agent with a dazzling smile. "You know I meant it in the relative sense. In fact, I'm sure you're thinner than the last time I saw you."

"I ate vegan on Earth—too many chemicals in everything else there," Judith replied grudgingly. "Hey. Do you know the story with Ambassador Aainda? She's making the local Vergallian intelligence people cooperate with us, and she even scrounged up some old surplus patrol craft and donated them to Flower's police academy."

"I've only met her once, but it was clear that she's from the group that opposes the main imperial faction. Her extended family controls three populated worlds, so she doesn't have to worry about somebody having her back."

"Too much talking, not enough trying-on," Dorothy interrupted impatiently. "This one is yours, Affie."

The women made the necessary exchanges and the two bridesmaids meekly shimmied their way into the dresses.

"Can you help with the back?" Judith requested.

"Sure. Put your hands on your waist like you do when you're looking tough for the recruits," Dorothy instructed her. "Now, exhale and squeeze." The bridesmaid-to-be followed her orders and the ambassador's daughter fastened the magnetic seal on the flaps. "You can breathe now."

"No, actually, I can't."

"Don't be a baby," Affie told her. "The dressing assistant at the modeling agency I worked for used to place her foot on our spines when she laced us in. I never figured out how she could do it standing on one leg."

"Are you sure the waistline won't simply burst?" Judith wheezed.

"I used the good carbon fiber thread. You could swallow a grenade and the dress would hold."

"Gross," Affie said, turning her back to the girl. "Do me, now."

Dorothy fastened the back of her alien friend's dress, and then ushered the two bridesmaids-to-be into the living area.

"Now dance together so I can see how the dresses move," she ordered.

"I'll lead," Judith said. "I don't know what I'm doing, but I always lead when I have to dance with Bob because he knows even less."

"Just wait until you have a few lessons with Marcus," Dorothy told her. "You'll be thanking me for the rest of your life."

Four

"Aren't you supposed to be at the Frunge coming-of-age ceremony on the park deck?" Donna asked Kelly.

"Czeros told me that they start by washing the dirt out of the vestigial root system on the children's feet and everybody gets good and muddy. Joe is picking me up in a few minutes and we're going for the festive meal after the clean-up."

"So why did you come into the embassy?"

"I thought you might let me take a peek at your sabbatical proposal. Don't worry, I'm not going to steal your idea," the ambassador added hastily. "I'm just really having trouble putting my concept into words and I thought that seeing yours might help me over the hump."

"What's your basic idea?"

"Mumble, mumble."

"Who over the age of ten actually says 'mumble'? You don't have an idea, do you?"

"I'm so desperate that I checked to see if there's a *Sabbaticals For Humans* book, but it's like the universe is conspiring against my getting a year of paid vacation. Hey, do you think that Chastity would hire me to write one?"

"What I think is that you're making a big deal over nothing," Donna said, activating the display desk and slipping out of her chair. "Feast your eyes."

Kelly sank into her best friend's chair and began reading the sabbatical proposal out loud.

"I am requesting a year-long leave at full pay from my position as embassy manager at Union Station after three decades of continuous service. My time away will be spent researching the best practices of alien diplomatic support staff through shadowing said employees at their embassies. In addition to retooling my own skill set, I will work with the EarthCent Embassies Employee Union to disseminate the results of my study, and I will make a presentation at a conference for embassy managers if funding can be found to hold one." Kelly paused and looked over at Donna. "Since when do we have a union?"

"It's only for the support employees—no diplomatic staff."

The ambassador shook her head and continued reading.

"I also want to take this time to thank EarthCent for its generous sabbatical policy. I feel honored to be part of a diplomatic organization that values the continuing professional development and mental equilibrium of its staff." Kelly pantomimed gagging before adding, "Don't you think you're laying it on just a bit thick?"

"Stanley wrote that part," Donna admitted. "You know he almost got trapped in academia when he was young and he says they all talk that way back on Earth. He helped a bit with the first section, too."

"I haven't seen Stan for a while," Kelly said disingenuously. "How about Joe and I treat you both to dinner?"

"You don't have to bribe him with food, Kelly. He's not a Cayl hound."

"You know, I'll bet they barely even look at these proposals in the president's office. If we changed a word here and there in yours..."

"Just come up with an idea. You'll feel better about yourself."

"I've got one. How about I study the sabbatical systems of alien diplomatic services?"

"Do they take sabbaticals?"

"I don't know, but if they don't, I can investigate the reason why. Libby?"

"You can try writing it up, but I'm not promising anything," the Stryx librarian said as the doors slid open and Joe entered the embassy.

"Write what up? Did Kelly finally have an idea? She's been driving me nuts about this sabbatical thing."

"I'm going to research alien sabbaticals," Kelly told him. "Are you ready for the Frunge party? Let's go."

"I told Clive we'd wait here until he and Blythe arrive," her husband replied. "The local head of Frunge Intelligence invited them because one of his shrubs is shaking the dirt out today."

"I thought they washed it out."

"They probably do both. Are you really set on studying alien sabbaticals?"

"Why do you ask?"

"Just seems a bit, I don't know," Joe said. "Wouldn't you rather learn something useful?"

Kelly glowered at her husband, and then her shoulders sagged. "I'm keeping it for a backup idea. When are you submitting yours, Donna?"

"Friday is the earliest date they're taking them, but with the time difference, I'm planning on transmitting mine before I go home Thursday evening so it will be at the top of their queue."

The embassy doors slid open again, and Clive, the director of EarthCent Intelligence, entered with Donna's older daughter.

"All ready to party with the Frunge?" Blythe asked.

"As ready as I'll ever be," the ambassador replied. "See you later, Donna."

The two couples exited the embassy and proceeded to the nearest lift tube, which Clive instructed to take them to the Frunge coming-of-age ceremony. A minute later, they exited onto a lush green park deck, planted with alien grasses and trees. Singing noise like the creaking of tree branches in a winter storm could be heard in the distance.

"Anybody else having problems with their implant's noise cancellation?" Clive asked.

"I bet you've never been to a Frunge ceremony before," Joe told him. "You have to enable the music override to get the songs translated."

"That's better. But now I can't tell which direction it's coming from."

"All of this technology has trade-offs," Kelly said, leading the group in the direction of the singing. "Lynx told me that she actually got to like Frunge singing after a while, but cultural attachés are weird like that. Speaking of which, when are you going to give me somebody to replace her? The president's office said that EarthCent Intelligence handles those assignments."

"The truth is that with our headquarters on Union Station, the cultural attaché position really isn't required here," Blythe replied.

"But every other embassy has one."

"And we pay all of their salaries. The Stryx don't object to us running intelligence agents out of our embassies because all of the other species do the same thing, but they aren't going to subsidize the cost."

"If I have to do Lynx's job and my job forever, I'm going to take early retirement," Kelly grumbled.

"How long do you have to go for that?" Clive asked.

"They keep raising it. Last time I had Donna check, early retirement was at seventy."

"Really? When's full retirement?"

"Seventy."

"Maybe we could get Judith to take over the slot," Blythe suggested. "Visiting alien cultural events isn't a full-time gig, and she's not getting forty hours a week at the training camp."

"That's a good idea," Joe said. "I know that the original thought was for her to replace my slot training recruits in hand-to-hand combat and eventually to take over from Thomas, but he says that she's even less interested in administrative work than Chance, if that's even possible."

The party was forced to proceed in single file to follow a dirt path through a dense hedge, but they were rewarded with a scene that might have taken place on the Frunge homeworld. The lighting had been altered to mimic the radiation of the Frunge sun, and hundreds of shrubs were playing a game of freeze tag, which to human eyes, looked like a poorly planned landscaping job. The parents were gathered around long stone tables piled high with raw vat-grown meats and platters of cheese, but there was also a wide variety of fruits and a full bar.

Czeros separated himself from the group of singers when he spotted the latest arrivals, causing the volume of sound to drop noticeably. "May the rains nourish your seedlings," the Frunge ambassador greeted his human friends.

"May the sun harden their bark," the visitors chorused.

"Mizash is playing with the children, Clive," Czeros continued once the formalities were out of the way. "He asked me to do double duty and host you spooks along with the McAllisters if you arrived before the game is over. Come, we have a table set up specifically for alien guests."

"Are we the only non-Frunge who were invited?" Blythe inquired as Czeros led them to an empty table.

"The others won't come until they know the singing is done," he told them, and hummed a few notes that reminded Joe of splitting cordwood. "I've had enough for the day, myself. They're all sentimental songs about parenting and none of my own offspring are here. Any luck with your sabbatical plans, Kelly?"

"I had an idea to study the sabbaticals of the other tunnel network diplomats but nobody else seems very enthusiastic about it."

"I understand the concept as my own people have always practiced something similar in regards to the land, but I'm not sure how lying fallow would benefit Humans," Czeros observed. "None of the tunnel network species I'm aware of grant extended leave to diplomats."

"Really? But some of you serve for hundreds of years at the same posting."

"There's plenty of time to relax during the petrification process," the Frunge replied with a shrug. "I thought you enjoyed your job."

"I do, but when somebody offers you a paid vacation, er, educational leave, you take it. Donna is going to be shadowing her counterparts in alien embassies to see how you all run things."

"The same way you do, through our bossy embassy managers," Czeros replied. "Why don't you sign up for the mediator list? According to my intelligence your merchant class has developed business relationships with many off-network aliens but your diplomats haven't kept up. I'm sure you'd learn quite a bit mediating local disputes."

"That's a great idea, Czeros," Blythe said. "Our business people are generally at a disadvantage because the aliens they do business with all insist that contracts must be adjudicated in the courts run by their respective species."

"I didn't quite finish my university education before I was recruited for EarthCent," Kelly admitted, not seeing the point in harping on the fact that she'd barely begun her second year of studies. "Wouldn't I need a law degree or some special training?"

"You need to be an ambassador or a retired ambassador," Czeros informed her. "It's one of the few perks that come with the job. Of course, you'll be graded by both parties based on your efforts, and since the mediation process is non-binding, any potential customers will be able to check the records for how many of your solutions were actually implemented. Nobody wants to pay a mediator today and an arbitrator tomorrow."

"I've never been really strong on business…"

"You have high-level negotiation experience, good common sense, and I've observed that you empathize well with aliens and AI. I believe you could earn a good living as a mediator, certainly more than your EarthCent is paying you."

"Libby? Could I get sabbatical credit mediating disputes on the station?" Kelly asked, reflexively glancing towards the high ceiling.

"Write it up," Libby replied, her voice materializing out of a space at the center of the group. "I strongly suspect it will be approved without a problem."

"I'm going to be a double-dipper," Kelly declared happily. "Joe, if it pays like Czeros says, we could take a luxury cruise to Earth and visit my mother."

"I'm afraid it doesn't work that way," the Stryx librarian told her. "The rules are still in flux, but the last draft in discussion limits the additional income of anybody on sabbatical to ten percent of their base salary before replacement occurs. Sabbatical is not intended to be an opportunity to supplement your income."

"What does replacement mean?"

"For each cred you earn above ten percent of your salary, a cred will be deducted from your sabbatical pay. If, as Czeros suggests is possible, you should earn more during your year as a mediator than you do as an ambassador, your sabbatical would be converted into unpaid leave."

"So I'd be working for nothing!"

"What difference does it make who pays?" Joe pointed out. "You get a chance to try working as a mediator, and if it turns out so well that the earnings replace your income, everybody wins."

"Or, just stop charging when you get near ten percent," the Frunge ambassador suggested.

"Would business people take me seriously if I worked for free?"

"Possibly not. But mediation isn't limited to contract disputes about business. The Frunge diplomatic service puts a strict limit on the number of hours I can moonlight, but I've mediated a number of family disputes for the Dollnicks, mainly to do with nesting rights."

"I'm surprised the Dollys would accept help from an outsider on such a sensitive issue," Clive said.

"It's precisely because passions run so high that an alien mediator is useful," Czeros explained. "To tell you the truth, Srythlan is much better at the work than I am. But the Dollnicks run out of patience waiting for him to say something, which is ironic, since the main part of the job is listening."

"What sort of advice do you give them?" Kelly asked.

"I don't really offer my own suggestions, or at least, I try not to. My goal is to get the clients talking in a civilized manner until they reach a solution on their own. Oftentimes, all it takes is keeping score."

"You assign points?"

"It's more like editing," the alien ambassador said thoughtfully. "I ensure that both sides have an ample opportunity to speak, and I continually refer back to their points of agreement, which usually outnumber their differences by a wide margin. I try to steer them away from legal jargon and keep them focused on a mutually beneficial outcome. If you let your clients focus on who's winning or losing, the mediation won't succeed."

"I'm going to try it, assuming my sabbatical request gets approved," Kelly declared. "Thank you, Czeros."

"You're very welcome. Shall we all celebrate your decision with this fine Cabernet Sauvignon from the new wine shop in your Little Apple? I think it's had sufficient time to breathe."

"It's a bit early for me, Czeros," Blythe begged off. "I have a strict rule about drinking alcohol before lunch." She rummaged through a deep tray full of chipped ice and bottled drinks, extracting an orange juice for herself and a Union Station Springs water for her husband.

"Oh dear. Does that go for all of you? Well, I've always said that the bottles are too small." The Frunge poured himself a large brandy snifter of wine and downed it with a sigh of satisfaction. "Excellent vintage. And how is your spring water?"

"It's cold," Clive said. "My daughter swears by this stuff, but Jeeves says it's the same water that comes out of the faucets."

Joe finished pouring himself a coffee from the large urn and found a teabag for Kelly before asking the Frunge, "Hear anything from your people on Flower?"

Czeros glanced over at the tag players. "Mizash would probably disapprove of my admitting that I'm in the loop. I've received several fascinating reports from a young metallurgist who we recruited directly out of the Open University when his proposal for a business on Flower was accepted."

"Razood?" Clive asked.

"That's him. It's very unusual for Frunge Intelligence to hire agents so young, but he had already created the perfect cover story. In addition to providing a tourist attraction with his old-fashioned blacksmithing shop, he's planning to set up a side-business doing certified assay work for your prospectors."

"Flower's first stop was the Break Rock mining colony, so he must have had plenty to say about it," Kelly speculated.

Czeros stole another look over to where his intelligence head was playing with the children before responding. "Actually, the most interesting parts of his reports are about Flower herself. For example, did you know that she's perfectly willing to play different music over each of her corridor speakers as long as everybody comes out of their cabins for morning calisthenics?"

"It must be pure cacophony," the EarthCent ambassador said, smiling to herself at the opportunity to use the word out loud.

"The Dollnicks are masters of acoustic suppression fields," Joe reminded her. "I imagine that Flower has pretty fine control over who hears what."

"He's also been full of praise for her cafeteria food," Czeros continued after refilling his brandy snifter with wine. "Apparently, most of the Humans prefer to prepare meals in their cabins or eat at restaurants and food stalls, but as I'm sure you are aware, male Frunge are not known for their skill in the kitchen."

"I don't remember Flower mentioning anything about a cafeteria during our negotiations," Blythe said. "I thought she was resistant to employing her bots to serve the passengers."

"Razood reports that the cafeteria is staffed by Humans who never prepared food for aliens prior to Flower employing them. It seems that the Dollnick AI is an excellent teacher, despite the fact she's never eaten herself. While she can directly synthesize any missing ingredients, it turns out that Flower is a bit of a purist when it comes to food, and she set aside ag deck space to grow staples for the various species as soon as she accepted this assignment."

"Do any of the other aliens eat there?" Clive asked.

"According to Razood, it's practically a spy convention when their meal times happen to coincide," Czeros answered. "Most of the aliens who joined your ship's maiden voyage are traveling alone, and even for those who know how to cook, it's not very much fun eating by yourself every meal. I understand that the Dollnicks who signed up to run a distribution business on Flower brought along their families, but the others are taking a wait-and-see approach. And that's how I got started on my diplomatic career," the Frunge ambassador concluded loudly.

Mizash shook his head in mock despair as he joined the group. "I take it I've interrupted the unauthorized sharing of information," he said. "Well, we're supposed to be cooperating so I can't get too angry, but if you tell them everything, I won't have anything to say to Clive at our scheduled meeting."

"We were just talking about the ambassador's sabbatical project," Czeros said. "She's going to be signing up for the mediator list."

"An excellent plan," the Frunge spy chief said. "There's no better way to study how the various species interact than by becoming involved in their disputes. If I could get anybody to accept my agents as mediators I'd provide their services for free, but unfortunately, nobody trusts spies to be unbiased."

Five

"This lighting is creepy," Vivian complained, holding up a pale blue hand in front of Samuel's face. "Are you sure the lift tube brought us to the right place?"

"We're early," Samuel said. "This place has that empty feel I remember from all of the hidden decks that Libby showed us back when she was starting Libbyland. I'll bet that the Stryx don't want people role-playing fantasy games in public areas. Do you want to warm up a bit while we're waiting for everybody else?"

"Sure," the girl replied, drawing her noodle sword from its scabbard and launching an attack on her companion, whose arms were still entangled in his backpack straps.

"Hey!" Samuel shouted, flinching as the blade made contact with his shoulder and instantly drooped like a strand of over-cooked spaghetti. "Stop doing that."

"It's so cool, I can't help it. With Jorb to tank for us, we're going to kill whoever we go up against."

"You invited Jorb?" Samuel finished shrugging off his pack and drew his own sword.

"He may act like the laziest Drazen in the Open University, but I stopped at the dojo to watch him teach, and he was throwing Dollnicks around like rag dolls. I've been studying up on LARPs with my brother, and if we outfit Jorb with a little armor and a few protective spells, he can be the first through the door to draw the enemy's fire while we flank them."

"But I invited Marilla," Samuel told her, and then executed a perfect lunge move at Vivian, who parried his thrust with her own weapon. The sound and feel of the blades clashing was so nearly identical to what the two teens were accustomed to from fencing with steel weapons that neither of them could help grinning. "Besides, Jorb is more of a berserker than a tank."

"I don't get why they hate each other," the girl said, giving ground as Samuel pressed the attack with his greater bulk and longer reach. "But if we come up against a Horten group, we'll have to worry about them wooing Marilla into changing sides."

"When Jorb sees her, he'll probably go over to the enemy without being asked."

Vivian escaped to the side as Samuel tried to back her into a wall, and glancing over his shoulder, said, "Hey, Marilla."

"You think I'm going to fall for that?" Samuel demanded, redoubling his efforts.

"Hey, Vivian. Hello, Samuel," the Horten student said. "Save something for the melee."

The teen dropped his guard and spun around to greet his classmate, giving his fencing opponent the opportunity to plunge the point of her sword into his side. It felt like being attacked with a cube of Jell-O.

"Marilla," Samuel welcomed her. "Great costume. Are you a Horten pirate princess?"

"Assassin," she informed him. "I couldn't find any information about what we'll be up against so I went with a stealthy character. The students who participate in these Open University LARPs all had to sign the same non-disclosure agreements that we did and nobody is talking. The funny thing is that I know Hortens who are really into role-playing and usually you can't get them to shut up about their latest adventure."

The lift tube doors slid open and a Drazen yodeling a war cry leapt out brandishing a battle axe. Then he caught sight of the Horten girl and he scowled. "What's she doing here?"

"Were you planning on chopping down some trees?" Marilla asked sweetly.

Jorb growled and slammed his axe down on the deck, where the head puddled like iron molasses. "If I didn't need the credit I'd be out of here. Where are we, anyway?"

"Samuel thinks it's one of the hidden decks," Vivian offered. "Maybe the gamemaster will know."

"And maybe he's not saying," a voice spoke from the opposite direction.

"Jeeves!" Samuel exclaimed. "Are you the gamemaster?"

"You may call me the orchestrator," the young Stryx said. "Follow me, and be aware that after I declare a start, you will be penalized for breaking character. As first-timers, you begin with twenty-five points each, and anybody with a negative total at the end of the experience receives no credit for participating."

"What is this?" Jorb grumbled to Vivian. "You said we were going on an adventure."

"That's what I thought it was."

"Now pay attention," Jeeves continued, leading them into a small room that was reminiscent of a ship's bridge. "There is a character sheet for each of you on the table. Do not look in anybody else's folder and do not share your personal characteristics or you will be playing at a disadvantage. You have five minutes to read your sheet and get into character before I give the starting instructions."

51

The four students retrieved the plastic folders with their names on the covers and opened them to find their character sheets, printed on the inside like an old-fashioned menu. To Vivian's dismay, there was no table listing starting values for health, strength, intelligence, or any other figures of merit, much less totals for leveling up. Instead, there were a few short paragraphs of text describing her personal characteristics and motivations. When she read that she would be playing a Stryx, she almost choked.

"How am I supposed to play a mage without a spell book?" Marilla demanded. "Do I just announce that I'm doing magic and then you say if it worked?"

"There's nothing here about the NPCs we're going to fight," Jorb complained.

"NPCs?" Samuel asked.

"Non-player characters," Vivian explained. "Jonah says that sometimes the gamemaster arranges for actors to take those roles, but most LARPs feature pre-programmed holograms."

"Four minutes," Jeeves announced. "I suggest you re-read your character sheets carefully before wasting your time asking irrelevant questions."

"This is all from history, isn't it?" Marilla demanded. "You're really asking us to reenact some turning point in the tunnel network's past, but without scripts. What kind of LARP is that?"

"An educational one," Jeeves replied. "Did you think that the Open University was going to give you credit for chasing each other around with fake swords?"

"This is supposed to be fun," Jorb said stubbornly, his indignation over being tricked into an educational experience overcoming his awe of the Stryx. "Live action role-playing. This scenario is just a bunch of blather about economics."

"I'm afraid there's been some misunderstanding," Jeeves said gleefully. "I've hired out instances of myself to orchestrate live *alien* role-playing. The point is to study the decision-making process on the tunnel network through the eyes of another species."

"This is all about that Verlock network that Kevin used to escape the pirates," Samuel said, putting together the clues from his character sheet.

"The Verlock Trading Guild's Emergency Recovery Network, better known as VTGERN."

"And I'm supposed to be the head of the Trader's Guild?"

"I bought all this stuff to play a Drazen berserker," Jorb said, shaking his axe. "The Verlock emperor doesn't even stand in the presence of subordinates."

Marilla brandished her character sheet at Jeeves and said, "According to this, if Jorb is the Verlock emperor, I'm the emperor's mage, and if Samuel is the Trader, Vivian must be—"

"Stryx Gryph," the girl said in a small voice. "How am I supposed to play any Stryx, much less Gryph?"

"One minute remaining," Jeeves warned them. "Do any of you have any practical questions you expect me to answer?"

"What did you mean when you said you were hired to provide instances of yourself?" Samuel asked.

"Surely you don't think that your lab fees cover two hours of my time. I'm currently engaged in orchestrating over a hundred LARPs through holo instances, while my physical instance is arguing with your sister about the cost of the cultured pearls she used in beading her wedding gown."

"So we just stand around talking based on our character sheets and then after an hour you grade us?"

"Time," Jeeves declared. "It is the three-hundred and fourteenth year in the reign of Shrynlenth the Two-Thousand and Seventh. Three Verlocks have gathered in the control room of the emergency recovery network to discuss its future—the emperor Shrynlenth, his chief mage, and the head of the Verlock Traders Guild. If you haven't reached a solution before the two-hour time limit, I will assign points or debits based on your progress and describe the alternative history that would have been the most likely result of your failure to act. You may begin."

The four students looked down at their character sheets again, but they had all been mentally prepared for a medieval adventure and none of them could think of anything to say. Jeeves, or his hologram, floated silently to the side, and Samuel started examining the various displays surrounding them.

"Hey. This must be a mock-up of the command center for the old Verlock recovery network," he said.

"Five-point penalty," Jeeves announced. "Going out of character."

The teen clamped his lips shut, and another minute ticked by before Jorb, operating on the description of his royal psyche given in the character sheet, declared, "VTGERN is the pride and joy of our people. The Grenouthians have their broadcast network, the Thark have their war fleets, the Cayl have their perfect interstellar combat record and their dogs. Without VTGERN, we will be perceived as just another slow-spoken species with a superior academy system."

"And the only practitioners of magic on the tunnel network," Marilla added, throwing in a series of impressive gestures as if she was causing something to occur some-where. A muffled explosion sounded outside the room.

"The recovery network has saved the lives of many traders," Jorb continued. "After ten thousand years of imperial subsidies, it's time for the Guild to shoulder the full expense."

"We can't afford this," Samuel declared, frowning at his character card as if it were a balance sheet. "Three quarters of our trading profits are spent on the recovery network's upkeep and it's only been accessed half-a-dozen times in the last century. According to my information, four of those retrievals weren't even true emergencies."

"Our people already pay an emperor's tithe that is higher than the family revenue-sharing scheme of our Grenouthian competitors," Marilla said. "The cost of maintaining VTGERN is producing a negative impact on our social cohesion. My prophecy cards tell me that funding VTGERN through public moneys will raise the chance of at least one member planet withdrawing from the empire in the next thousand years by fourteen per-cent."

"An increase of around one in seven doesn't sound so bad," Jorb mused.

"Five-point penalty," Jeeves declared. "The Verlock em-peror would never speak in such imprecise terms about mathematics."

The Drazen shot a sour glance at the Stryx's hologram, but he mastered his desire to say something in response and instead continued arguing his character's position. "There are millions of VTGERN devices installed on our ships and all of them were sold under royal charter. If we begin buying back the hardware tomorrow, it will still take many years before we can start dismantling the network, and even then, there will certainly be some stray devices that we miss. Our honor is at stake here."

Marilla played the trump card from the list of magical objects on her character sheet. "I have here an astral projector that allows instantaneous communication with the Stryx," she said, holding out an empty hand. "I have spoken to them about the problem—"

"Without our permission?" Jorb thundered, staring daggers at the Horten girl, who actually flinched.

"Let us hear what the Stryx have to offer," Samuel wheedled the emperor. "They are generous when it comes to achieving their ends, and it's possible they feel threatened by our technological prowess."

"Ten-point penalty," Jeeves announced.

"Timeout," Samuel called, making the classical "T" shape with his hands. "I'm not saying the Stryx feel threatened by the Verlock network. I'm saying it as the head of the Traders Guild to sweet talk the emperor into listening."

The hologram of Jeeves muttered, "Yeah, right," and then added. "Penalty rescinded."

"Don't try to sweet-talk us," Jorb roared majestically. "We will listen to the Stryx's proposal, but only as a sign of our deep respect for our AI friends."

"Five-point bonus," Jeeves announced.

"I have consulted with the other first generation Stryx and we are willing to assume responsibility for your recovery network on three conditions," Vivian said, attempting to lower her voice to sound more like Gryph when he made the occasional public announcement in English. "First, you will attempt to buy back all existing VTGERN devices. Second, any crew using a VTGERN device in the future will be asked to pay actual costs for their recovery or forfeit that device. Third, we want one favor to be exercised at a future time."

"You, want a favor from us?" Jorb declared in disbelief.

"The Stryx have no magic," Marilla reminded her emperor.

"The Stryx don't need magic," he retorted, and even though Gryph was supposed to be communicating through his mage's magic box, he couldn't help looking at Vivian as he spoke. "Are you aware what we are spending—of course you are, but have you considered—of course you have, but—"

"Emperor," Samuel interrupted him. "I counsel accepting the Stryx offer.

"But an open favor?" Jorb gripped his axe and frowned. "A wise leader would never commit his people to such a condition."

"If you don't accept the offer, our only option will be to close the network while there are still devices in circulation," Samuel argued. "The Stryx are effectively guaranteeing your honor in perpetuity."

"In return for our future in perpetuity. We cannot agree without conditions on this favor."

"The emperor is correct," Marilla said, her voice betraying the reluctance she felt in giving Jorb any credit. "Your offer is most generous, Stryx Gryph, but Shrynlenth the Two-Thousand and Seventh is unwilling to commit our people to an unrestricted promise."

"Do you trust us so little?" Vivian asked.

"In the calculation of statecraft, as in battle, one must take all possible outcomes into account," Jorb replied slowly, almost at the glacial pace of a real Verlock. "If any other species offered us the same deal, we would accept, because if the favor turned out to be too dear, we could sacrifice our imperial honor for the good of our race and refuse. Although we are confident that you would never make an unreasonable demand on us, in the face of Stryx power, we would have no alternative other than to comply. We cannot gamble with our future in that way."

"I accept your modification," Vivian said. "The third condition is removed."

"Winner," Jeeves announced, pointing at Jorb with his pincer. "When the first-generation Stryx took over responsibility for the recovery network, the emperor negotiated nearly identical conditions."

"But there was only one possible outcome," Samuel objected. "What's the point of playing through when it was going to end with the Stryx assuming responsibility?"

"This particular scenario has been adopted as the standard introduction to LARPing for the Open University and has been played by more groups than you could count in a month," Jeeves retorted. "The outcomes have ranged from the bankruptcy of the Verlock Empire to the first assassination in the history of the royal family. Fewer than three percent of players who stay on track long enough to hear the Stryx offer even try to negotiate the terms."

"Familiarity breeds contempt," Vivian suggested.

"What?" Marilla asked.

"Jorb has met Jeeves before and seen Samuel and I arguing with him. The members of most tunnel network species go through their lives without ever encountering a Stryx in person, and when they do, they duck their heads and turn down a corridor."

"An interesting explanation," Jeeves said. "Now that the LARP is complete I will be leaving, but I can inform you that you've all received full credit. One-hundred bonus points will be added to your personal accounts and are convertible into gold coins for purchasing gear at a one-to-one ratio. You may share the private motivations from your character sheets now if you wish."

The Stryx vanished in an ostentatious puff of holographic smoke, leaving the students with over an hour and a half open on their schedules.

"Does anybody want to stop in the university cafeteria?" Jorb asked. "I'm buying."

"You've studied the Verlock history," Marilla said in accusation. "You must have known the solution in advance."

"I never even heard of VTGERN before, and the only thing I know about Verlock history is that they've been around longer than any of the other oxygen breathers on the tunnel network."

"So how did you know to reject the offer?"

"It said on my character sheet that I live for my people and that the long-term viability of our species was my utmost goal. I wasn't about to make the same mistake as the boy in the dragon fable."

"What fable is that?" Vivian asked.

"You know, the dragon who offers to save the boy from drowning in return for three wishes."

"How can a boy grant wishes to a dragon?"

"He was a magical boy. You guys don't have that fable?"

"So what happened?" Samuel asked.

"I don't remember all of the details because it's been a while since I heard the women sing it, but I know that in the end the boy threw himself into the sea, so granting the wishes couldn't have worked out very well."

"Why were you so willing to take the Stryx's first offer?' Marilla asked Samuel.

"My character sheet said that I had gone deeply into debt and I needed a remission from taxes to restore my fortunes. I'd pledged my wife's assets without her knowledge so I was desperate. What did your character sheet say?"

"The subsidy for VTGERN included funds that had been redirected from mage academies, so I wanted to see it end, but I also had to protect the emperor's honor because I was his best friend."

"How about your character sheet, Vivian?" Jorb asked. "What was Stryx Gryph's motivation?"

"It just said that I respected the Verlocks and would act in the normal Stryx fashion. My initial offer had to be made without changes, but after that I was free to negotiate."

"Why did the Stryx demand the open favor in the first place?"

"It didn't say, but my guess is that they wanted to preserve the emperor's pride. The deal we arrived at was basically charity if you think about it."

"Let's go have a snack and then we can stop by the bookstore and see if there's anything worth spending our points on," Samuel suggested. "Jeeves did say this was just the introductory LARP, so maybe the next one we'll get to fight."

Six

Dorothy danced into the living room of the ice harvester and cried, "We have a date!"

"Finally," Kelly said. "When is it?"

"Second Sunday of next cycle," her daughter replied. "We only have six weeks left to get ready."

"How will Kevin's sister make it here on time to do the ceremony? I thought that New Kasil wasn't on the tunnel network."

"They get visited by a mall ship like once a month. With a couple of connections, Becky and the rest of Kevin's family should be here two days before the wedding."

"I don't understand why she's cutting it so close. What's wrong with the following Sunday?"

"She had a vision," Dorothy said gleefully. "Becky saw my wedding picture on the front page of the Galactic Free Press."

"And she was able to read off the date in her vision?" Kelly asked skeptically.

"No, but she noticed the blue box at the top where the paper lists which aliens are having holidays, and it was Volcano Day. The Verlocks only celebrate it like once a decade."

"But our days aren't the same length."

"I know, but I checked with Libby and Volcano Day overlaps with the Frunge celebration of Grass Day next

61

cycle. Since Becky didn't see Grass Day listed, it means it could only be that Sunday."

"Beowulf," Kelly called to the dog. "Can you tell Dring we have a date?"

The giant Cayl hound rolled off the couch, stretched, and then trotted out of the ice harvester.

"You have to reserve the hall right away, Mom," Dorothy told her mother. "And there's Ian, and the florist, and the baker. Six weeks is barely enough time. I'll have to take a vacation from work."

"I've already talked to everybody so all I have to do is ping them," Kelly said, attempting to hide her own excitement. "Just think of it as a big party, and you know how many of those we've thrown."

"Party! I almost forgot. I have to see Flazint and Affie right away."

"Affie will be asleep," the ambassador cautioned. "Aainda stopped in the embassy today to ask if Donna wanted to spend her entire sabbatical on the Vergallian embassy's staff, and she mentioned that it was late evening on their clock."

"Affie won't mind if I wake her," Dorothy said confidently. "This is important."

"Where is Kevin?"

"He's helping Dad and Paul swap engines in an old scout ship. I was hanging out watching them when Jeeves came and brought the news. Becky is a prophetess of Nabay, you know, so she was able to contact the Stryx using the High Priest's link."

Kelly smiled indulgently when she noticed that her daughter was edging towards the ramp, so impatient was Dorothy to run off and tell her friends.

"Go, and don't worry about the arrangements. As soon as Dring has time we'll finish up the invitations, and then it's mainly a lot of waiting."

Dorothy almost collided with the Maker as she fled down the ramp. "Sorry, Dring," she said, dodging to avoid the chubby reptilian shapeshifter. "We have a date."

"So Beowulf informed me," Dring replied. "Congratulations. I had a premonition and was already on my way here."

"I didn't expect you to drop everything and come right away," Kelly said, sticking her head out of the ice harvester when she heard the conversation. "Are you sure we aren't taking you from anything?"

"If I've learned one thing in my long life it's that you can never give everyone enough time to make plans. The sooner I finish the invitations and you get them delivered, the easier it will be for the guests to attend."

"What he said," Dorothy called over her shoulder as she ran for the exit from Mac's Bones.

"Come in, then," Kelly said. "All of the non-electronic invitations are just waiting for you to add the date. Are those your calligraphy supplies?"

"Yes," Dring said, brandishing a small metal briefcase. "I brought quick-drying ink for both paper and plastic. I believe you said there weren't any metal invitations that would require acid etching."

"Not that I'm aware of. We only got the plastic printed for the Frunge and the Hortens."

"But the Hortens produce fine parchment."

"Joe suggested plastic in case they want to disinfect the invitations before handling them. Do you need help figuring out the date in all of the alien languages? I mean, I could ask Libby."

"I've always had an excellent memory for calendars, probably because I see them as an art form," the Maker said. "Are you going to employ delivery bots?"

"I'm hiring Aisha's daughter and her friend Mike for the job, and Spinner will probably go along for free," Kelly told him. "If you want to get started, the boxes are on the table and the date is set for—"

"The second Sunday of next cycle," Dring cut her off. "Beowulf told me, though he held out for all of the treats I had with me. I'll start with the invitations for the species that are currently awake."

"I'll just stop next door and see if Aisha is home, then," Kelly said, finding herself edging towards the door with the desire to give Paul's wife the news before she found out from somebody else. "It's still early in the evening, so maybe Fenna can get a start on the deliveries."

Dring whistled to himself as he set out his calligraphy supplies and began grinding powder on his inkstone. The ambassador headed down the ramp and then turned immediately for the habitat that Paul and Aisha had converted into a home. Before she could reach the door, Fenna ran past her into the house yelling to her mother that Dorothy had a wedding date.

"Congratulations," Aisha greeted the ambassador when Kelly stepped into the habitat. "It's been a long time in the making."

"Yes, it has. Dring just started adding dates to the invitations, and if Fenna and Mike are available, maybe they could deliver a few before bedtime."

"Oh, please," Fenna begged, making doe eyes at her mother. "I've never delivered an invitation before."

"If Mike is available," Aisha replied. "I don't want you running around the station alone."

64

"I'll ask Libby to ping him," the girl said, and turning away from the adults, called for the station librarian to contact the Cohans.

"Have you decided yet when to get her an implant?" Kelly asked Fenna's mother.

"I'd have done it when she turned eight, but Paul was against it. He thinks it's good for children to hear alien languages while they're young, rather than getting everything seamlessly translated, and Fenna talks to Libby enough without having a direct connection. Besides, she and Mike spend most of their time with Spinner, and he seems to enjoy translating for them."

"Well, I don't suppose Samuel would ever have become fluent in Vergallian if we had given him an implant early."

"Daniel and Shaina are making Mike wait for his thirteenth birthday, so that gives us another four years before Fenna would start feeling left out."

"Mikey's on his way," Fenna informed them, after finishing her conversation by way of the station librarian. "His mother is sending the dog with him to keep an eye on us because Spinner is stuck doing multiverse math homework."

"Come over when he gets here," the ambassador instructed the girl. "I should go make a vegetable smoothie for Dring so he knows how much we appreciate his help."

By the time Kelly put her words into action and emerged from the kitchen with the Maker's favorite celery and carrot tonic, Fenna and Mike were impatiently awaiting their first consignment of invitations and arguing over delivery techniques.

"It will be funny if we ring the doorbells and then run away," Mike insisted. "Me and Spinner do it all the time."

"You're making it up," Fenna said confidently, "Spinner would never play pranks. Besides, how can we give them the invitations if we run away."

"I forgot," the boy admitted, and thought for a moment. "We could leave it in front of the door. Then they'll think that a ghost brought it."

"Or, you could just wait for them to answer the door and then say, 'Special delivery from the McAllisters,'" Kelly suggested, placing the Maker's slushy beverage on the table a safe distance from the invitations. "How are they coming, Dring?"

"I just finished the first batch of Frunge invitations," he said, pushing a folded piece of plastic in front of the ambassador. "Don't worry, the ink dries as soon as I blow on it."

"That's fantastic, Dring. I can't tell your calligraphy from the print shop's."

"It's all in the wrist. I also printed the addresses in English on the backs. All seven of these apartments are on the same corridor so it shouldn't take the children more than fifteen minutes to deliver them."

"We could run," Mike offered.

"That won't be necessary," Kelly said. "How about Fenna carries the invitations and you lead the way?"

"I could ring the doorbells too."

"That sounds fair. But come back as soon as you finish and we'll give you another batch if it's not too late."

As soon as Mike and Fenna were down the ice harvester's ramp, they broke into a run despite the ambassador's instructions. Three Cayl hounds chased after them like a small herd of ponies, but the two males halted at the exit from Mac's Bones, and Queenie alone continued along to supervise the children.

"Frunge deck," Mike told the lift tube as if he visited there every day. "Who's the first one, Fen?"

"Flazint," the girl replied. "Uncle Czeros and the older Frunge with families all live in groves, but the ones Dorothy's age have apartments like everybody else."

The capsule came to a halt and the doors slid open, but before exiting, Mike asked, "Which way, Libby?"

"Flazint's residence is down the corridor on your right," the station librarian informed them. "You can count eleven doors or just look for Dorothy's shoes."

The children took off running again, and as neither of them remembered to count doors or pay attention to the shoes, they would have missed the apartment if their chaperone hadn't skidded to a halt and barked. The children stopped, turned, and saw Queenie pointing at a pair of shoes with a bent paw.

"Thanks," Mike said. "Those must be Dorothy's."

"They are," Fenna confirmed. "I wonder why they're here?"

"Maybe Flazint borrowed them?"

"I don't think they'd fit her. Ring the bell."

The boy waved his hand over the pad next to the door and a voice asked something in Frunge. The dog barked in response. A moment later, the door slid open and Flazint emerged.

"Hi, kids. What are you doing here?" the Frunge girl asked as she reached out to scratch behind the dog's ears.

"We brought you this," Fenna declared proudly, handing the top invitation to the alien.

"A hand-delivered wedding invitation?" Flazint marveled. "Wait here for a minute, let me get you something," she said, and called over her shoulder, "Dorothy. Your niece is here with your invitation."

67

The ambassador's daughter came to the door in her stockings and stopped Mike, who was inching forward to get a look inside the alien's apartment. "The Frunge don't wear shoes in their homes," she reminded him.

"I forgot. We brought your invitation all by ourselves."

"I'll bet Queenie helped," Dorothy said, reflexively giving the Cayl hound a little attention.

"She smelled your shoes for us. Why are you here?"

"We're planning my Jack-and-Jill party," Dorothy told them.

"Can we come?" Fenna pleaded. "I know the rhyme."

"There's going to be a big wedding party for everybody and you'll both be there. The Jack-and-Jill is a different thing, for grown-ups."

"But you're not a grown-up," Mike pointed out. "You're just old."

Flazint returned with her purse and gave the children a fifty centee tip. "Thank you for the invitation and for bringing the dog to see me."

"You're welcome," the children chorused, and after a quick consultation with Libby, hurried off to the next destination and the potential for more tips.

"You spoil the children," Dorothy told her Frunge friend. "I'm sure my mom is paying them."

"You're only a shrub once in life. Besides, it's hard for the little ones to earn money, and they're inundated with advertisements whenever they walk the corridors."

"Why do you think it's taking Affie so long to get here?" the girl fretted. "We have to plan my party."

"You did say she was sleeping when you called," Flazint said, drawing Dorothy back into the apartment. "Is it normal with you guys for the bride and her friends to plan a pre-wedding party?"

"Sometimes the best man and the maid of honor do it, but that's Samuel and Vivian for us, and they're too young to know anything about parties."

"Aren't they too young to play such an important part in a marriage ceremony?"

"Kevin doesn't have any unmarried friends, and Samuel wouldn't do it unless I asked Vivian because she'd never let him hear the end of it if he danced with somebody else. Anyway, the important thing is that they look good together."

"Didn't you say you wanted the same number of bridesmaids and groomsmen?"

"It's critical to the aesthetic." Dorothy gripped her friend's arm and fixed her with an intent stare. "You have to find a guy to go with you."

"You know we don't work like that. I mean, maybe my parents would give me permission to go with somebody from the office if we employed any Frunge guys, but—"

"I'll get Jeeves to hire a temp. Maybe there's like a catalog and we can pick out a guy who looks good in black."

"I'm NOT getting a wedding date from a catalog," Flazint stated firmly. A bell chimed, and after glancing at the security feed on her entertainment system and confirming it was Affie, she called out, "Open door."

The Vergallian girl entered, looking both half-asleep and half-dressed. "Congratulations," she yawned. "I'll give you a pass this time, but if you start having a wedding every year, I'm going to stop answering your middle-of-the-night pings."

"Don't you always wear a shawl with that top?" Flazint asked.

"Didn't I—Oh no!"

69

"Are you actually blushing?" Dorothy demanded. "I didn't even know you could."

"You'll have to loan me something to go home in, Flazz," Affie said. "I hope a bunch of guys didn't follow me here."

"You must have had a long night to be this out of it," the Frunge said sympathetically.

"We went to some party where everybody was burning sticks and you know I have no head for the stuff. By the way, Dorothy, Stick agreed to be in the wedding party."

"Great! It will give me something to tell my grand-children." The ambassador's daughter pantomimed opening an old-fashioned photo album and pointing out people. "And the Vergallian guy next to your grand-uncle Sammy was a recreational drug dealer. He cleaned up at my wedding selling Kraaken Red sticks to all of the kids."

"The Stryx would kick him off the station if he sold to underage aliens, but it's your wedding, so if you want me to find somebody else…"

"No, Stick's the right height and he's not a bad dancer. Does he have any Frunge buddies we can draft to go with Flazint?"

"Don't push her," Affie advised, settling cross-legged onto a giant pillow. "We can always ask Jeeves to rent us a hologram from their advertising system."

"I am NOT going to a wedding with a holographic date," Flazint retorted, though her emphasis on 'not' wasn't as strong as it had been in the previous usage. "You know, holographic escorts on call would really come in handy sometimes. We should suggest it to Jeeves."

"How about going with Metoo?" Dorothy said. "He promised to come to my wedding and I know he wouldn't mind disguising himself as a Frunge for you."

"Let me talk to my ancestors," Flazint said with a groan. "Maybe they'll give me a waiver since your mom is so well connected and all."

"What about the urgent party you said we have to plan?" Affie asked.

"Right. It's just for our friends and I want it to be really memorable. And it can't be too close to the wedding, so we have to hurry up and sell tickets."

"Oh, Dorothy," Flazint said. "Do you have money problems? I know Jeeves keeps threatening to withhold your pay unless you stop buying whatever you want on the company's programmable cred, but do we really need to do a fundraiser for your wedding?"

"It's not like that, though I guess back on Earth some people raised money for their honeymoon that way. We take the cash upfront so nobody has to spend anything at the party."

"Oh, maybe we can rent a dance club with an open bar," Affie said. "But how many people are you going to invite?"

"Not that many, though you're welcome to ask your friends. We go to dance parties all the time, though, and the guys don't really like it. I want everybody to have a good time."

"How about bowling?" Flazint suggested.

"No, no, I've got it," Affie said. "Have either of you been watching the new fantasy role-playing league? They do really cool adventures with magical creatures and treasures."

"People watch that?" Dorothy asked doubtfully.

"Sure, but that's not the point. We could figure out a time that everybody is free and reserve studio space for our own adventure."

"Military training was part of your royal upbringing," the Frunge girl objected. "Some of Dorothy's friends would be sitting ducks."

"It's not just warriors, you can play all sorts of characters. You could be a healer, Flazz, and Dorothy could be a mage or a minstrel."

"Can we get my brother and Vivian on our team?" Dorothy asked. "They're both really good fencers."

"I only know about this stuff from watching a couple of league LARPs with Stick, but they don't always have teams play against each other. Some adventures are all about defeating pre-programmed characters, so the teams get ranked on the time it takes them to complete the quest."

"Would we need to buy a lot of gear?"

"Stick said they do rentals, and he's been pestering me to try it with him."

"I guess that would be different, at least, I've never been invited to one before," Dorothy mused. "Libby? Is there a time in the next month when I can schedule my Jack-and-Jill party without making my friends get up in the middle of their night or miss work?"

"Three weeks from Tuesday, though you'll have to eat dinner early," the station librarian replied without hesitation. "I think it's an excellent idea."

Seven

"Good morning, Donna," Kelly announced herself and deposited the box of Friday donuts on the embassy manager's display desk. "Do we have another pair of stranded travelers?" she added in an undertone, nodding at the nervous-looking couple who were sitting on a pile of luggage near the kitchenette sink, engrossed in something on their tabs.

"You'll never guess in a million years."

The ambassador studied her friend's excited face and tried to come up with the most outlandish explanation for the waiting couple she could imagine.

"More lost relatives for Clive? Vergallian face dancers defecting to EarthCent intelligence? Another new species that looks exactly like humans?"

"They're our replacements, Kelly. Both of our sabbatical proposals were accepted!"

"What? Nobody notified me."

"Janice is the replacement embassy manager and Phillip is filling in for you. Daniel barely had time to greet them before he had to run into his office to take a call from Flower, but he said he wouldn't be long."

Kelly stared for a moment while the embassy manager's words sank in, and then her face lit up with a smile as big as her friend's. She strode over to the replacement staffers, both of whom appeared to be in their mid-thirties, and offered her hand.

"I'm Ambassador McAllister, but please call me Kelly. If you'll just give me a minute to grab a few personal items from my display desk, the embassy is yours."

The newcomers froze for a moment, and then they burst out laughing. "The president warned us that you were a great kidder," Phillip said. "I'm Bench Ambassador Hartley and my associate is Bench Embassy Manager Smitts. Reporting for spring training."

"Spring training?" Kelly's smile slipped a bit at the corners. "I've never heard the 'Bench' designation before. What does it mean?"

"The president told us that we're your creation, or at least, it was your idea. The two of us are the first replacement team for ambassadors and embassy managers who go out on sabbatical together. The idea is that we come in off the bench to replace the first-stringers. It's a sports analogy."

"I see. The president's office didn't bother keeping us in the loop, so could you tell me a little about your backgrounds? No, wait. Let me see if Daniel is off his conference call and then the five of us can sit down together and you won't have to repeat yourselves."

Kelly turned to approach the associate ambassador's office but the door slid open before she could take a single step.

"Lynx sends her regards," Daniel said. "Did you remember that today was your turn to bring donuts?"

"I did. Let's grab some chairs and all go in my office where we can talk. Do you want to hang the 'Out to lunch' sign on the door, Donna?"

"I'll just ask Libby to interrupt us if anybody comes in," the office manager said.

Five people with three extra chairs filed into the ambassador's office and parked themselves in a loose circle around the display desk.

"There's not much to tell," Phillip said in response to Kelly's question. "I've been the consul at Sharf Prime for the last three years, but EarthCent decided to downgrade the post from a consulate to a business office."

"I never knew we had a diplomatic presence in Sharf space."

"Neither did they, at least not officially. I think it might have gone better if our primary mission hadn't been so diametrically opposed to their interests."

"Establishing formal relations?" Kelly guessed.

"Representing warranty claims," Janice said. "The Sharf have sold tens of thousands of second-hand spacecraft to humans, mainly two-man traders and small prospecting vessels, and a lot of them came with what the buyers thought were generous warranties. But the fine print makes clear that claims have to be filed on Sharf Prime, and when you consider the cost of going there and providing all the necessary documentation from a certified repair facility, most ship owners who get stuck with a lemon don't bother."

"We were able to get compensation for some of the more spectacular failures, but it didn't make us any friends in the Sharf establishment," Phillip picked up the thread. "The Drazens tipped us off that second-hand ship warranties are funded by a small percentage of the purchase price that is paid up front to punters who take on the risk. There's a single agency that's responsible, and every cred they pay out is a cred less profit for the investors."

"I'm glad to hear that you have experience with the Drazens as they're our closest allies on the station. Where were you posted before Sharf Prime?"

"I ran a construction crew for the Dollnicks before EarthCent tapped me for the consul job. I grew up on a Dolly ag world where my parents were in a labor contract."

"So EarthCent has finally started recruiting diplomatic staff from humans who weren't born on Earth," Kelly observed. "That's good news, and I'm glad to hear that they gave you credit for your professional experience rather than starting you at the bottom."

"I took a big pay cut, but I want to be part of the solution, and they assured me that the benefits are improving."

"I was employed as a counselor in a Verlock academy on Earth when I was recruited," Janice added. "It was tough giving up working with children, but the principal promised she'd hire me back if I didn't like the EarthCent job. They were very supportive."

"Do you have any secretarial experience?" Donna asked.

"I'm a whiz at anything involving warranties," the woman said with a shy smile. "When this opportunity came up and they explained the job, the main thing that worried me was planning functions."

"That's perfect. Event planning is the only reason I'm still working, so I'll be happy to come in and help," Donna offered.

"About your training," Kelly said. "Do we have any guidelines or are we just going to wing it?"

"The president's office sent us this," Janice said, and passed Donna her tab.

"Training instructions for EarthCent bench personnel," the embassy manager read out loud. "Your training will be spent researching the best practices of EarthCent diplomatic support staff through shadowing employees at our embassy. In addition to retooling your skill set, you will work with the EarthCent Embassies Employee Union to disseminate the results of your experience, to include a conference for embassy managers if funding can be found." She looked up, bemused. "They stole my sabbatical proposal and changed the pronouns."

"How about yours?" Kelly asked her replacement. "I don't see how my proposal could have been repurposed that way."

"Mine is the same as Janice's, except for the stuff about the union," Phillip said. "Sometimes I'm not sure whether to take EarthCent seriously. We thought we were just transferring at Union Station—me on my way to an assistant ambassador gig at Middle Station, and Janice heading back to Earth for additional training. All of a sudden, a steward escorts us up to the bridge for a holoconference call from the president's office, and a robot shows up with our checked baggage that was pulled out of the hold. The Dollnicks sure didn't do business this way."

"Shadowing us for a few weeks really isn't a bad idea," Donna told Kelly. "That's enough time for Janice to see most of what happens in the office, except for the special events, and you can take Phillip around to meet all the other ambassadors."

"You're welcome to sit in on one of my conference calls with the Sovereign Human Communities Conference members any time," Daniel offered the bench ambassador. "We do one every time Flower arrives at and departs from each stop on her circuit, to review the mission's progress."

"Are there any alien functions coming up where I can introduce Phillip to the other ambassadors?" Kelly asked.

"Lynx never turned down an invitation to anything," Donna said, activating the ambassador's display desk from the opposite side and flipping the calendar orientation with a gesture. "There's a Horten open meeting this afternoon seeking community input on their upcoming Gortunda revival. Have you ever been to one of those?"

"The religious revival or the planning meeting?"

"The meeting. I remember Lynx accepting this invitation when it was extended last year, but I guess the Hortens kept putting it off for some reason. I don't understand why they're open to input from the other species."

"It's probably an excuse for proselytizing," Daniel said. "There's a human colony on one of the few Horten open worlds where half of the people have joined up. I heard that the local revival offered a fifty-year remission on tithing for new converts, and with our lifespans, that's like getting something for nothing."

"I'm sure we can make it through one meeting without succumbing," Kelly said, giving Phillip a playful smile. "But I should have asked if the two of you are tired. With all that luggage, I assume you came straight here from the passenger liner."

"We both did stasis for the first leg of the trip so we're fine," Phillip said. "We would have dropped our luggage off at our quarters if we knew where they were."

"Didn't you ask?"

"Ask who?"

"Libby. Our Stryx librarian."

"I've never spent time on a Stryx station before. Do I make contact through my implant?"

"You can, but most of us just talk unless we want privacy. Libby. I'd like to introduce my sabbatical replacement, Phillip, uh…"

"Hartley," the Stryx prompted her.

"Right. And Janice Smith."

"Smitts," Donna's replacement and Libby said at the same time.

"I'm very pleased to meet you both," the station librarian said, causing Phillip and Janice to look around the office for a hidden speaker. "I often use field projections to create interference patterns that produce localized speech at an appropriate volume. I hope the two of you will feel free to ask me anything."

"Do you know where our quarters are?" Phillip inquired.

"The ambassador has a budget for temporary lodging of replacement staff," Libby replied. "It was applied to the embassy account when you arrived."

"Donna?" Kelly asked.

The office manager pulled up an accounting display on Kelly's desk and whistled. "This will cover two weeks in a luxury hotel or six weeks in a bed and breakfast."

"If it's alright with Phillip, why don't you and Janice pick a place?" Kelly suggested. "It will give you a chance to get her started on learning your display desk's reservation system."

"Good idea," Donna said, getting to her feet. "Bring your chair, Janice. It's the one that goes next to my desk."

"I should get back to work myself," Daniel said. He stood up and lifted his own chair while offering his free hand to the newcomers. "Nice to meet you both, I'm sure we'll enjoy working together."

As soon as he was alone in the office with Kelly, Phillip lowered his voice to a loud whisper and said, "I have an ears-only communication from the president."

"I thought there might be something," the ambassador said, and moved to the door. "My standard procedure is to engage the security lock when discussing confidential business. You can ask Libby to do it, but I think that locking it myself helps me to keep track of what's on and off the record. With the home office of the Galactic Free Press on the station, we get reporters in and out of the embassy all the time."

"I thought the job was going to be complicated enough just with EarthCent Intelligence. You're sure you'll be available on the station if I need to consult?"

"I'm not going anywhere, and to be perfectly honest, Daniel is more than capable of replacing me if he wasn't so busy building a network of commercial trade agreements for his sovereign communities."

"That's one of the things that the president told me. He said that even though I'll be officially batting for you, Associate Ambassador Cohan will be the team captain during your sabbatical. He also said that you'll be continuing as the Minister of Intelligence, so you might kick me out of your office from time to time for secure conferences."

"More sports analogies?"

"Sorry. We played a lot of baseball on the ag world where I grew up because it was the closest we could come to paddle-cup-mitt-ball."

"I understand. Did you have a display desk on Sharf Prime?"

"No, but we had something similar in the Dolly construction trailer for scheduling and checking the holographic blueprints. May I?"

"Please," the ambassador said, rolling her chair to the side to make room for Phillip to slide his in. Her replacement swiped his hand down the desk's surface to clear the calendar Donna had brought up, but nothing happened.

"Is it ignoring me?" he asked.

"You need to authorize Phillip to access your desk," the Stryx librarian informed Kelly. "The current user list is limited to Donna, Daniel, and Lynx."

"How do I do that?"

"You ask me to register him."

"I remember now. It's just that it's been years since we added Daniel. Please register Bench Ambassador Hartley for my display desk and any other embassy controls, like the door locks."

"Could you place both of your hands on the desk, Phillip?" Libby requested. A hologram full of geometric shapes appeared over the desk as soon as he complied. "Initiating the calibration process. Please begin by moving all of the blue spheres into the centers of the red cubes, alternating hands after each."

Phillip reached out and pinched a blue sphere between his right thumb and forefinger. "It's hard to tell where the edges are," he commented. "The Dollnick desk had a modeling function that worked with special gloves."

"I could provide you with tactile feedback, but the point of the calibration process is to allow the desk to align your spatial perception with your fine motor control."

"I get it," Phillip said, and after placing the first blue sphere, switched to his left hand for the next. "How's that?"

"You have a good eye and excellent depth perception," the station librarian complimented him. "One more time with each hand should do it."

"I don't remember going through this," Kelly said.

"You initially chose to postpone completing the calibration process as you were satisfied with the default settings, and then you asked me to hide the weekly reminders generated by the desk," Libby told her.

"I did? When did it stop generating them?"

"It never stops. You have over a thousand reminders, which I believe is a record for a tunnel network ambassador. You never completed the eye-tracking calibration for your heads-up display, either."

"Oh. It's always worked really well without it."

"What's next?" Phillip asked.

"Tie a square knot in the yellow line segment," Libby instructed him. "That's very good. Now, do you see the green isosceles triangle?"

Kelly's replacement said "Yes," at the same time she asked, "The what?"

"Using both hands, stretch the base until it becomes an equilateral triangle."

"Now I remember why I postponed it," Kelly said. "I had to keep asking about which shapes you meant."

"It's not me, it's the desk," Libby told her. "I'm just inserting myself into the process to be sociable."

A few minutes later, after correctly manipulating the legs of a parabola to move the black dot representing the focus along the axis of symmetry until it covered a white dot, Phillip asked, "Is that everything?"

"Yes. And Kelly, you have a call coming in from the president's office."

82

A hologram of the president of EarthCent sitting at his desk replaced the calibration pattern. As soon as he saw Kelly and Phillip in the projection above his own display desk, he shouted, "Surprise!"

"It certainly is, Stephen," Kelly acknowledged. "My question is why?"

"I thought you liked surprises," the president replied. "Besides, it came together very quickly. The Stryx still have approval over all of our tunnel network appointments, and I was in a meeting this afternoon when the word came through that Phillip and Janice had been accepted as the first replacement team. I just wanted to check in before I head home for the day."

"I'm not complaining, I just thought it was a bit odd. And thank you for approving my sabbatical."

"If anybody deserves one, you do," the president told her. "Have you checked your embassy accounts? I pushed through a little housing bonus for your replacements."

"Yes, thank you. As a matter of fact, Donna and Janice are looking through the listings for temporary lodging as we speak."

"I'll leave you to it, then," Stephen said, his eyes shifting away from the ambassador's. "Coming, Hildy." The hologram went dark.

"Janice is waiting at the door," Libby announced.

"Why doesn't she—oh, right." Kelly got up and went to disarm the security lock. "Did you see how I did that, Phillip?"

"Yes," he said, having followed behind her. "What's up, Janice?"

"Donna found us super-discounted rooms at a Vergallian resort providing we get there in the next twenty minutes," she said excitedly. "Libby said that they're trying

83

to raise their occupancy for the final quarter of the chain's fiscal year."

"Do you mind if I run out?" Phillip asked Kelly.

"Not at all. You should settle in and have lunch. Just be back for the Horten thing this afternoon. And don't drag your luggage with you while you're in a hurry. You can pick it up later."

"Thank you," Phillip said, and the two newcomers headed off to claim their discounted rooms.

Kelly glanced over at Donna, but her friend was busily sorting through holographic spreadsheets and the ambassador knew better than to interrupt her just to chat about their replacements. She returned to her desk, thinking about something Phillip had said.

"The two of them were really just here to transfer ships on their way for different assignments when you approved them as our sabbatical replacements?"

"Quite a coincidence," Libby acknowledged.

"And when did our sabbatical requests get Stryx approval?"

"That happened a few seconds earlier, contingent on the availability of replacements."

"Who just happened to be available," Kelly said dryly.

"Don't you think the two of them make a nice couple?" the Stryx matchmaker asked.

"You're incorrigible, and you've rubbed off on Dorothy. She made me pester Ambassador Ortha until he agreed to meet the parents of a Horten girl from Samuel's student committee."

"Mornich and Marilla are almost through the initial screening process so an official introduction isn't far off. If your daughter hadn't put them together, I would have had a go at it myself."

Eight

"I thought I'd seen everything in this place, but those guys are grossing me out," Vivian said, pushing away her soup. "Do you want this?"

"Sure, give me your spoon." Samuel pulled the bowl to his side of the cafeteria table and looked around to see who the girl was complaining about. "Which guys? The zombies?"

"Yes, the zombies. Ugh, they're adding ketchup to their brains."

"Those are just cauliflower heads. The zombies must have bribed one of the kitchen staff for whole ones."

"I think this LARPing craze is getting out of hand. After Tinka announced her new InstaSitter league, kids started applying for babysitting jobs just so they can join."

"I want to know why they get to be zombies and we're stuck playing historical characters," Samuel complained. Then he noticed that Vivian was staring in rapt attention at the costumed role-players who were carving their ketch-up-drenched cauliflowers, so he lifted the soup bowl and drank off the contents in a few gulps.

"Way to go, Human," Jorb said, setting his tray on the table and pulling out the chair next to Vivian. "You've finally learned something from your dogs."

"Drazens are the last biologicals that have any right to criticize anybody's table manners," Marilla shot back, settling into the chair next to Samuel.

"The zombies must be in the intramural league," Vivian finally replied to her boyfriend's question, still unable to tear her gaze away from the heavily made-up students in their faux-tattered clothing. "They don't receive any university credit."

"But they get to have lots of fun," the Drazen said, using his elbow to create a depression in a loaf of hard alien bread. He shoveled all of the contents from his plate into the crater and topped it off with hot sauce from his personal bottle. "The dojo was half empty this morning because everybody is off having real adventures."

"Maybe Jeeves will let us do something other than talk after today," Marilla said. "Some of the students who started before us said the for-credit LARPs get better as they go along."

The Horten student's words finally pulled Vivian's attention away from the disgusting vegan feast taking place across the aisle. "I'm glad you've finally stopped saying 'Stryx Jeeves' all the time, like being a Stryx is a medical condition or something. Jeeves is a sentient, just like you and me. He's actually younger than my father."

"I admire your self-esteem, but I don't have such a high opinion of myself or my species," Marilla replied, and then turned an odd shade of orange. "Do you have to eat with your tentacle in front of me, Drazen?"

"It's the only way to keep the loaf from falling apart," Jorb said unapologetically. "The crust got soggy too fast because the cafeteria bakers don't know how to make good bread."

"It's the closest thing to an all-species loaf they can manage," Samuel told him. "I think it's mainly synthesized."

"Did you guys all study the material Jeeves sent us?" Vivian asked.

"Of course," Marilla said.

"I looked at it," Samuel replied, and dug into his pudding in hopes of avoiding follow-up questions.

Jorb made a noncommittal noise and then shoved enough of the Drazen-style sandwich into his mouth to remove himself from the conversation.

"We should just replace both of them with girls," Marilla suggested to Vivian. "Why is it that men will stay up all night programming a new game, but if you ask them to learn anything useful, all of a sudden they suffer from some sort of collective attention deficit disorder."

"Samuel's not *that* bad," Vivian defended her boyfriend. "He's just not a big history fan. He used to take a double major in Vergallian studies and they overloaded him with a million years of imperial genealogy. That's enough to make anybody hate history."

"You know that Jorb isn't going to do any preparation so you might as well just tell us," Samuel suggested hopefully.

"I'll read it to you," Vivian said, pulling out her tab. "It will give me something to concentrate on so I don't keep looking at the corpse-twins there."

"Skip past the intro," Marilla told her. "I think it was written for students who didn't grow up on the station."

"All right. The date is, it doesn't matter, it's in Grenouthian, and the bunny network has signed its first deal for Stryxnet access, making the dream of a live news broadcast to all members of the tunnel network and beyond a reality. Unconfirmed reports have started coming in about Chert refugees arriving at Stryx stations in the tens of millions, but it's not known who they are fleeing or if they are being pursued. A meeting is taking place at the Grenouthian network headquarters during which it will be decided whether to push the story, including exclusive footage of the normally elusive Cherts."

"That's our LARP? We're going to stand around and talk about whether or not to run a news story?"

"It's not just a story, Samuel. It's Chert history."

"So what did the Grenouthians decide?"

"The introduction said we shouldn't do any research because it would prejudice our role-playing," Vivian said. "Unlike the last LARP we did, in this one the characters all have a solid understanding of each other's positions and motivations, so Jeeves sent us the character sheets ahead of time. He said we can all read them and decide who we want to play, but not to discuss the Chert story until our session."

"Which starts in twenty minutes," Marilla reminded them, before taking a dainty bite of her popover.

Jorb shifted his current mouthful into his cheek and said, "I dibs the top executive."

"You haven't even heard the character traits yet," Vivian said in exasperation.

"I know bunnies, and I know there's going to be an alpha fur-ball, so I want to be it," Jorb reiterated stubbornly.

"Fine by me," Samuel said. "Who else is there?"

"A young correspondent, an editor, and the network ombudsman."

"What's that last one?"

"The Grenouthians appoint a sort of roving official do-gooder to make sure the network serves the public interest," Vivian explained. "It's required by their contract for Stryx bandwidth."

"So the ombudsman was new when this happened."

"Yes," Vivian said after glancing at her tab. "I don't know how I missed that."

"And who do you and Marilla want to be?"

"Editor," the Horten replied, watching Vivian out of the corner of her eye to see if the other girl reacted. "I've already applied to the student news show as an assistant editor so it would be good practice."

"Take it," Vivian said. "I was going to try to get the ombudsman role, but if it means playing a newbie, I'd rather be the correspondent."

"Fine, I'll be the ombudsman," Samuel agreed. "Does the LARP have a time limit?"

"It's just one hour or until we reach a conclusion, after which the orchestrator is supposed to take a few minutes to tell us how everything would have worked out based on our role play. So let's try not to start a war."

Fifteen minutes later, the four students found themselves seated around a table in a room that wouldn't have looked out of place at the Grenouthian network offices on Union Station. Jeeves, or a holographic instance of the Stryx, finished giving them the pre-LARP instructions, and then with a flourish of his pincer, declared, "Go!"

"What are you wasting my time with now?" Jorb inquired in a bored voice, but he was unable to keep from grinning at having the opportunity to play an alpha-bunny.

"Cherts," Marilla replied in her role as the editor. "They're pouring into the tunnel network. None of the competing news services have picked up on it yet because they think it's just a local story, but our intelligence indicates that Cherts are showing up at all of the Stryx stations. This is confirmed by our intercepts of intelligence reports from the less advanced species."

"Run it," Jorb barked. "Where's my yellow tea?"

"I'm sure you've already considered the matter of our Stryxnet contract, but perhaps we should talk it through so I can understand the implications," Samuel said deferentially.

Jorb glared at the ombudsman. "Idiot. What difference does it make whether or not you understand what's going on? You're here as a sop to the Stryx and nothing more."

"Microseconds are wasting," Vivian added. "We're talking about a scoop, and I have plans for my bonus."

"It just seems to me that there may be some degree of prearrangement in operation here," Samuel said. "Everybody knows that the Cherts have been on the move across the galaxy for millions of years, but I can't believe they would start showing up at Stryx stations in such large numbers without an invitation. Doesn't anybody else find it strange that they're getting their own deck right away, rather than milling around looking to rent temporary quarters."

"Stop beating around the bush," Jorb growled.

"If the Stryx arranged for the Cherts to move onto tunnel network stations all at once, they may have a reason for secrecy."

"Haven't you been listening?" Marilla said scornfully. "It's not a secret. It just hasn't broken as a galactic story yet."

"What if their safety is at stake?" Samuel asked.

"How can they be in danger when they're already here?" Vivian exploded. "The whole point is that the entire population of Cherts in the galaxy has suddenly pulled up stakes again and moved to Stryx stations."

"But doesn't that mean they're running from something?"

"Of course they're running from something. That's why it's news!"

"Now, wait a minute," Jorb said, leaning forward. "Do we have any facts to substantiate that claim?"

"It's obvious," Vivian said stubbornly. "Why else would they show up with nothing more than their personal belongings? Those transports they arrived on are basically jump-capable dormitories with ship-wide stasis fields. They're barely worth their weight in scrap."

"That's supposition," the Drazen said in his role as the network executive. He leaned forward and pointed at Marilla. "What can we prove?"

The Horten student looked uncomfortable and glanced at her tab to see if her character sheet provided any hints on conducting herself in this situation. "Counting ships and estimating the capacities, we're confident that this migration constitutes the bulk of the known Chert population, possibly including all of their members."

"And their motivation for leaving their homes and moving to Stryx stations?"

"That's, uh, not entirely clear yet," Marilla said. She cringed as Jorb began tapping his fingers on his belly in a perfect imitation of how the Grenouthian on their student committee used to act before he lost his temper. "They, uh, nobody really knows that much about the Cherts as they previously stayed away from the tunnel network and their technology is concentrated on stealth ships and personal invisibility projectors. Our profilers say they must have been traumatized by—"

"More supposition," Jorb shouted, slamming a fist on the table. He spun towards Vivian and ordered, "Tell me the story!"

"What?" the girl asked, obviously confused by the direction the LARP was taking.

"Pretend we're on a lift tube and you have thirty seconds to tell me your scoop."

"But the immersive footage is the—"

"Have I sinned?" Jorb inquired acerbically, looking up at the ceiling. "Is there something I did to offend the universe that I'm cursed with such incompetent subordinates?"

"Five-point penalty," Jeeves announced. "Cultural mismatch."

"Timeout," Jorb said. "What did I do wrong?"

"Grenouthians have approval over their subordinates at all levels so they would never accuse them of being incompetent," Jeeves explained. "It would be the same as publicly admitting your own failure for hiring them. Now play on."

Vivian glanced at Marilla to see if any support was forthcoming from her editor and then began her lift-tube pitch. "A wave of Chert refugees has poured onto Stryx stations around the tunnel network. They arrived in obsolete transports, carrying with them little more than their personal belongings, and appear to constitute the entire—"

"Appear?" Jorb interrupted.

"She's young," Marilla said apologetically. "The fault is mine for rushing ahead with the story based on phenomenal visuals."

"If you could interview a Chert on the record," Samuel suggested.

"Now the ombudsman is going to tell us how to report a story," Jorb said disdainfully.

"It's just that if we had their side, we might figure out what the Stryx would want us to do."

"Do the Stryx pay your salary?" the Drazen asked in a tired voice. "Do they pay my salary, or hers, or hers? I have a news show to run and I'll broadcast whatever is newsworthy."

"The story is newsworthy," Vivian began, but Marilla cut her off.

"We could do it as a special item from the shipping news," the Horten suggested. "It would still be a scoop, and we could shift it to the political news later if the facts warrant a higher slot."

"Have the announcer keep the tone light," Jorb instructed her. "For all we know the Cherts may be taking advantage of some Stryx special offer for cheap deck space."

"Just the facts," Marilla promised.

Nobody spoke for a few moments, and then Jeeves announced, "Not very original, but I'll give you a pass."

"That's it?" Samuel asked. "What did the Grenouthians really do back when it happened for real?"

"They made it the top story on their network for a cycle. Endless speculation about who the Cherts were fleeing and whether their presence would impact the economy on the stations. I've reviewed the historical records and the Cherts were happy to grant interviews, though they never said anything noteworthy."

"So what was the outcome?"

"The correspondent won their 'Best new reporter of the cycle,' award, advertising rates crept up, and viewership hit a new peak. It turned out that a good mystery made better news than a presentation of known facts. The Grenouthian network has become progressively more sensationalistic ever since."

"I thought you were supposed to tell us what the outcome would have been for the Cherts if the Grenouthians had followed our solution."

"No difference," Jeeves said. "Whether the Grenouthians pushed the story at the top of their news, as they did, or whether they ignored it completely, it would have had no impact on the Cherts."

"It was a trick LARP?" Marilla asked.

"So what's the point?" Jorb demanded.

"Did you ever stop to think how the Grenouthians go about selecting which stories to run on their network and what impact that has on the galaxy at large?" Jeeves shot back.

"No, but you're saying it doesn't even matter."

"I'm saying that in this instance it didn't matter because nobody was going to chase the Cherts onto Stryx stations and they're welcome to stay as long as they want. The point of this exercise was to put yourself in the shoes of another species which happens to control the most popular news network in the galaxy and to take responsibility for your actions."

"Which didn't matter in the end," Jorb muttered stubbornly.

"I learned what an ombudsman is and that the Grenouthian network has one, though they probably ignore him," Samuel said. "I get why somebody thought these might be good scenarios for alien role-playing, but don't you have anything where we could at least get some exercise, Jeeves?"

"I'd like to fight some zombies," Vivian said.

"Next week," their orchestrator told them. "I'm not promising any zombies, but there will be plenty of opportunity for rough-housing depending on your actions." Then the holographic instance of the Stryx vanished before the students could ask any questions.

"So how many gold coins do you guys have left?" Marilla asked.

"I've got two hundred," Vivian said after checking her university LARP account.

"One-eighty," Samuel reported.

"Why do you want to know?" Jorb asked suspiciously.

"I saw a notification in the Galactic Free Press that there's a traveling LARP fair coming to the station this weekend on the Human calendar. They're going to have all sorts of enchanted weapons and costumes for sale, and the Open University is a sponsor so they'll accept our virtual gold."

"You still take the Galactic Free Press?" Vivian asked.

"I got used to reading it when we were running the committee for refitting Flower, and they had a super discount deal for students to subscribe to the ad-free edition that was too good to pass up," the Horten admitted. "Anyway, I think we should all go to the fair together and pool our gold if there's something that will help the whole team."

"Can we use the stuff we buy outside of the Open University LARPs?" Jorb asked. "If Jeeves keeps giving us these talking roles to play, I'm going to look into signing up for a league that will let me swing my noodle axe."

"All purchases are guaranteed to work on the stations," Marilla informed them. "The Stryx librarians provide the back-office support for the leagues, including handling the non-player characters and all of that."

"I still think we should outfit Jorb as our tank," Vivian said. "When the game gets physical, the outcome is based as much on our actual ability as on the point system."

Marilla scowled. "You want me to spend my gold making the Drazen stronger?"

"Just so we can send him through the door first to take all the damage. While he's getting pounded, we can stay back at a safe distance and deal with the attackers."

"Oh, that doesn't sound so bad then," the Horten girl said.

"Do I get a say in all this?" Jorb asked.

"If you don't want to do it, I can," Samuel offered. "It's just that I'm only good with the one weapon, while you're used to fighting guys with four arms."

"I just wanted to be asked. But the deal is, if Jeeves doesn't find us a fight soon, I get to use the stuff in another LARP league, even if you guys don't join."

"And what if you get killed there?" Marilla asked.

"It's just a game," Samuel pointed out. "He won't really be dead."

"I don't care about that, I'm talking about the gear. If you get killed in a role-playing game, don't you drop all of your possessions?"

"So he'll pick them up."

"No, she's talking about something else," Vivian said. "The Hortens have role-playing games where you sit around a table and the outcomes of encounters are determined by random number generators. All of your gear is imaginary, and sometimes you drop stuff when you get killed and you don't get it back. My brother says they do something similar in the professional LARPing league, except you only lose the stuff that you found on the current quest if you die."

"Thank you all for your concern about my equipment should I be killed outside of your service," Jorb said as he rose to leave. "Ping me when we're meeting for the fair."

Nine

Affie lounged against the wall in the lobby of the practice space, dressed in a molded one-piece combat suit that left nothing to the imagination. A group of human teenagers emerged from the virtual stage and stopped to stare at her, wondering if they had somehow been trapped in an alternate fantasy reality. Brandishing her noodle sword wasn't enough to get the boys moving, so she offered them a dazzling smile and said, "I haven't had a chance to test my pheromone control on Humans lately. Who wants to act like a chicken for the next twenty-four hours?"

The heavily armed adventurers fled, almost trampling a figure wearing an odd patchwork dress in their rush for the exit. "What was their hurry?" Dorothy asked the Vergallian when she finally made it into the room. Then her eyes narrowed with suspicion. "Did you just threaten those boys with chemical warfare?"

"It seemed like the right thing to do before they could get themselves into trouble," Affie replied innocently. "What are you supposed to be?"

"A seamstress," Dorothy declared, showing off her cloth workbag. "I have pincushions, needle assortments, and a selection of thread, plus all of my scissors."

"You were supposed to stop at the rental counter for an outfit. I reserved a complete mage setup for you."

"But I don't know anything about being a mage. Why is it that everybody who plays these games has to be a swordsman or a priest in some made-up cult? I don't want to be a minstrel or a dwarf or any of that. I'm sure that wherever our adventure takes place they'll need seam-stresses."

"Not in combat," Affie said with an exaggerated sigh. "I thought I explained to you that all the normal occupations are reserved for non-player characters. That includes shopkeepers, monsters, castle guards—"

"Since when are monsters normal?"

"Since fantasy role-playing games made them normal. We need to slay them in order to earn gold and level up, and real players don't want to dress up as monsters just to get killed. Monsters are all holographic glamour layered onto constructs."

"Huh?"

"You didn't watch the introduction holo, did you?"

"I meant to, but I got caught up working on my outfit."

"You're lucky we're both here early. Constructs are dumb mechanicals that are controlled by the game. Rather than building different types of brainless robots for every character you can imagine, there's a standard model with attachments for different types of limbs and weapons, but it's only there for the sake of giving the real players some-thing solid to hit. The constructs are always wrapped in holograms so you think you're fighting a Dollnick assassin or giant snake, and the studio effects make everything super realistic."

"Wait. Did you say they're going to attack us with real weapons?"

"They won't break your skin," the Vergallian girl as-sured her. "The constructs are all variations on the basic dueling bots people use for practicing their combat skills, and they use noodle weapons as well."

Flazint entered the studio waiting room, a longbow in one hand and a wicked dagger thrust through her belt.

"What are you?" Dorothy asked.

"Forest Ranger. I did archery in school for my physical ed requirement."

"What about the knife?"

"It's an honor dagger. I thought every girl knew how to use one. Why are you dressed like a rag doll?"

"I'm a seamstress," Dorothy replied, sounding a little less confident in her choice. "I mean, a ninja seamstress."

"What's that?"

"I have secret assassin training," the girl replied, glancing furtively in Affie's direction.

"So secret she didn't know about it herself two minutes ago," Affie said. "Listen. I had to charm the clerk into accepting our reservation because he said that subletting is actually against their policy."

"You rented us time in another group's LARP?" Flazint asked.

"It's a big studio space. They'll be on their quest and we'll be on ours. If we run into them, just make sure they know we're players so they don't get us confused with NPCs and attack."

"That sounds kind of dangerous."

"I doubt we'll come across them," Affie reassured her. "Players prefer big groups to get the studio cost down and to cover all the skill sets that are needed for complicated quests. The gamemaster always keeps track of the real players and acts to prevent them from hurting each other. It's easy to mix up who's who in a skirmish."

"So let's get this show on the road," Dorothy said in a show of false bravado. "At least we don't have to worry about making fools out of ourselves in front of the boys."

"There's nothing in there we can't handle," Affie proclaimed confidently. "It's just an entry level simulation that gives us the chance to kill lots of NPCs to level up. This way we'll be prepared to do something more interesting at your Jack-and-Jill. Some of the friends we've invited have been playing for a while, and it would be too boring for them if it was your first time."

The three women headed through the portal into the playing space, Affie in the lead, Flazint following with her bow held loose in her hand, and Dorothy bringing up the rear with her sewing kit. If the ambassador's daughter hadn't known she was entering a holographically enhanced game space, she would have thought she had just stepped into a small clearing on the surface of a planet overgrown by jungle. Ruins of stone towers poked through the vegetation in places, but there were no signs of the original builders.

"Spooky," Flazint said, as an animal screeched in the distance. "So we're supposed to hunt monsters or something?"

"I can't believe that's not really a sun." Dorothy squinted at the giant orb where the ceiling should have been and inhaled deeply through her nose. "The air is different from the station, too. It's like we really have been transported to a new world."

"Get in character," Affie warned them in a whisper. "Monsters have ears, you know."

Dorothy climbed up on a flat stone that may have once served as a sacrificial altar and swatted at a mosquito. "I hope all the bugs are holograms," she said in a low voice,

101

and took a moment to survey the clearing. "What does it mean when the grass rustles and there's no wind?"

"Where?" Affie demanded, clambering onto the rock to look in the direction the girl pointed. "Whatever it is, it can't be very tall. Flazz, get up here and load an arrow."

"Nock," the Frunge girl corrected the Vergallian's terminology. She removed an arrow from her quiver and carefully placed the notch in the fletched end on her bowstring.

"Why aren't you pulling it back?" Dorothy asked.

"Never draw a bow until you have a target," Flazint recited from rote. "It has to come out of that grass if it's going to attack."

Affie cut an impressive pattern through the air with her sword and declared, "Whatever it is, we'll make it sorry it met us."

The grass parted and a twitching nose emerged, followed by large whiskers and a pair of beady black eyes. Then the shoulders pushed through the grass and the animal stepped out into the open, sniffing at the air.

"It's a giant rat!" the Frunge girl screamed, retreating behind the other two.

"Shoot it, Flazint," Dorothy said, closing one eye in hopes of seeing less of the jumbo rodent.

"I'm not shooting THAT," the forest ranger replied. "It's gross."

"Can you kill it with your sword, Affie?"

"Not from here," the Vergallian royal replied in a tone that made it clear she wouldn't be budging from the spot. "Ugh, why is it squealing so loud when we aren't bothering it?"

The answer quickly became apparent as the tall grass began rustling all the way back to the forest.

"It must be calling its friends," Dorothy whispered. "How can rats be so big?"

"That one must be the size of a dog," Flazint said, peeking over Dorothy's shoulder. "Not a Cayl hound," she added hastily as the human girl's knees buckled. "Just a regular dog."

"I count five of them already, and more are coming," Affie told the Frunge girl. "If you can't shoot them we're going to have to make a run for it."

"Do you think they can get up here?" Dorothy asked.

"We did."

"Oh no!" the Frunge girl cried, her head twisting around like it was on a pivot. "They're coming out of the jungle all around us."

"Get the station librarian to make them go away," Affie begged the ambassador's daughter. "You're friends with her."

The rats grew bolder, risking themselves in the open. They crept closer and began circling the rock the girls were standing on, occasionally making little feints towards the players, testing for a response.

"You have to shoot them, Flazint," Dorothy pleaded with her friend. "I can't get eaten by rats before my wedding."

"Remember, they can't hurt us," Affie said. "They're just constructs wrapped in holograms. Get the station librarian to call them off already."

"My implant isn't working. I just get a message that outgoing communications are forbidden in LARP space."

"I'm going to try to kill one," the Frunge girl announced, and drawing back her bowstring, let fly an arrow towards the biggest of the rodents. The rat twisted faster than the eye could see and caught the shaft in its teeth, shattering the arrow with a loud crunch. The three friends looked at each other and screamed.

Almost immediately, their chorus was drowned out by an even higher-pitched squeal, and squinting through half-shut eyes, Dorothy saw a fountain of gore shooting into the air where the king rat had stood. It was replaced by a balloon showing two gold coins, which quickly faded. This was immediately followed by more squeals and more balloons, though the latter were mainly for one gold coin. The rats fought valiantly with their attackers, but the three men, whooping battle cries, made short work of the pack.

"Playing through," the tallest of their saviors called to the huddled girls. "Sorry about skimming off your easy kills, but they were in the way."

"Hold up, Boz," one of the warriors called. "Stupid rat took a chunk out of me."

"So take a healing potion, Zach. We're already late for the rendezvous."

"It's not my body I'm worried about. I can't play like this," Zach complained, and turning his back towards the other two men, showed that the seat of his pants was hanging in a large flap below his belt, exposing colorful boxer shorts.

A tremendous explosion sounded in the distance, and then bits of jungle and less savory items began raining out of the sky.

"They blew the mine," the leader shouted in disbelief. "I can't raise any of our guys on my telepathic link."

"Look at my magical map," the third man cried, holding up the square of tanned leather for Boz to see. "Their avatars are all gone."

"That's it, then," Zach said, edging around the clearing towards his friends while keeping his face towards the women. "We may as well just work on our stats. Without a necromancer and mage, it would be suicide to try to invade the underground kingdom."

"Not to mention that it just got blown to high heavens," Boz pointed out.

"Uh, excuse me," Dorothy called from her perch on the altar. "Does that mean you guys can stick around in case the rats come back?"

"You three are doing the entry level quest, right?" the map owner asked.

"Yes, " Affie replied, stepping out from behind Dorothy and Flazint. "We've never LARPed before."

"You only get one chance at the easy points, so the rats won't be back. If I remember, it's zombies next. Right, Zach?"

"It may have been great-billed woodpeckers."

Flazint let out a strange hiss and nocked another arrow.

"We should introduce ourselves," the tallest warrior said, leading the others over to the altar, but stopping several paces away so he wouldn't have to tilt his head way back to talk to the girls. "I'm Boz, the guy with the map is Funt, and the Frunge mooning the jungle is Zach."

"Tzachan, but these Drazen idiots can't pronounce it," Zach said, and removing his helmet, performed a sweeping bow.

"But where are your tentacles and your hair vines?" Dorothy asked the aliens in disbelief.

"We're playing Humans," Zach told her. "It's the Cursed Earth adventure. And what made you guys decide to play a Vergallian, a Frunge and a Human on an entry level quest? It's a weird combo, and those glamour potions must have cost a fortune in gold."

"We aren't glamoured," Flazint said, and her hair vines turned dark green.

"You mean the three of you actually look like that in real life?"

"Well, we usually dress better," Dorothy told them. "Speaking of which, if you give me your pants I can fix them in a jiff. I'm a ninja seamstress."

Zach looked from Flazint to Dorothy and back again, and to everybody's amazement, the holographic overlay that made him appear human blushed bright red.

"Just go behind that collapsed tower and give your pants to Funt," the tall Drazen instructed the embarrassed Frunge. "We've already blown the adventure so we may as well hang around and pick up some points helping the newbs."

"I'm sorry we're pulling you out of character," Affie said, clambering down from the altar. "We just weren't prepared for giant rats."

"Everybody has something that creeps them out," Boz said agreeably. "For me, it's the vampire slugs. There's just something about looking down at your legs after wading through a swamp and finding that half of your blood—"

"Too much information," Dorothy interrupted. "I wanted to do something cool for my Jack-and-Jill party, but I didn't realize it would be this gross. Are there any adventures where we won't have to fight for our lives against nightmarish creatures?"

"Sure. There are LARPs where you basically spend all of your time trading or working at crafts to earn gold, but most players only do that to buy magical weapons and other stuff that will help them on quests."

"Aren't there any peaceful quests?"

"You mean like tourism or something?" The tall Drazen's holographic wrapping looked puzzled, but Dorothy suspected that beneath it all, he was scratching his head with his tentacle. "I've never heard of any. I mean, if you want to just go for a walk in the woods, the park decks are free."

"Here you are," Funt said, passing Dorothy the unfortunate Frunge's pants. "Zach told me to say that he'll pay you the fourteen gold he earned killing your rats for the job. It's only fair."

"This will only take me a couple of minutes," the ninja seamstress replied, sitting down on the altar stone and spreading her sewing supplies on the surface. "Are you guys sure he's alright over there by himself without any pants? What if a monster comes?"

"He'll be fine," the Drazen said dismissively. "He can always take off the rest of his clothes, cancel his glamour, and blend into the jungle. Frunge are great at camouflage."

"Maybe you should go over there and keep him company, Flazint," Dorothy needled her friend.

"That'll chase him off for sure," Boz said, and lowered his voice confidentially. "He's pretty shy around the ladies in real life. We all work at the same inter-species law office and the poor sap doesn't have a life outside of intellectual property rights. Talk to him about trademarks or copyright and he's as confident as a Grenouthian, but send him to entertain clients and he goes all Chert on you. We kind of hoped that LARPing would help him shed some inhibitions, but as soon as he takes off the glamour, it's back to the old Tzachan."

"He said you couldn't pronounce his name," Flazint accused the Drazen.

"We just like teasing him," Funt said. "He's really easy." The Drazen looked down at Dorothy's flying hands and stared. "Did you drink a 'speedy action' potion or something?"

"None of us have any potions," Affie said. "We just wanted to see what LARPing was like before the party."

"So we wouldn't look foolish running from giant rats," Flazint added dryly.

"Everybody starts with at least one magic potion," Boz informed them. "You have to check your inventory."

"I thought that was only for gold," Affie said, and her eyes began tracking something invisible on her heads-up display. "We're such idiots! I have a magic rat repellant potion."

"And I have a bracer that will increase the accuracy of my archery by forty percent." Flazint concentrated for a moment and a leather bracer materialized on her bow-hand's wrist and forearm. "Nice. I swear I can even feel it. What do you have, Dorothy?"

"Done," the ambassador's daughter announced, holding up the Frunge's pants. The repair would have been invisible except for the colorfully embroidered SBJ Fashions logo she had sewn onto the back pocket. "Advertising," she explained. "This way Jeeves can't complain because I charged the LARP on my company cred."

Funt took the pants back to the Frunge, who hurriedly dressed and rejoined the others.

"Pay fourteen gold to Ninja Seamstress," he said out loud, and a little cartoon balloon showing fourteen gold coins appeared over Dorothy's head, and then quickly faded out.

"This is great," she thanked him, checking her inventory. "Does anybody else need any costume repairs?"

"I could go for one of those designer labels," Boz said. "I'm only a paralegal so I can't afford to shop in boutiques."

"About that," Zach said, and his holographic wrapping again showed the blood rushing to his face. "I'm not going to report you or anything, but you really can't go around creating knock-offs by adding fashion tags to clothes. Those companies invest a lot of money and intellectual capital to build their brands, and the label is more than just a way to demand a higher price. It shows pride in craftsmanship and a culture of innovation."

"Wow," Affie said. "We should make Jeeves hire this guy, Dorothy. I've never heard it put so well."

"Don't worry," Flazint told the Frunge lawyer. "The three of us are the design team for SBJ Fashions. "Dorothy adds a tag to everything she touches for, uh…"

"To justify my expenses," the ninja seamstress said.

"You've got something in your hair, Dory," Affie said, and leaning close to the ambassador's daughter to pluck out an imaginary speck, whispered, "Let's get him for Flazz."

Dorothy looked at her friend questioningly, and then her eyes lit up. "We just heard from our friends on EarthCent's circuit ship that their flea market is flooded with fashion knock-offs," she exaggerated. "How do we hire somebody like you?"

"SBJ Fashions," the Frunge said hesitantly. "Isn't the majority owner a Stryx? There's not much I can do that—"

"Jeeves believes in empowering biologicals to solve their own problems," the seamstress said, laying it on thick. "Do we have to visit your office or can you come to us?"

"I generally like to meet new clients in their workplace to get a feel for the business."

"Perfect," Dorothy said. "Arrange a time with Flazint. She can show you the ropes, and then one of the Hadad sisters, they're the co-owners with Jeeves, can fill you in on what we know about the knock-offs. Any idea what size you are?"

"My parents buy my suits for work," the shy lawyer mumbled. "My mother brought me to a Vergallian fitting room but she kept the sizing chit."

"Get it from her, or I'll measure you myself when you visit," Dorothy directed him imperiously. "Our custom at SBJ Fashions is to make a new outfit for everybody we work with, just to stay in practice." Then she turned to Affie and the two girls exchanged a high-five.

Ten

Kelly led Phillip into the Drazen ambassador's office where her sabbatical replacement stared at all of the bladed weapons decorating the walls. Finally, he asked, "Is the ambassador a role-player?"

"Don't let him hear you say that," Kelly whispered. "He's a historical reenactor, and he's been in a number of Drazen immersive productions as a background actor in fight scenes. Reenactors hate role-players."

"What's the difference?"

"What's the difference?" Bork repeated, entering his office with a tray on which rested the drink orders he had insisted on taking from the EarthCent diplomats. "How can you possibly confuse the two? Reenactors replicate the past as closely as possible while role-players invent a bunch of twaddle about magic weapons and fantasy skills. Most of them can't even handle a real weapon without chopping off somebody's tentacle by accident."

"Sorry, I didn't know." Phillip inspected the coffee presented to him by the Drazen ambassador carefully before tasting it. "Hey, this is the best coffee I've ever had!"

"We grind fresh coffee beans that Drazen Foods roasts on Earth and sends directly to the station," Bork told him. "After young Drazen parents learned that sucking on the beans calms finicky babies, coffee has turned into almost as big a money maker as hot sauce." He gave Kelly her usual mug of herbal tea and then settled behind his desk with a steaming metal cup of some beverage that would no doubt have proved fatal to the humans if they took the smallest sip. "Please explain this 'bench ambassador' concept to me again. It sounded intriguing."

"It was my idea," Kelly said. "I wanted to go on sabbatical and I knew that Daniel was too busy to take on my workload. We don't have a big pool of diplomatic trainees in EarthCent, and I thought that rather than appointing temporary acting ambassadors every time somebody goes on a long vacation, we should have some roving ambassadors who can fit into any empty slot."

"And running from post to post so frequently is acceptable to you?" the Drazen asked Phillip.

"A year isn't that short to us," the human reminded the alien. "It's a great way to see more of the galaxy, and now that I've spent a few days on Union Station, I suspect that settling into a new posting with the help of a Stryx librarian won't be that big a deal."

"I understand. I'm sure that Kelly has told you that my door is always open, and I would be honored if you come to me first with any questions you might have about our various interspecies committees."

"She has," Phillip confirmed. "I—"

A piercing claxon drowned out his words, and Bork leapt up from his chair and grabbed a great two-headed battle axe from the wall. "I'm so sorry, duty calls," he cried over his shoulder. "Take your time, Kelly. Security will lock up after you leave."

The EarthCent ambassador, holding both hands over her ears, rose from her seat and went around the Drazen's desk to a light sconce which was flashing red. Then, with a pained look, she removed one of her hands from over an ear and used it to fumble around the bottom of the fixture until the light went out and the claxon cut off.

"What was that all about?" Phillip asked.

"The difference between reenacting and role-playing," Kelly told him with a wry smile. "That's the ambassador's special gig alert. It might be anything from a children's party to a castle assault in Libbyland."

"And the ambassador drops everything and runs when he gets an acting gig?"

"Not during office hours. I don't think he's even officially here today. It's their long weekend, if I recall."

"You're right. Every sixth weekend on the Drazen calendar they take the whole week off," Phillip recalled. "And he just leaves you in his office?"

"Well, I'm certainly not going to steal any of his weapons, and I'm hardly going to plant bugs. EarthCent cooperates with the Drazen Intelligence at our highest level, though I wouldn't be surprised if their home office, as they call their central government, is barely aware of our existence. And unlike EarthCent, the Drazen embassy is staffed by security around the clock. I have no doubt that somebody is watching us as we speak." She paused and pointed at her ear. "Clive and Blythe are asking to meet us for lunch back at the embassy. They're offering take-out for everybody."

"That's the—" Philip lowered his voice, "EarthCent Intelligence people?"

"You don't have to whisper, the Drazens know who they are. In fact, I'm sure that one of these days Clive will be introducing you to Herl, the head of Drazen Intelligence."

A bell sounded and a hologram popped up over Bork's desk showing a figure standing in the corridor outside the

Drazen embassy's doors. The visitor gave up trying to spot the security imaging hardware and settled for lifting the laminated pass that hung from a lanyard around his neck and slowly moving it through an arc above his head.

"For you, Ambassador," a Drazen's voice announced over a hidden speaker.

"Are you talking to me?" Kelly asked.

"There's a Human reporter at our front door requesting to see Bork," the security guard informed her. "I'm not authorized to invite aliens into the embassy when none of the diplomatic staff are present. Perhaps you can go out and talk to him, allowing me to resume my nap."

"Got it." Kelly took a final sip from her tea and motioned to Phillip. "Bring your mug, there's a sink in the hall on our way to the exit."

The main door to the embassy slid open when the two EarthCent diplomats approached. "Bob Steelforth, Galactic Free Press," the waiting reporter identified himself, holding his press pass out for Kelly to inspect. Then his brain caught up with his eyes and he let the badge drop back to his chest on its lanyard.

"You can't come in, they're closed," Kelly said, blocking Bob's attempt to step into the reception area. "Phillip and I were just leaving."

"Then what are you doing here?"

"Ambassador Bork came in specially to meet us but something, uh, urgent came up and he had to run out."

"I was counting on him for a pull-quote," Bob said, his face falling. "I'm writing a feature about your sabbatical, and a comment from an alien ambassador would give me a shot at the full distribution rather than just the Union Station edition."

"I'm a bit surprised you didn't come see me first," Kelly told him as she started for the nearest lift tube.

"I like getting the hard part of the job out of the way before I start writing," Bob said. "I even tried getting a comment from the Fillinducks on my way here, though they rarely talk to reporters, and I got as far as the ambassador's assistant before they showed me the door."

"Don't tell me that the Fillinducks have a problem with your Galactic Free Press credentials?"

"No. The assistant did the old, "What's EarthCent?' routine, and then she said they didn't have time for such foolishness."

"I've never met a Fillinduck," Phillip ventured as the three entered the lift tube.

"EarthCent embassy," Kelly instructed the capsule. "They really don't like us and I don't buy that it's just the way we smell. The Fillinduck ambassador usually skips the interspecies meetings that I attend. Maybe you'll have better luck."

"So as long as I've got you both, how about an interview?" Bob suggested. "I can always try Czeros for a quote later, or maybe I can catch the Vergallian ambassador when their embassy opens. But the truth is, I've been hitting her up for content so often lately that it's hardly newsworthy anymore."

"Why not Srythlan?" Kelly asked. "He practically lives in his office."

"The Verlock ambassador is nice enough, but I can't listen to him for hours just to get a quote. I have deadlines, you know."

"What's your angle for the piece?" Phillip inquired as they exited the lift tube down the corridor from the EarthCent embassy. "Janice showed me the official announcement of our appointment, the one your paper published before we even checked into our hotel, so the ambassador's sabbatical is hardly breaking news."

"I figure I'll make the article a sort of a retrospective on Ambassador McAllister's service, and then I can get a follow-up piece out of your background. You can't be too careful in my business about running out of news."

"I could give you a half an hour later today, Bob, but we're meeting Clive and Blythe at the embassy for an early lunch," Kelly told the reporter. "We need to get Phillip up to speed on EarthCent Intelligence."

"Can I come?" the reporter asked hopefully.

"Don't be greedy. You already have the best intelligence source of any reporter on the paper."

"You?"

Kelly stopped at the door of the EarthCent embassy and shook her head at Bob's innocent look. "This is exactly why you have to be careful around reporters, Phillip. Flattery and obfuscation."

"Did you mean Judith?" Bob asked incredulously. "She never tells me anything. When she gets home from the training camp and I ask her how her day was, she tells me that information is on a need-to-know basis."

"I forgot how gung-ho she is," the ambassador said with a chuckle. "Other than that, any progress in your relationship?"

The reporter glanced over at Phillip before replying. "I think I'll go and see if I can get a pull-quote now, and then I can interview you alone later and not waste Bench Ambassador Hartley's time. Will you be free after lunch?"

"Donna is planning on showing both Phillip and Janice how the embassy accounting system works this afternoon, so an hour from now should be fine."

"Great. I'll ping you," Bob said, and headed back towards the lift tube.

"Seems like a nice guy," Phillip commented. "Is the embassy his beat?"

"Bob's the senior reporter for Union Station so you'll see a lot of him. He lives with Judith, who you'll meet when you come to the training camp." Kelly led Phillip past Donna and Janice, who were up to their elbows in the holographic directory for station services, and continued talking on the way into her office. "Clive is the director of EarthCent Intelligence, and he's married to Blythe, who is Donna's elder daughter. She isn't on the payroll because she bankrolls a good portion of the intelligence budget, but everybody knows she's second in command. Our friend Lynx used to be third, but she sort of lost interest and left on Flower with her husband, Woojin, who I believe is still in charge of strategic planning. Judith used to be a field agent, but she took over from my husband as a training camp instructor, and she does some of Woojin's stuff too. Got it?"

"Are you kidding? I'm still stuck on the fact that your office manager's daughter is funding our intelligence service!"

"She's rich, you know. Blythe founded InstaSitter with her sister Chastity, who owns the Galactic Free Press."

Phillip plopped down in the chair next to Kelly's desk and said, "I need an instant replay here. Who's on third?"

"Lynx used to be on third, but now it's Thomas, an artificial person and a good friend of ours. You'll meet him with Judith when you visit the camp, and I can introduce you to Dring afterward."

"Dring? The Maker?" Phillip asked, his voice rising.

"He lives in our junkyard. Well, it's not a junkyard anymore, more like a second-hand alien spaceship business since Aisha bought a lot of abandoned ships at a Stryx auction. Our whole family lives there."

"The Aisha from the children's show?"

The office doors slid open and Blythe stuck her head in. "Busy? We walked right past mom without her even seeing us."

"Come right in. Bring chairs."

Blythe continued into the office first, and Clive appeared a few seconds later, carrying a spare chair from the reception area under each arm. "With all the meetings you have in here you could buy a few more chairs," he suggested. "It's not like you're using the space for anything else."

"But I don't want my office to become the default meeting room," Kelly said. "Libby promised to hold the space next door when the travel agency moves. Then we can finally expand and have a real conference room like all the other embassies. I just have to convince the president to raise our budget. Hey, where's the food?"

"I'm pretty sure that's what mom and her understudy were busy doing when we came in. I pinged her right after we talked to you, and she's probably showing Janice every place we've ever ordered from on the station."

"Oh, that makes sense. I was just getting Phillip up to speed on who everybody is. Maybe I should give him a week to recover before I bring him home and introduce him around Mac's Bones."

"Don't feel bad if you're a bit overwhelmed," Clive told Kelly's replacement. "I married into this mess and I still can't believe it at times."

118

"So speaks the man who just found out he has a long-lost sister," Blythe retorted.

"My mind went into overload back when the ambassador said that the Galactic Free Press belongs to your sister and that the two of you founded InstaSitter," Phillip said. "I just don't see the connection between babysitting, spying, and journalism."

"Intelligence work and newspaper reporting are practically the same things, and Chastity is always poaching our agents. Babysitting pays the bills, plus it gets the aliens to take us seriously."

"Come again?"

"I don't want to steal Kelly's thunder, but you're going to find that when the other ambassadors contact you, there's usually a business issue at the bottom of it."

"And it's the aliens we're here to talk to you about," Clive added. "Kelly said you were in Bork's office when we pinged, so what did you make of him?"

"We barely had a chance to sit down before he grabbed an axe and ran off somewhere," Phillip said. "He did make a great cup of coffee."

"His friend, Glunk, was one of the first alien entrepreneurs to open a major business on Earth. Drazen Foods is the largest exporter of agricultural products on the planet today. If you need something shipped out from Earth that the Stryx won't accept for the diplomatic bag, the president's office can usually get the Drazens to throw it in with a cargo of hot sauce or coffee beans."

"Didn't I hear something about our people reverse-engineering a Drazen jump ship?"

"An early one, under contract to the Drazen museum for the history of space travel, though our people have to do the work at Glunk's factory city because the museum's board insists that the ship remains in Drazen custody."

"So what can you tell me about Bork?" the bench ambassador asked.

"Very sympathetic to humanity, but as with the other species, business always comes first with the Drazens," Clive said. "While he's a fanatic for battle reenactments, he's also convinced that there are ample opportunities to keep his people challenged for the foreseeable future within the bounds of the tunnel network, so he doesn't favor pouring funds into colony ships. That puts him at odds with the majority of the Drazen diplomatic corps who see expanding their area of control as the easiest way to create economic activity."

"I thought that the tunnel network rules prohibit conquest."

"They do, but the galaxy is full of unoccupied or abandoned worlds that can be terraformed. It's mainly a question of economic justification, especially when the Dollnicks can probably do a better job for less money."

"I'll bet they can," Phillip proudly said of his former employers. "How are our official relations with the Dollnicks on the station?"

"Reasonable," Kelly told him. "I don't think that Crute ever took me seriously, in part because I'm female, but he hasn't actively opposed our interests in years. They didn't object to the Stryx arranging for us to lease Flower, and I know that the factory on Earth licensed to produce human-optimized floaters with Dollnick technology runs around the clock."

"We're hoping Phillip will be able to help us cultivate a closer relationship with Dollnick Intelligence," Blythe said. "We're trying to crack down on corrupt labor contractors, and if we could get the Dollys to play along rather than refusing shady deals outright, it would make it easier to build court cases."

"You want the Dollnicks to negotiate with the bad guys?"

"We want to stamp out the practice before the crooked human agencies figure out a way around alien ethical standards through creating mazes of subcontractors or falsifying balloon payments. Our greatest fear is that our crooks hook up with pirates to send human laborers beyond the tunnel network where protections are spotty at best."

"I can whistle a couple hundred words in Dollnick and I participated in labor negotiations when I ran a crew, so maybe I'll have better luck with Crute than Ambassador McAllister," Phillip said. "What kind of budget do we have for bribes?"

Kelly laughed outright at her replacement's sense of humor, and then realized she was the only one doing so. "Are you serious?"

"Showing up empty-handed to ask a favor from a Dolly is like saying that you consider his status to be so low that you can boss him around," Phillip explained. "I always carried a tin of Sheezle larvae on the job site, just to have a little something to offer the equipment operators to chew on if I had to ask them to do anything that wasn't specifically included in the work order."

"I can give you a budget for gifts related to EarthCent Intelligence activities," Blythe said. "Just don't put anybody on retainer without checking with us first. We consider that to be recruitment and we'd need to assign a handler, especially since you'll only be on the station for the length of Kelly's sabbatical."

"If the Dollnicks are willing to play along and pass us recordings of meetings with dirty labor contractors as evidence, do we even have jurisdiction to do anything?"

"Possession is nine-tenths of the law," Clive said. "As long as we can grab the bad actors and get them back to Earth, the court system there can deal with them. The president's office always had authority to create a judiciary for dealing with interstellar crimes, but until we started building up EarthCent Intelligence, there wasn't any enforcement mechanism. Now we're pushing ahead with it, and the alien businesses on Earth are helping where they can because criminal activity is bad for their profits."

Eleven

"How cool is this?" Jonah demanded and made a fist. The chunky memory-metal bracelet on his right wrist instantly transformed itself into a small, round shield. "And it's been ensorcelled by a Verlock mage to attract missile weapons!"

"It would have to be," Vivian told her twin brother. "I've been reading through the LARPing catalogs, and while bucklers are handy for dueling, you'd need incredibly fast reactions to deflect an arrow with one."

"How many gold coins?" Samuel asked.

Jonah relaxed his fist and the buckler shrank back down into a bracelet. "Thirty thousand," he said. "Did anybody check the virtual gold to creds exchange rate?"

"It's just over a hundred to one, so you're talking three hundred creds. I wonder why it's so expensive?"

"Must be the enchantment," Vivian said. "It's no good for us anyway because it's not a noodle shield. You can't mix noodle weapons and real weapons in LARPs or somebody could really get hurt."

"Who uses real weapons in LARPs?" Jonah asked.

"Verlocks, when they play by themselves. Of course, they fight in slow motion, so maybe it doesn't matter."

"Hey, Humans," Jorb said, joining the group. "Looks like I'm not the late one for a change."

123

"Marilla is in the changing room trying on a blouse with scale armor," Vivian informed him.

"Noodle?" the Drazen asked.

"Yes, and it's actually pretty cheap."

"I wouldn't mind picking up a chainmail tentacle sheath if anybody sees one. I tried an old-style scale one, basically bits of noodle plate sewn onto a sleeve, but it wasn't flexible enough."

"There's something funny about all of this stuff," Samuel observed from where he was crouched sorting through a bargain bin of supposedly enchanted objects. "It reminds me of the collection of random household junk they keep at the training camp to teach trading basics to potential field agents."

"Ask the woman running the booth," Vivian suggested.

"She was here a minute ago," Jonah said, looking around. "Oh, there she is, in front of the next booth over."

A tall female humanoid dressed in a loose-fitting housecoat and wearing a beekeeper's hat with black netting elbowed a Grenouthian out of the way and approached the teens. A long straw pierced the lid of the oversized takeout coffee she had just purchased from the pushcart stand which was operated by students in the intramural LARPing league to raise funds for studio time.

"Excuse me," Samuel asked politely. "I was wondering if you could tell me what these objects do?" He held up the last item he had examined, a plastic ladle.

The vendor turned to the ambassador's son and seemed to freeze for a moment. Then she reached up and touched the heavy veil obscuring her features as if to make sure it was still in place before answering, "You serve soup with that one."

"Yes, I know that, but the sign says it's enchanted."

"Anybody who eats the soup will fall into a deep sleep."

"Really? How about this," he asked, holding up what appeared to be a box of tissue.

"That shouldn't be in there," the woman said, snatching it away from the teen. As the vendor extended her arm, Vivian thought she caught a glimpse of feathers beneath the cuff of the housecoat's sleeve.

"And this pot lid?" Samuel inquired, holding up the cheap aluminum item by the little round handle.

"A magical shield. It reflects any curse back on the caster at twice the potency."

"Then why is it in the bargain bin?" Vivian demanded.

"Because my brief time on the LARP fair circuit has taught me that you silly players care more about appearances than results," the vendor replied bitterly. "If I had known, I never would have wasted my time and talents enchanting this garbage."

"You're a mage? I thought the Verlocks were the only ones who can perform magic."

"Ha!" the woman barked, and then shocked her audience by blinking out of existence and reappearing on the other side of the table. "Now are you going to buy something or shall I turn you all into newts?" As she raised both of her hands to shoulder height and began to perform some intricate casting, her sleeves fell back to reveal fully feathered arms and a dark black bracelet on her wrist.

"Baa?" Samuel asked, attempting to make out her features by squinting through the heavy netting suspended from the brim of her hat. "Is that you?"

"Keep it down," the Teragram mage hissed, dropping her arms and her voice simultaneously. "None of these superstitious twits will buy my stuff if they find out what I am."

125

"I don't get it. Jeeves still complains about the size of the bribe Libby made him pay you to vacate our couch after my mom invited you to stay. We thought you left for some primitive planet to buy your way into a pantheon."

"I was betrayed," Baa said mournfully, her hands involuntarily clenching into fists as she spoke. She motioned for the young people to approach closer and then she touched her bracelet. The background sound from all of the visitors and vendors at the LARP fair faded away as they stepped into the acoustic bubble that formed, and then the Teragram mage triggered some kind of recording to play back.

"It's a sure thing," a honeyed male voice said persuasively. "With the creds you extorted from that Stryx youngster, I can finally perfect my inter-dimensional displacer and we'll be the most powerful techno-mages in history."

"You got conned?" Jorb asked.

"Watch your mouth, boy, or I'll turn your tentacle into a trunk." The Drazen covered his nose with his hand and tucked his tentacle down the back of his jacket.

"Was the mage your boyfriend?" Vivian asked.

"If you could only see him when he fans his feathers…" Baa said in a dreamy voice, which trailed off as her whole body shivered from the sense memory.

"Aren't you worried about Jeeves finding out that you're back on the station?" Samuel asked.

"That child?" Baa sniffed. "We've already met and come to an amicable arrangement to share the galaxy between us. I'm just here to sell off my stock so I can be finished with this miserable retail existence."

"And this stuff really works?"

126

"Guaranteed. Go ahead, pick something out for yourself. I've been here for hours and nobody is buying from the bargain bin anyway."

"Does the little backpack on the table do anything?" Vivian asked, pointing at a small leather bag featuring straps studded with metal rivets.

"I'm only giving away the things in the bin," Baa told her. "I paid forty creds for that pack before enchanting it."

"I have virtual gold, money too," Vivian said. "What does it do other than holding stuff."

"Nothing," the mage said. "I'll let you have it for two hundred creds."

"What? You just said you paid forty!"

"And in any LARP on the tunnel network that pack will hold fifty different items with no limit on the quantity of each item."

"She means it's a bag of holding," Jonah said. "They're pretty valuable."

"What do you mean about no limit on quantity?" Vivian asked.

"Exactly what I said. The pack holds fifty unique items in any quantity, so whether you put in one spear or a thousand, it's all the same." Baa picked up the small black pack by one of its straps and began swinging it slowly back and forth like a pendulum, perhaps attempting to hypnotize the girl. "Did I mention that it preserves all of your possessions if you die? You want this."

"Buy it if you like it, Viv," her twin advised. "I can loan you the money if you're short. Tinka just paid me for the time I spent beta-testing."

"I have the money, but it feels like cheating," the girl said. "I mean, two hundred creds is twenty thousand in virtual gold. We've done two of the university LARPs and we haven't earned a thousand between us."

"Gold is much easier to make in normal role-playing games where there are plenty of monsters to kill," Jonah told her. "You'll probably be the only one at your university LARPs with a bag of holding."

"One-eighty," Baa offered.

"Go ahead, Vivian," Samuel said. "You can carry all of our stuff for us."

"What about the weight?" the girl asked suspiciously. "Will I be able to lift it with a thousand spears inside?"

"Make it two hundred and I'll throw in a ninety percent weight reduction," Baa replied, and stopped swinging the pack. "Just give me a minute." The mage put both of her hands on the leather backpack and began mumbling under her breath. The runes inscribed in her bracelet began to glow and the lights in the exhibition hall briefly dimmed. "There," she said, tossing the pack to Vivian.

"Did you just tap into the station's power grid to enchant my pack?" the girl asked.

"Maybe. Where's my two hundred creds?"

"In my purse," Vivian said. She glanced inside the pack to make sure that Baa wasn't sticking her with a dead body or somebody's recycling and then slipped into the shoulder straps, so it hung in the middle of her back. Then she unsnapped the flap on her SBJ Fashions purse and fished out her programmable cred from its special pocket. "Here."

"I don't have a register," the mage informed her. "You'll have to get cash somewhere."

"Any suggestions?" Samuel asked.

"The coffee cart is charging one percent to—oh, what is it now?" Baa demanded in irritation as Jeeves appeared with an audible pop.

"It seems that somebody borrowed a cup of gigawatts from the station grid and I instantly thought of you. Gryph sent me to warn you not to do it again."

"My booth rental included power," she shot back.

"Read the fine print," Jeeves retorted, and projected a dense block of holographic text. "Power draw not to exceed three billion joules/second for longer than one second. Surcharges may apply."

"You know I'm broke," Baa said sullenly. "Besides, it was for the Human. You Stryx like them."

"Maybe we like them because they don't place reckless demands on our infrastructure. Gryph will let it go this time, but if you try it again without notifying him, you won't enjoy the results."

"Hey, Marilla," Samuel said, intentionally stepping into the path of the staring match between the Stryx and the Teragram mage as he greeted the girl. "That armor looks great on you."

"I think it's too restrictive," the girl complained. "The elbows are all right, but when I try to rotate my shoulders, the scales kind of bunch up." She demonstrated the issue by wind-milling both of her arms, forcing Jorb to jump back to avoid getting hit. "But it was really a bargain, so I bought it, and I'm going to cut off some of the shoulder scales."

"I can fix that," Baa offered. "Twenty creds."

"The blouse only cost thirty," the Horten girl retorted.

"Five," the mage counter-offered. "And I'll throw in any single object from the bargain bin."

"Deal," Marilla said. "I'll go take it off."

"You don't have to remove it. Just come closer."

"Remember," Jeeves said in warning.

"Resizing a few hundred noodle scales won't require more than a couple gazillion electrons," the mage said, placing her hands on the Horten's shoulders. The black bracelet flared to life and the lights in the exhibition hall remained steady. "Five creds," Baa demanded, holding out her hand.

Marilla swung her arms to rotate her shoulders through their full range of motion and even tried a move that looked like a baseball pitch. "Great. Do you take programmable creds?"

"I'll get it," Samuel said, moving in front of the Horten girl and handing the glowering mage a coin. "Are you going to pick something from the bin? I've got a magical curse deflector," he added, displaying his dented pot lid.

"No, you take mine. It's only fair since you paid for my fitting."

"May I examine that?" Jeeves asked, extending his pincer towards Samuel. The ambassador's son handed the Stryx the pot lid and returned to rummaging through the bin. "Interesting. May I inquire why you chose this particular probability density?" he inquired of the mage.

"For a thousand creds," Baa said immediately.

"It's not that interesting," Jeeves told her, dropping the lid like a hot coal.

"What does this do?" Samuel asked, holding up an enormous pink rubber eraser.

"In my experience it creates gouges in paper even if I'm being gentle," the mage replied.

"I mean the magic effect."

"It removes curses from certain object classes."

"Does that include circlets?"

"Not if they're made from precious metals."

"I think it's pure iron."

"Then the eraser will do the job," Baa said. "It does, however, require a short recharge cycle between uses."

"How long is short?" Samuel asked, recalling that the Teragram mage had spent almost six thousand years sleeping off a broken heart before being discovered in the wall of Paul's newly acquired habitat.

"A century in your years, but consider the price."

"She's got a point," Jorb said. "If you can clear the curse from the circlet of power you showed us, I'll wear it if you won't."

"Here," Vivian said to Baa, returning from the coffee cart with a handful of twenty-cred coins. "What are you doing with the giant eraser, Sam?"

"It's Marilla's freebie. I'm going to use it to de-curse the circlet, though after that it's worthless for a hundred years."

"When's the last time it was used?" she asked, counting out two hundred creds for the mage.

"I don't know." Samuel turned back to Baa. "When was the last time it was used?"

"Give it here," the Teragram said with a sigh. "I'll just need a minute to reset the timer."

"Is that Yvandi with Grude trying out those broadswords?" Vivian asked Jorb.

"Sure is," the Drazen replied, and putting two fingers in his mouth, gave a piercing whistle. The Dollnick student immediately looked over, giving the tall Sharf girl the opportunity she needed to behead him, except the noodle weapon merely wrapped around his neck and drooped down his chest. Then the two aliens handed the swords to the next pair of students waiting to have a go, and made their way over to Baa's booth.

"Hello, Sir Jeeves," Grude greeted the Stryx, who he had met while serving on Samuel and Vivian's student committee for Flower. "Hey, guys. Sorry I've been skipping the dojo lately, Jorb, but I signed up for a LARP with Yvandi and some friends of hers and I barely have time to get my homework done these days."

"Medieval quest?" the Drazen asked enviously.

"Capture the Queen," Yvandi told him. "It's an old Horten table game based on raiding a Vergallian tech-ban world, but it's recently been adopted for LARPing. What are you guys playing?"

"We're not," Jorb responded bitterly. "We signed up for the LARP elective and it's just Jeeves—"

"Remember your non-disclosure agreement," Vivian cautioned him, indicating the Stryx with a nod of her head.

"Well, I can say that it's not fun, can't I?"

"You get university credit?" Grude asked.

"It's a regular course," Vivian told him. "They're starting new ones all the time. You guys can sign up too, but you need a group of four."

Jorb shook his head vigorously in the negative.

The Dollnick student took the hint and said, "Uh, maybe next year. Why don't you guys come on one of our raids? We've got a big enough group so that it's down to twenty creds an hour each, and it only gets cheaper when more players sign up."

"Twenty creds an hour?" Samuel asked in dismay. "That's what I earn for a full shift at my work/study job, though tips are up because we've been getting more customers since the LARPing craze hit the station. The weapons dropped in the league studios are brought to the lost-and-found."

"I seem to have misplaced a number of things myself recently," Baa said innocently. "Can I just come in and browse through the inventory?"

"You have to be able to describe the item to whoever is working. Only employees are allowed behind the counter, and the Stryx security imaging for the station is available to confirm claims."

"Never mind."

"You're a Teragram mage, I just paid you two hundred creds in cash, and you've probably been selling stuff all morning," Vivian said in exasperation. "Why are you talking like some centee-less labor contract runaway?"

Yvandi and Grude both flinched at the girl's words, and the Dollnick reached in a belt pouch and threw a pinch of a white crystalline substance that might have been salt over his shoulder.

"Keep it to yourselves," Baa growled at the aliens. "And you," she turned to Vivian, "are you trying to put me out of business? I just gave you a great deal on that pack."

"Sorry, I forgot they were all scared of your kind. I just don't get why somebody with your obvious abilities would be reduced to making false claims at the lost-and-found."

"If you had lived as long as I have you'd know that multi-species lost-and-founds are a great place to refresh your wardrobe. Everything is always in fashion somewhere."

"You sound like my sister," Samuel said, and then he burst out laughing.

"What's so funny," Vivian asked him.

"I just had a thought," the teen said. "Rather than avoiding Jeeves for the rest of your life, Baa, why don't you make a deal to pay him back with work? I'm not into clothes myself, but SBJ Fashions has all sorts of stuff you could cast spells on. I'll bet there are plenty of players with money who would rather wear a designer cloak that protects them from arrows than some stiff leather armor."

"I almost bought a brand-name hat that offered a ten percent increase in intelligence for stats-based games, but it cost way too much, and I already have a game hat that I like," Yvandi said, touching the brim of her headgear. "How much would you charge for an enchantment like that?"

"A hundred creds," Baa replied promptly.

"Oh, I was hoping more like twenty."

"Twenty," the mage agreed. "Toss me the hat."

"Wait a minute," Jeeves said, intercepting the hat with his pincer and spinning to face the mage. "Let's get a few things straight. If you're going to work for SBJ Fashions, we require exclusivity."

"We can discuss that right after I complete my contractual bargain with the young Sharf," Baa said, holding out her hand for the hat. "I haven't agreed to anything yet, and I need to earn some more ready money if I'm going to be able to retain an attorney to review whatever ridiculous employment contract you ask me to sign."

"She's pretty sharp," Jonah commented to his sister. "Mom would like her."

Twelve

"Come in, come in," Dorothy greeted the Frunge attorney. "You've got great timing."

"Flazint appears to be busy," Tzachan mumbled, tightening his grip on an ancient valise that looked like it had been passed down from his ancestors. "I could come back in—"

"Nonsense," the ambassador's daughter interrupted, and grabbing his free arm, dragged the shy alien into the design room. A rarely used 3D modeling machine languished in the corner, and Flazint had a small metallurgical laboratory set up against one wall. "She's just experimenting with coatings for silver thread to keep it shiny or something."

"I wouldn't want to interfere with—"

"Flazint!" Dorothy called loudly, and followed up by throwing a pincushion at the back of her fellow designer's lab coat. "Company's here."

The Frunge girl carefully set down the beaker of bubbling liquid she had been about to pour and pulled off the head-and-shoulders shroud that she wore for protection while working with chemicals. Her hair vines were wrapped in a tight bun to reduce the chance of accidental damage, and her hands and arms were covered with heavy gauntlets.

"You have to stop throwing pincushions at me while I'm working," she complained, while lowering a metal hood down over her experiment. "Just ping me."

"Tzachan is here," Dorothy repeated, maintaining a tight grip on the attorney's wrist. "I'm going to go get the conference room ready and find Shaina and Brinda, so you show him what we do. Don't forget to see me for a fitting before you go," she instructed the alien, and then slipped past him into the reception area.

"I'm sorry for interrupting your work," Tzachan apologized. He suddenly realized that his newly freed hand had nothing to do, and he vacillated between moving it behind his back and attempting to strike a casual pose like the models he had seen in corridor advertisements. After a moment's hesitation, he tried to insert the hand into his suit jacket pocket, but it seemed to be sewed closed just below the flap. To the Frunge girl, it looked like he was scratching himself below the ribs.

"I wasn't doing anything important," she said, taking a small step in his direction and accidentally kicking the pincushion, which bounced off a stool and rolled to a stop between the attorney's shoes. The hair vines of both of the Frunge turned dark green in embarrassment. Then Flazint's eyes went wide with horror. "Dorothy closed the door on her way out?"

The attorney spun around and stared at the offending door. The ambassador's daughter had waved it shut as she left, meaning that he was alone in an enclosed space with an unmarried woman who wasn't a family member.

"I'm so sorry," he apologized, frantically waving at the door, which didn't respond since he was too far inside the room. "What's wrong with the thing? Is it locked?"

"Even Dorothy wouldn't do this intentionally," Flazint said, unwilling to accept that her friend's alien sense of humor might indeed stoop so low. "Try stepping closer. We keep the proximity fields tight so that the door doesn't slide open every time somebody visits the business office."

Tzachan practically leapt into the door, which responded by sliding open on an empty hallway. He stuck his head out and looked both ways. "I don't think anybody saw," he told the girl.

"Then it didn't happen," Flazint said. "Humans have a different sense of propriety than we do, but we're friends, and she doesn't mean anything by it."

The Frunge attorney relaxed a little on hearing how sensibly the girl was behaving. He'd heard of cases where a male had entered a room unaware that a female was present and ended up in honor court over damages to her reputation, though of course, that could only happen if there were witnesses. "You're dressed very differently than the last time I saw you," he said in an attempt at small talk.

"That was my first time in a LARP, you know," she replied, her hair vines coloring up again. "I didn't know anybody would see me, other than my friends."

Tzachan suddenly recalled that she had seen him with the seat torn out of his pants, and he cursed himself for having brought up the subject. The two Frunge stood silently for a minute, trying to figure out how they should act in the absence of a chaperone, and then Dorothy returned.

"Brinda is ready, and Shaina isn't coming in because it's Parents Day at Mikey's school, so we can start the meeting as soon as Jeeves gets here."

"Stryx Jeeves will be attending our meeting?" Tzachan asked, snapping out of his haze of social confusion.

137

"He's the majority owner and we all find that life goes smoother if we pretend that he's running everything. Did you give Zach the grand tour, Flazint?"

"I was just about to start, it took me a minute to clean up," she said, gesturing at her work area. "Tzachan waited in the doorway," she added for the sake of propriety.

"Don't let her ignore you, Zach," Dorothy said, giving the attorney a playful push in her friend's direction. "I'll just run out and—"

"NO!" both of the Frunge cried at the same time, and then tried to cover up with nervous laughter.

"I guess I can stay if you're having trouble controlling yourselves," the human girl teased the aliens, but immediately felt bad when she saw the expression of shocked disbelief on Flazint's face. "I'm just kidding. Come over here, Zach, and I'll get a start on your fitting while she changes. You're still wearing a lab coat, Flazz."

Flazint fled behind the changing partition to recover her wits while the alien attorney followed Dorothy to the fitting area. The corner of the room used for taking measurements was empty except for a grid painted on both walls and a device reminiscent of a periscope that came down from the ceiling. "Do I have to empty my pockets?" he asked nervously.

"No, it's a completely passive scan, but don't ask me how it works. Flazint could probably explain it. Just hold your arms out from your sides—it would be better if you put down your briefcase—that's it, and turn around slowly."

"You caught me by surprise earlier with your offer of a suit of clothes. As much as I appreciate the gesture, I don't think it's appropriate, especially since I haven't been officially retained yet. I hope you aren't offended."

"That's fine, I just like getting everybody's measurements," Dorothy said brightly. "So what kind of dancing do you prefer?"

"Excuse me?"

"It's a hypothetical question. Say you were at an alien wedding and there was a Horten band playing Vergallian ballroom instrumentals. Would you be freaked out if you had to dance?"

"My parents made me attend Astria's Academy of Dance on the station when I was a shrub," Tzachan admitted. "I was the only Frunge in the class."

"Ahhh," Dorothy breathed, rapidly formulating a psychoanalytic profile for the shy lawyer. "You must have been traumatized trying to keep up with the steps while wearing those boots with the dirt in them."

"It wasn't much fun," the alien acknowledged. "Do you have everything you need?"

"Yes, you can put your arms down. Flazint? Are you coming out or do I have to send this brave man in to fetch you?"

"Stop being a brat," the Frunge girl called back, "I'll just be another minute."

"Actually, I have a question for you," Tzachan said, trying to buy time for the Frunge girl so that Dorothy wouldn't say something else inappropriate. "I noticed earlier today that there's something wrong with my suit pocket. I suppose I never had a reason to use it before."

"Let me see," the ambassador's daughter said, and before the attorney could remove the jacket and hand it over, she was examining the garment as if he were a mannequin. "Oh, this is hilarious. The pocket doesn't work because there isn't one. The maker just sewed a flap to the front of your jacket. Is this a Frunge style?"

"I wouldn't know," Tzachan said. "My parents buy my clothes."

"Stop torturing him," Flazint said, stepping out from behind the changing screen. Her lab coat was gone and she had freed her hair vines from the tight bun and somehow woven them through a modest trellis in record time. "Don't let her upset you, Tzachan. She's like that with everybody."

"Is Dorothy giving our prospective legal representative a hard time?" Jeeves demanded as he floated through the door.

"They're ganging up on me," the ambassador's daughter said innocently. "You know how clubby the Frunge are."

"Brinda is waiting in the conference room so let's get started." Jeeves put his words into action by leading the way out of the design room. "Dorothy and Affie tell me that you're a genius with intellectual property, Tzachan."

"I don't know where they got that idea, sir. We've only met once and—"

"His philosophy on brand value is inspiring," Dorothy interrupted. "Tell him, Zach."

"It's just that I believe creators should be rewarded for their investment," the attorney said. "I've represented clients whose businesses were on the brink of failing due to brand piracy even as their innovations were coming to dominate the markets. My firm recently hired an artificial private detective on Chintoo to look into the less reputable manufacturing operations, but I find it difficult to imagine that they would attempt to cheat you, sir."

Jeeves acknowledged this observation with a little bobbing motion and floated to his place at the head of the conference room table as the others filed in behind him.

Tzachan took the seat Dorothy indicated, and Flazint brought him a cup of Frunge tea from the sideboard. The attorney accepted the drink and even smacked his lips politely with the first sip, despite the fact he never drank the stuff because it bothered his digestion. Then he set the cup aside and drew a bonded tab and stylus from his valise, enabling the confidential note-taking mode.

"My partners in SBJ Fashions, Shaina and Brinda, handle our marketing and sales," Jeeves began. "Our contracted manufacturing facility is on Chintoo, though our bespoke lines are hand-finished here on the station. As you correctly observed, my involvement in the business keeps our contractors from manufacturing goods for the piracy markets. Unfortunately, my elders made it clear to me when I entered this business that it would be inappropriate for me to take an active role in any type of enforcement activity, whether collecting unpaid bills or protecting our intellectual property."

"We do see a little leakage of factory seconds, but that's figured into the bid cost," Brinda added. "Our main problem has been with look-alikes as opposed to direct piracy. For example, some of the bazaar sellers on Flower, EarthCent's circuit ship, have been selling knock-offs of our basic items branded with a '581' tag."

"By basic, you mean…"

"Travel cloaks, hats with ribbons, tube dresses. Styles that aren't unique to our brand, though we like to think that we do them better."

"I know we do," Dorothy interjected.

"And the '581' tag?" Tzachan asked.

"Here are a few images our friends on Flower have forwarded to us," Brinda continued, and activated the conference room screen. "You see that the '5' is a bit rounded, like the 'S' in our logo, the '8' is kind of flattened on the left side, so you could mistake it for a 'B', and there's just enough of a bump on the base of the '1' that you could easily take it as a 'J', especially if that's what you're expecting."

"I see where that would present confusion, especially for non-Humanese readers," the Frunge attorney concurred. "That bump on the last digit—"

"They make it look like a sewing glitch," Dorothy said angrily. "It's really just one thick piece of thread that gets looped over and stitched down, as if somebody pulled the label out before the machine controller completed the sequence."

"Have any of these knock-offs showed up on the stations?"

"Not yet," Brinda said. "The boutiques wouldn't touch them in any case since their business model depends on brands. My father works on the open market deck and he's been keeping an eye out for us, but it seems like the 581 crowd are avoiding the Stryx stations."

"That makes sense," Tzachan said. "I reviewed the intellectual property treaty to which Earth is a party before coming today, and your protections are limited as contrasted to the other species. This is due in part to your status as probationary members of the tunnel network, and in part because of your failures to meet your obligations under the existing treaty."

"Could you give some examples?"

"Certainly," the attorney said, and switched screens on his tab. "The numbers involved make me suspicious that Humans are blissfully unaware that the alien home entertainment systems they are purchasing are required by tunnel network law to log viewings of pirated content for reporting. The current tally of pending complaints is in the hundreds of trillions, which is quite impressive for a species that barely numbers ten billion."

"Why would the home entertainment systems show pirated content in the first place?' Dorothy asked. "It's almost like entrapment."

"Precisely," Tzachan said. "Tunnel network species abandoned encryption for protecting intellectual content many millions of years ago, since it only pushed the problem underground. The bulk of the complaints I've seen filed against humanity are coming from the Vergallian Guild of Drama Producers for back-episodes of some of their longer running serials."

"So the Vergallians will hardly be in the mood to cooperate if we need their help with trademark dilution," Brinda concluded.

"Despite the treaty, intellectual property protection has always been hit-or-miss, even with the advanced species. For example, we have a client who writes a bestselling book about low-temperature welding that has been widely pirated by several species, both on and off the tunnel network. Our most successful enforcement efforts occur where we can offer something in return. While the Hortens have a treaty obligation to cooperate with our enforcement efforts, we didn't make any headway until one of their publishers of gaming guides approached us for help when they realized how many unauthorized copies were being made by Frunge. In the end, we negotiated a cross-licensing deal, so our client now publishes a local version of the gaming guides and the Horten publisher started a sideline in metal fabrication techniques."

"But we don't want another fashion house producing our clothes," Dorothy pointed out. "It's not just about the label, we really do make clothes differently. Our heels have more patents pending than some spaceships."

"I wasn't suggesting cross-licensing agreements for your business, just giving an example," Tzachan said. "In the light of what Stryx Jeeves told me about his artificially imposed limitations in this matter and the generally poor behavior of Humans vis-a-vis the intellectual property of other species, I would recommend that we concentrate on protecting your brand on the stations. If we start now, we can stay ahead of the curve, and playing catch-up is nearly impossible in these cases. Unless I'm mistaken about the scale of your operations, you have plenty of room to grow on Stryx stations before it becomes an issue."

"That's exactly what Shaina and I have been discussing," Brinda said. "Our market research shows that we have growing brand recognition on the stations, thanks to a giveaway we staged with InstaSitter a couple of years ago, but the follow-on sales were mainly through our catalog operation. We have a long way to go with getting our full line into boutiques on every station, and we've been hesitating over making that investment for fear of wide-spread knock-offs."

"Has anybody duplicated these heels you mentioned?" the attorney asked, turning to Dorothy.

"I'd like to see them try," she said. "The Verlock scientist who designed—"

"Verlock?" Tzachan interrupted. "Did he take out the patents?"

"His name is on all of them, even the gathering mechanism for long dresses that was my idea."

"But were the patents filed in Verlock courts or here on the station?"

"Jeeves?" Brinda asked.

"Both," the Stryx replied. "Drilyenth had already filed patents on his homeworld for the basic heel innovations before we acquired them, and he insisted that we continue to file Verlock patents for any technology he licenses to us exclusively."

"That's fantastic news," Tzachan told them. "Everybody is afraid of offending the Verlocks, even the Vergallians, so we should be safe on that front. I'd like to draw up a campaign for protecting your brand on the stations, starting with logo education, and if possible, including your personal stories. If you provide customers of your bespoke line with immersive footage of your design process, you add value and piracy protection at the same time."

"How will holographic video protect us from piracy?" Flazint asked.

"Your customers will play back the immersive footage on their home entertainment systems," the attorney explained. "If the source is copied, we'll get a report, just as if we were producing dramas."

"That's settled, then," Jeeves announced. "Brinda will handle your retainer, Tzachan, and I look forward to seeing the details of your campaign when you draw it up."

"An honor, Stryx Jeeves," the attorney replied, and stood while his new client exited the conference room.

"How about a little privacy while I discuss Tzachan's billing arrangements with him," Brinda hinted.

"Right," Dorothy said, popping up from her chair. "Come on, Flazint. You don't want him to think that we're nosey."

"I would never make that error," the attorney said, bowing slightly in the Frunge girl's direction as she followed Dorothy out.

"Well?" the ambassador's daughter demanded as soon as the door closed behind them. "What do you think?"

"Everything he said made a great deal of sense to me, and I think it would be neat for our customers to see us working on new designs."

"Not that," Dorothy moaned in frustration. "I mean, what do you think about *him*?"

"He seemed very professional."

"Are you trying to irritate me? Didn't I tell you everything about David and Kevin?"

"I just met him, Dorothy. Well, twice, but I don't know anything about his family—"

"His parents buy his suits," Dorothy interrupted. "How much more do you need to know?"

"—and my own family doesn't even know he exists. We don't rush these things."

"Oh, sure. My wedding is only four weeks away, but you just take your time. Maybe you'll have a date by the time my daughter's wedding rolls around."

Flazint fled into the design room and triggered the door lock, leaving Dorothy standing alone in the hall. A wicked smile crossed the girl's face, and instead of calling Libby to override the lock, she slipped out of the SBJ Fashions office and began studying the ads on the display panels as if she didn't have a care in the world. A few minutes later, her patience was rewarded as she heard Brinda bidding the Frunge goodbye at the door. Dorothy intercepted the attorney on his way to the lift tube.

"So?" she demanded.

"In reference to?" he asked in reply, obviously puzzled.

"Flazint," Dorothy said. "Do you like her?"

The Frunge stared for a moment, and then looked down at his feet as if he was wondering why they didn't take him away from the crazy woman, but they betrayed him.

"She's very nice," he admitted.

"Here," Dorothy said, pushing a custom-made ticket to her Jack-and-Jill party into his hand. "If any of your overbearing relatives give you grief, you can tell them that I invited all of the attorneys representing SBJ Fashions."

"A LARP party?" he asked, impressing Dorothy with his ability to read the invitation, though it was likely that as an inter-species attorney, his implant would be loaded with translation algorithms. "That's very kind of you, but—"

"Flazint will be there, guaranteed."

"Oh." He raised his head, really looking Dorothy in the eyes for the first time. "Thank you."

Thirteen

"Phillip. Come in," Kelly greeted her replacement. "I was just about to make tea, but Joe has coffee brewing if you prefer."

"Is that really a dog?" the bench ambassador asked, holding his position in the door of the ice harvester and pointing at Beowulf. "More importantly, has it eaten anybody yet today?"

"He's a Cayl hound, but his spirit was reincarnated from a genetically engineered cross with a mastiff, and there are times you could almost mistake him for an Earth dog," Joe said.

"Except for being twice the size of the biggest dog I've ever seen," Phillip pointed out without moving from his spot.

"Just walk around him," Kelly said. "He doesn't eat people even when he's hungry, and I know that for a fact because he's always hungry."

"Welcome to Union Station," Joe added. "My wife tells me that you're her ticket to a year's vacation, and she's certainly earned it by now. I figure you for a coffee man."

"You figure correct," Phillip confirmed, taking the seat indicated by the ambassador's husband. "Interesting place you have here."

"Thanks, it's a work in progress. Take anything in your coffee?"

"Black."

"Don't get up, Joe," Kelly said. "I'll bring it in." She disappeared into the kitchen and returned a minute later with a tray holding two steaming mugs of black coffee, a small tea kettle with a cup and saucer, and a plate of flatbreads with some colorful side dishes. "Try the roti, Phillip. Aisha has been teaching her daughter to cook and they always make too much. There was a giant plateful waiting in the kitchen when I got up this morning."

"I had something before I came," Phillip said, but not wanting to give offense, spread a little of the most familiar-looking substance on a flatbread and took a bite. "Hey, this is pretty good."

"Joe and I already ate," Kelly encouraged him. "The kids were out before I even got up. I can't tell you how much I'm enjoying not having to rush to the office every morning."

"Does that mean there's a particular time I should be there?"

"I'm not sure, really," Kelly admitted. "Donna was already the embassy manager when I came to Union Station so I just started going in the same hours that she worked. Of course, all of the aliens on the station live by their own clocks, so most of the meetings and functions you'll attend in my place will take place outside of the embassy's normal hours."

"Do we get paid overtime?" Phillip asked.

Joe swallowed a gulp of coffee the wrong way and began choking, the only thing that kept Kelly from bursting out in laughter. "Not exactly," she said, "but then again, the station librarian is the only one who knows how many hours you're working, and she's not going to say anything as long as you're doing your job."

149

"I've been wanting to ask you about, uh, Libby." The bench ambassador didn't seem to be aware of the fact that his hands were making a sandwich from two pieces of roti and a spoonful of whatever was in each of the dishes. He took a bite and then spent a few seconds chewing before he continued. "The conversation that Janice and I had with President Beyer when we were reassigned here during our stopover was a bit vague at best. Who are we working for, exactly?"

"For humanity," Kelly replied. "It's in the oath."

"Yes, I remember the oath," Phillip said, and interrupted himself with a larger bite of the sandwich and an even longer break from the conversation "Did I already say that this is really good? Anyway, what I meant is, who determines what's good for humanity?"

"That's the question," Joe told him, casually snagging the last piece of flatbread from the dish while studiously avoiding his wife's look of disapproval. "As our daughter was fond of saying when she was young, it's complicated."

"It *is* complicated," Kelly told the bench ambassador. "In one sense, the Stryx are willing to let us make our own mistakes, but in another sense, they don't like seeing us wasting a lot of effort and causing ourselves or others needless suffering. The advanced species on the station don't like talking about how much of our autonomy is real and how much is an illusion, but the one thing everybody agrees on is that there's no point worrying about it."

"Seems a little fatalistic," Phillip observed.

"You said you've never lived on a station. When you've seen the Stryx in action a few times, you'll realize that a hundred seemingly unrelated decisions taken by dozens of different actors have somehow inevitably led to a predetermined outcome that you didn't see coming. The

150

aliens even developed a sort of mathematical philosophy to describe how all of our actions result in the same conclusion, but I can never remember—"

"Convergence Theory," Joe contributed.

"Right, but it rarely comes up unless somebody has had too much to drink at a diplomatic reception."

A long whistle sounded from somewhere outside the ice harvester and the Cayl hound unfolded himself from the floor and shot out the door.

"That's Paul," Joe said, rising from his place at the table. "We're resealing the hull of a Grenouthian yacht and Beowulf is in charge of making sure we get the epoxy mixed consistently every day so it dries the same color. His nose is better than a chemical lab."

"Paul is Joe's adopted son," Kelly informed Phillip after her husband left. "He's married to Aisha, and they live in the habitat next door with their daughter Fenna and a new baby boy."

"I hope it doesn't sound like I'm prying, but don't the Grenouthians pay her enough to live somewhere a little more upscale?"

"Aisha has gone through enough contract renegotiations by this point to be a wealthy woman, but living here suits them. Paul and Joe are always around working, Dring and Aisha share sprouts from their vegetable gardens, and there's plenty of space for the children and their friends." Kelly looked around the room and smiled. "I wasn't sure I'd ever get used to it when Joe first brought me home after our wedding, but now I couldn't imagine living any other way."

"I guess it is pretty spacious for a space station. Is that how you ended up with the EarthCent Intelligence training camp in your backyard?"

"My husband had a career in the mercenaries before coming to Union Station, though he doesn't like talking about it, and he helped run the training camp until recently. I don't remember whose idea it was to have the camp here rather than renting space elsewhere, but it's worked out well. I thought we might run out of space when Aisha bought Paul a fleet of abandoned ships from Stryx long-term parking, but he and Joe can only work on a few projects at a time. Are you ready to meet the staff?"

Phillip glanced at the plate to confirm the roti was all gone before replying. "Yes, though the truth is, I'm not sure why you're bringing me into the loop. Do all of our ambassadors work so closely with EarthCent Intelligence?"

"The cultural attaché is the main intelligence contact at most embassies, but all ambassadors receive regular briefings," Kelly explained as she led Phillip out of the ice harvester and turned towards the training camp area. "You'll be seeing more of Judith now that she's handling some of that work in place of Lynx. I'll just introduce you and observe until my clients get here."

"You've already started with the mediation thing?"

"As soon as I added my name to the list I got swamped with requests. The other ambassadors warned me about holding a session on the home turf of one or the other of the parties, which of course they all requested, so I decided to do it here. Some ambassadors use their embassy office to add gravitas to the process, but that didn't feel right to me, especially since I'm on sabbatical."

"Who are your first clients?"

"You'll laugh, but it's a Sharf used ship dealer and a Dollnick repair facility operator. Who'd have thought that used spaceships would be involved in so much legal wrangling?"

"I'll have to tell Janice that one. She must have filed over a thousand warranty claims during our time on Sharf Prime." Phillip paused and squinted as though he couldn't believe his eyes. "Is that woman sword-fighting without any protective gear?"

"Yes. Thomas is an artificial person and he has fine enough motor control to keep from making contact with Judith's skin even if she makes a mistake."

"But he's wearing a facemask and a vest!"

"He has to protect himself. Artificial people have limited self-repair capacity and some of their parts are pretty expensive."

"It's exactly the opposite of what I would have expected," Phillip admitted. The two diplomats stopped at the edge of a white circle painted on the deck where Chance had posted herself, calling contradictory advice to both fighters.

"Good morning, Ambassadors," she greeted the newcomers and introduced herself to Phillip. "They'll just be another minute. Thomas has been trying a mercenary enhancement from QuickU, but the personality donor was a cavalryman, and dueling from the saddle and the ground are two very different things."

As if to confirm Chance's assessment, Judith neatly deflected a slashing stroke from the artificial person's heavier sword and buried the point of her rapier in his chest protector.

"Three!" she called out triumphantly. "I win again!"

Thomas returned his saber to its scabbard and removed his mask. "We all win when one of us improves," he said. "That's the whole point of training."

"What a great philosophy. Did you just make that up?"

"I've always believed that teamwork—you're taunting me, aren't you?" Thomas cut himself short.

The swordswoman just smiled and went over to meet Kelly's replacement. "Hi, I'm Judith. I'll be available to attend functions that you and Daniel don't have time for, and Daniel never has time for anything that isn't connected to his sovereign human communities."

"Thomas," the artificial person introduced himself as he removed the bulky chest protector. "If you have an intelligence emergency and you can't reach Clive or Blythe, I'm available 24/7."

"Thank you both," the newly minted ambassador said. "I understand that you'll be briefing me about interspecies police agency cooperation."

"That's correct," Thomas affirmed. "The process of sharing information is heavy on protocol, even at the level of individual requests, and ambassadorial approval is required for deep data mining."

"Do we have any such issues pending?"

"As soon as you're ready to support us. We're working with Earth and our people on Flower to crack down on unethical labor contractors. The aliens we brought in to train our personnel on the system informed us that they log all complaints in their jurisdictions, even those from other species. It could be that half of our job has already been done for us and all we need to do is submit the proper requests. Unfortunately, there isn't a single form covering all of the law enforcement entities participating in the Inter-Species Police Operations Agency."

"No acronym?" Phillip asked.

"ISPOA," Judith replied. "Thomas doesn't like using it because he says the sound reminds him of a hydraulic leak."

"You have to be an artificial person to understand," Chance contributed.

"If this is a training camp, where are all the trainees?" the bench ambassador asked.

"We have a dynamic schedule with different length courses and sometimes it leads to utilization gaps," Thomas explained. "We just finished with a couple of new law enforcement support groups, and tomorrow we're starting a batch of newspaper reporters through their kidnap avoidance training. That's why today was ideal for you to come in. Filling out the forms should only take a few hours."

"That's my cue to get going," Kelly said. "I gave my first clients instructions to find Dring's, but if you see an angry Sharf or Dollnick wandering around, send them over."

Phillip blinked at her announcement. "You won't meet clients at the embassy but you asked the Maker to help with your sabbatical business?"

"He offered his garden space as a tranquil setting. He won't be participating in the session, but I'm hoping that having a Maker working on his sculptures in the background will be conducive to a calm meeting."

"You mean they'll be intimidated by Dring's presence," Judith translated.

"One can only hope. Oh, I see a Sharf heading that way so I better get going."

The three EarthCent Intelligence trainers led Phillip off to their makeshift office area while Kelly skirted around the assortment of parked ships and headed for the break in the old mound of scrap that concealed Dring's corner of Mac's Bones. She saw the Sharf disappear into the narrow passage ahead of her and was surprised that he had located it without help. The ambassador hurried after him and found that Dring had already introduced himself to her client and led him to the garden, inviting the Sharf to take a seat on what Kelly had always thought was a piece of abstract sculpture.

"Yzonge?" she ventured.

"What?" the Sharf asked distractedly, still staring after the Maker. "Say, do you think you could get an image of us together?"

"I can ask the station librarian to make one with the security system right now," Kelly replied, approaching her client. "You're so tall that it would probably work better with me standing and you seated."

"You misunderstood," Yzonge told her bluntly. "I meant an image of myself with the Maker, but only if you're sure he wouldn't consider it an imposition. He seemed very friendly."

Kelly took this rejection in stride and made a mental note of how it might prove useful in her mediation toolkit. "We'll see how the session goes first," she told him with a smile.

A heavyset Dollnick carrying a travel desk on his shoulder emerged from the short tunnel through the scrap mound and looked carefully in every direction. His eyes lingered on Dring, who was welding an alloy that gave off a bright purple flame, and he nodded his approval at the technique. Then he approached Kelly and the Sharf, set down his burden, and extended his two lower hands to the ambassador.

"You must be Mrs. McAllister," he greeted her, and clasping her hand in both of his own giant mitts, gave her a politician's handshake. "I'm sorry if I ran a little behind, but I was just chatting with your husband about some work I hope to give him."

"Did you just offer her a bribe?" the Sharf demanded. "We both know that your complaint has no merit, Pruke, but I thought you'd at least pretend to present your argument before getting down to brass tacks and bidding on her cooperation."

The Dollnick unfolded his travel desk and settled his large frame onto the fabric seat, which must have been capable of carrying a heavy load. Then he passed each of his four palms in front of a glowing electronic eye, unlocking the desk's drawer, from which he drew out a high-tech whiteboard of the type that his species used as a substitute for paper. Finally, he deigned to acknowledge the Sharf's insinuation.

"I've done business with the ambassador's husband for years, there's nothing nefarious about my statement. What would be the point of bribing a mediator? You know as well as I that the process is non-binding."

"Gentlemen, please. It's clear that you two are well-acquainted, and Yzonge, I apologize for not knowing that my husband has had financial dealings with Pruke."

"It's been a while, actually," the Dollnick said. "Last job I did for them was painting a habitat a few years back."

"You're the one who delivered Paul and Aisha's home with a Teragram mage sleeping in the wall?"

The Dollnick stuttered a series of untranslatable whistles and the Sharf burst out laughing. "Cancel my objection," Yzonge wheezed when he finally caught his breath. "Shall we proceed to our arguments?"

"Just a moment," Kelly said, deploying a tactic Czeros had coached her to try. "Before we get to the bone of contention, why not start by telling me what you agree on?"

Both aliens looked surprised by the mediator's approach, but Pruke nodded grudgingly, and setting aside his Dolly board, placed a hand on each of his hearts and began to speak.

"The Sharf dealer known as Yzonge hired my shipyard to refurbish forty-eight ships of the mid-level prospector class for sale at his dealership. At the time our agreement was made, he promised that the ships had been lightly used by retirees in a fantasy asteroid mining operation."

"Excuse me," Kelly interjected. "Could one of you explain what fantasy has to do with mining?"

"Think of it as an adventure vacation for Sharf who spent their lives in desk jobs," Yzonge told her. "I saw an advertisement for vacation packages on Earth that offered an analogous activity which involved sitting on trained animals and chasing untrained animals around the countryside."

"A dude ranch," the ambassador told them. "I believe all of the animals in question are highly trained."

The Sharf and the Dollnick shared a look over the bizarre Human vacation concept, and then Pruke continued.

"I based my cost estimates on the sample ship he brought which supposedly was representative of the whole lot. When the remaining forty-seven ships arrived, it turned out that none of them were in as good a shape as the first ship."

"Do you agree to this point?" Kelly asked the Sharf, who nodded distractedly, his eyes on the Maker. "Could you sum up the difference in condition between the initial ship and the later deliveries, Pruke?"

"Certainly. They were filthy. My shipyard employees are highly trained engineers and technicians, not janitors. I was forced to hire a Gem cleaning contractor to come in and prep the ships prior to beginning the work. I run a tight schedule, and a three-day delay to thoroughly clean forty-seven ships is nothing to laugh at."

"Yzonge?" Kelly asked.

"Yes, yes," the Sharf responded without looking over. "The ships were dirty. Get on with it."

"As I was saying, the Gem cleaners had me over a barrel due to a bottleneck in my schedule, and the bill for cleaning forty-seven ships came to twenty-three thousand, five hundred creds," Pruke said, though it was clear that the Sharf's apparent lack of interest in the proceedings was beginning to get to him. "In addition, I was forced to turn down a lucrative engine overhaul job on a Class 2 freighter for lack of space to do the work. In short, I put my total damages at," he hesitated for a moment, "one million creds."

"A million creds?" Kelly asked incredulously. "What was the value of the engine overhaul job you passed on?"

"Twelve thousand," the Dollnick asserted.

"Eight," Yzonge said, proving that he was paying attention after all.

"Let's say ten for the sake of making the math easier," Kelly suggested, leading the aliens to exchange another look at her expense. "So you suffered less than thirty-five thousand creds in extra expenses and lost business, Pruke, but you want a million in damages?"

"My reputation suffered when I turned down the engine overhaul," the Dollnick explained. "And when I pinged Yzonge and demanded that he cover my losses, he refused to pay."

"Now that's not true," the Sharf said, finally tearing his eyes away from the Maker. "I offered to assume the Gem bill, which I would have negotiated down to a more reasonable amount, but I see no reason to compensate the Dollnick for his own scheduling errors. Then he started whistling about his attorney and I broke off the call."

"Wait, wait," Kelly spoke over the Dolly, who had begun an angry rebuttal to the Sharf's claims. "Let's go back to what you both agreed on. The ships were delivered in a state that required you, Pruke, to hire a Gem cleaning crew. Yzonge offered to settle the contractor's bill, but was unwilling to pay for your lost business opportunity. Is this correct?"

"If you put it like that," the Dollnick grumbled.

"May I ask you gentlemen the total value of the refurbishing contract?"

"Two million creds," the Sharf offered promptly. "And that's more business than—"

"Thank you," Kelly interrupted, holding up her hand. "Is there something you aren't telling me, Pruke?"

"He won't apologize," the Dollnick said angrily.

"I'm sorry?"

"I'd have accepted his offer to take care of the Gem and eaten the lost work myself if Yzonge would have come to the shipyard and apologized for dumping a bunch of dirty ships on us without warning. He shamed me in front of my workers."

"I understand," Kelly said, knowing full well how important such matters were in Dollnick society. "I'm not as familiar with your species as I am with members of the tunnel network, Yzonge. Was an apology out of the question?"

"We're not as sensitive as the Dollnicks, if that's what you mean. But if word got out that I'd apologized to a four-armed shipyard owner in front of his staff, I'd be the one to take a reputational hit. The wholesale used ship market is a cut-throat business with thin margins, and my ability to buy new stock at a price that will let me profit depends on my reputation as a tough customer."

"I see. Would you gentlemen excuse me for a moment?" Kelly requested, and getting to her feet, began a short circle around the garden, as if she was lost deep in thought. When she reached the farthest point from her clients, she called in a loud whisper, "Dring, don't look over. Can you hear me?"

"Yes, Ambassador," the Maker responded as he took a file to some unseen defect in the metal sculpture he was currently constructing.

"Would it be a great imposition if I asked you to have your image taken with one of my clients? I think it would help settle their dispute."

"I'd be happy to oblige," Dring said, returning the file to his utility belt. "Is now a good time?"

"Just give me a minute to close the deal," Kelly said, and hurried back to the aliens in a straight line. "Yzonge. Would a high-resolution image of you with the Maker outweigh any reputational damage you would suffer from apologizing to Pruke?"

"Done," the Sharf declared.

Five minutes later, after agreeing that Kelly was the best mediator on Union Station, her first clients left Dring's garden on their way to the Dollnick's shipyard to take care of the apology and discuss a new business deal.

161

"Thank you," Kelly told the Maker again. "I'm not sure I could have settled their dispute without your help, and I really wanted to get off on the right foot."

"It was good practice posing," Dring told her. "You know I'm not the most outgoing sentient in the galaxy and I expect there will be plenty of requests for images from the guests at Dorothy's wedding."

Fourteen

"I can't believe I'm finally going to get to use my axe," Jorb exclaimed gleefully. "What's taking Jeeves so long to get here?"

"We're early, and he'll probably send a holographic instance of himself right on time," Samuel said. "I'm looking forward to our first real studio experience. Vivian's brother says that the holographic overlays on the standard robotic NPCs are so real that you can't tell the difference."

"I wish Jeeves had sent us something to prepare, even if it was just character sheets," Marilla said. "He could be dropping us into the middle of the Battle of Scort Woods for all we know."

"Then we'll be all set," the Drazen replied. "I probably know as much about that battle as a historian."

"Watching a lot of immersives doesn't mean you know what really went on," the Horten shot back.

"I read some books too. I even wrote a paper about the Pullrips when I was a kid. I always wanted to visit their empire."

"Don't they attack Drazens and Hortens on sight?" Vivian asked.

"Come on, that battle was like a half a million years ago," Jorb said. "They've probably gotten over it by now."

"My dad visited the planet when he was a kid," Vivian told them. "Whoever won, the Stryx declared it a galactic historical site and you can't take anything from the surface."

"I don't think there is anything on the surface, other than woods," the Drazen said. "That's why the Frunge got involved in the first place."

"Except they aren't trees in any normal sense of the word, more like crystalline growths, and they don't burn," Marilla contributed. "Which was lucky, because the Pullrips are fire-breathers."

"The Pullrips are softies," Jorb insisted, taking a few trial cuts at the empty air with his noodle axe. "I say we do a commando raid."

"I tried to get some details out of Jeeves last night when he came by Mac's Bones to help reprogram an old Grenouthian security system on a ship my dad and brother are restoring," Samuel informed the others. "All he'd say is that we'd get all the action we can handle."

"And I intend to keep my word," the Stryx promised.

"Jeeves! How long have you been floating there?"

"Long enough to know that your imaginations are running away with you. In this educational LARP, you will all be playing Vergallian mercenaries working at a Frunge mining cooperative in the asteroid belts of Callizack Six."

"Vergallian?" Vivian asked in dismay. "Can't we be ourselves? I've never even heard of Vergallian mercenaries."

"This particular scenario takes place before any of your species joined the tunnel network," Jeeves told her. "The Frunge normally policed their own mining habitats, but in this case, the ore was so rich that their law enforcement officers kept quitting to stake their own claims."

"So our mission is to protect the miners and prospectors from claim jumpers?" Jorb asked eagerly.

"Not this evening."

"Is there some kind of civil war going on?" Samuel asked.

"I wouldn't put it that way, exactly," the Stryx hedged.

"Come on, Jeeves. What's the deal then?"

"The four of you are employed by an establishment known as the Gold Vault."

"So we're bank guards," Jorb concluded. "That's cool, as long as somebody actually tries to rob us."

"Your boss is Razel, a Frunge woman who inherited the business from her father. The mission is to keep the Gold Vault peaceful for two hours without killing anybody."

"WHAT!" the Drazen exploded in disbelief.

"If there are no further questions," Jeeves said, and without waiting for a response, engaged the holographic virtual reality system of the studio space.

The four students found themselves standing on the curved deck of a standard spinning habitat of the sort towed into position for medium-term mining or space construction activities. Looking at each other, they found that their features had been partially obscured with overlays, rendering the four of them as Vergallians. For Samuel and Vivian, the main difference was they had aged ten or fifteen years, though they also sported military hairstyles and higher cheekbones. Jorb was missing his tentacle and extra thumbs, and Marilla looked like a rebel princess in a Vergallian drama.

"We better find this vault place," Samuel said, knowing that arguing with the invisible Stryx would only result in lost points for breaking character. "Does anybody read Frunge?"

"I can manage the basic stuff," Marilla told him, stepping aside to avoid a drunken miner lurching out of the noisy bar in front of them. "Oh, no!"

"What?" Jorb demanded.

"It's here. This bar is named the Gold Vault."

"We're bouncers?"

"Look sharp," Vivian warned them. "I think our boss is waving at us and she doesn't look happy."

"Get your lazy Vergallian butts over here," a middle-aged Frunge woman shouted at them. "The mercenary guild must have fallen on hard times if you're the best they can send me on Seedling Day."

"We're bouncing for the Frunge miners on Seedling Day?" Jorb said in dismay. "They're all going to be loaded!"

"I'll assume you know how to use those weapons, but everybody here is a customer, so you stick with bare hands unless they can't pay the bill," the alien proprietress barked. She shook her head at the students, who looked more like models than crowd-control specialists. "You ladies handle credit checks at the entrance and the seating, and don't accept any guff about friends coming later. These scanners read the credit balance and nobody gets in with less than twenty unless they have cash to make up the difference." Razel handed each of the girls what looked like a secret decoder ring from a box of breakfast cereal.

"So we show the new customers to an empty table?" Vivian asked.

"Haven't you ever worked bar detail before? We save the empty tables for large groups. Your job is to seat the newcomers wherever they fit, and start filling the tables nearest to the bar first because it's a shorter trip for the waitresses."

166

"We seat them with strangers?"

"If they were friends, I wouldn't have to pay you to make them sit together, now would I?" the owner replied sarcastically. "You males," she continued with a sneer that showed what she thought of pretty-boy Vergallians, "are going to be my sorry excuse for a flying squad. If anybody starts fighting, you get there and turf them out before they start putting dents in the furniture. But make sure you don't interrupt a drinking game by mistake or you'll be the ones going home early. Got it?"

"Drinking game?" Samuel asked.

"I'll explain," Jorb volunteered. "Thank you for hiring us."

The Frunge woman gave them all a final disgusted look and then stalked back through the maze of tables to resume her place behind the bar. The four students took a minute to survey the interior of the Gold Vault, which was furnished with hundreds of black-painted metal chairs and perhaps forty tables of various sizes and shapes.

"A couple of Frunge who work out at the dojo invited me to a Seedling Day party last time it came around," Jorb told the others. "They aren't bad drunks, like Dollnicks or Humans, but once they get started on these awful drinking songs that go in rounds, you'll wish they were brawlers. And they play this game where they punch each other in the shoulder and whoever flinches first has to drink. Frunge are wiry, but they're tough."

"I can't believe we're supposed to seat people with strangers," the shy Horten girl said. "What if they refuse?"

"Here's your chance to find out," Samuel told her as a couple of miners sauntered up to the entrance.

"Uh, credit check," Vivian said, stepping in front of the two Frunge. Neither of them showed any surprise at the request, and one who was faster at opening his belt pouch extended some sort of payment chit. Unsure what to do, she reached to take it, and the ring she had slipped onto her finger lit up with a three-digit number. At the same time, the miner jerked his hand back.

"Were you about to touch my chit?" he demanded incredulously.

"Sorry, it's my first time," Vivian apologized.

Next to her, Marilla hastily shoved her ring onto a finger and carefully extended it over the chit presented by the other miner. The tiny screen again lit up with a three-figure sum. "He's all set," she said.

"Great," Vivian said. "If you gentlemen would come with me."

"Gentlemen," one of the miners repeated to the other with comic politeness, and instead of a nudge, threw a hard punch at his friend's shoulder. The Frunge on the receiving end didn't even turn his head at the impact and followed the girl into the bar.

Vivian cringed as she led them past a number of empty tables and up to a round table with four chairs, two of which were already occupied by a pair of older aliens who had obviously been drinking for some time. Unsure what to say, she indicated the empty seats with an open hand.

"Thanks, but we'll just take one of the open tables we passed back there," one of the miners said.

"I'm sorry, but all of our tables seat a minimum of four," Vivian said as firmly as she could. "You know the rules."

"Rules?" the miner drawled, winking at his friend. "We don't need no stinking rules."

"Oh, shut up and plant it," one of the seated Frunge said. "You're buying the next round for making us listen to that immature backtalk. You'd think they never worked on a habitat before," he concluded, though it was unclear to Vivian whether he was addressing her or his companion.

"That didn't look so bad," Samuel said when the girl returned to the entrance.

"One of them started to say something but the older guys shut him down."

"Is the habitat failing?" Marilla asked, as loud creaking sounds suddenly began.

"They're singing, 'My Green Forest' already," Jorb groaned. "It has like a hundred verses, and the only saving grace is that they pause for a couple minutes between each round to symbolize growth."

"Are those guys playing or fighting?" Samuel asked the Drazen, pointing to a pair of Frunge in the corner of the bar who appeared to be trading blows.

"We're on," Jorb replied, and dashed off in the direction of the combatants. It only took the student bouncers a moment to separate the battling miners, much to the disappointment of the Frunge seated nearby. Samuel couldn't help marveling over how real it all felt, even though he knew that he was restraining a robot wrapped in a hologram.

"What seems to be the problem?" he asked the construct, which continued trying to slip by him to get to the other miner.

"I was next in line for the bathroom and that rotten stump tried to sneak past me."

"You can't fight in here. The owner doesn't want the furniture getting banged up."

"I wasn't hurting the furniture," the miner complained. "And save the lecture, I still have to water the grass."

A commotion broke out near the door, and Samuel looked over to see Vivian and Marilla arguing with a pair of Frunge females who sported towering trellis work.

"Don't make me come over here again," he warned the miner, and sprinted back towards the entrance. Jorb delayed a minute, allowing the miner Samuel had released to enter the restroom and latch the door before setting his own catch free with a similar admonition. By the time he made it to the entrance, the owner was there shouting at the two girls while Samuel tried to restrain her.

"How many females do you see in the bar?" Razel demanded, and then proceeded to answer her own question. "There's me, my three waitresses, and the four ore graders sitting together who haven't spent a cred on drinks all night. Why haven't they bought any drinks? Because the miners keep sending them my best wines, that's why. And you tried to run a credit check on two single girls from station administration who took the trouble to put up their hair vines before coming out?"

"But you said there was a twenty-cred minimum," Vivian protested weakly.

"Use your brains, Vergallian," the Frunge proprietress practically howled. "It's a bar. If these miners just wanted to sit around and drink, they could do it in their quarters for a fraction of the cost."

"No credit checks for females," Marilla said, doing her best to suppress her own anger over being yelled at. "Got it, boss."

Razel snorted and turned her attention to Samuel. "And why didn't I see you hauling those brawlers out the door?"

"They were just arguing over the bathroom, they didn't seem that drunk."

"Mine was carrying a couple hundred in cash," Jorb added.

"All right, then," the Frunge said, sounding slightly mollified. "At least somebody has their head screwed on straight. One of you grab a mop out of the utility closet behind the bar and clean up over near the waitress station where somebody spilled a drink."

"I'll do it," Samuel volunteered, and followed Razel back to the bar.

"This isn't what I was thinking about when Jeeves promised us an action LARP," Jorb complained to the girls.

"Ten-point penalty for going out of character," the Stryx's voice came out of thin air.

"Timeout," Vivian requested, and the noise from the bar halted as if somebody had hit a mute button. "Is there really a point to this exercise or are you just showing off the technology? I'm not even old enough to be in a place like this."

"All the more reason you should see what they're like now before you get into the habit," the disembodied voice replied. "And let me remind you that patience is a virtue. Timeout over."

"What do you think he—" Jorb began, but swallowed whatever he was going to ask about Jeeves when he remembered the ten-point penalty, and instead improvised, "—is going to use to squeeze out the mop?"

"It's the sponge type," Marilla said, looking over as Samuel pulled that tool from the utility closet. "I guess he'll just wring it out over the slop sink."

"Credit check," Vivian announced to a new trio of miners who had just arrived. As they reached for their chits, another round of "My Green Forest" started up, and the three new arrivals creaked along with the others at the top of their lungs.

"I'll seat this batch," Marilla offered, and led the customers into the bar. Jorb stood like a sentry at the entrance, studying the customers inside while Vivian watched for new arrivals. It wasn't long before an artificial Sharf appeared, his non-biological status made obvious by the lack of a covering on his robotic right arm, which had obviously been damaged in some kind of mining accident.

"Credit check," Vivian told the ragged artificial person, though she felt terrible about asking.

The Sharf produced a pay chit without a word, and the girl's scanner ring showed that he had just eighteen creds, assuming that was currency displayed.

"I'm sorry, there's a twenty-credit minimum tonight," she said. "It's Seedling Day."

"My power pack is dead," the artificial person told her. "I really need some alcohol for my backup turbine or I'm going to collapse somewhere."

"I'm sorry," she repeated. "Do you have any cash to round up?"

"Cash?" He gave a bitter laugh. "Since my hand got skinned in a crusher feed the Frunge won't hire me. I'm just trying to stay on my feet until the next supply ship comes in so I can beg them to take me on as an indentured worker."

Vivian felt for her purse, but something seemed to push her hand away and guide it towards the belt pouch of her holographic uniform. She opened the flap and saw a few coins gleaming inside. "Here," she said, offering the artificial Sharf a five cred piece. "Now you've got twenty-three and you can go in."

"I'll return this," he said, his voice choked with feeling. But two steps into the bar, several drunken Frunge lunged up from their table to block his path.

"Who let the robot in here?" the biggest one demanded, poking the artificial person in the chest. "We don't need your kind on this habitat."

"Take it easy," Jorb growled, pushing between them. "He just wants to have a drink, the same as everybody."

"Robots steal our jobs," another Frunge said in an ugly tone, and a few more miners rose from their tables when they figured out what was happening.

"Don't call me a robot," the Sharf retorted, his head turning in the direction of the new accusation. "I'm an artificial person, and my people were building faster-than-light ships back when you were—"

"Throw him out!" Razel ordered, pushing through the growing mob and glaring daggers at Jorb. "The four of you must be the stupidest Vergallians in history. You want to turn away single females and then you invite in broken-down robot trash?"

"That's not right," Jorb began, but the Frunge proprietress didn't give him a chance to continue.

"MOVE!" she thundered, shoving the Drazen so hard that he stumbled into the artificial person. "Are both of you brain dead?" Razel hissed as she continued shoving them back towards the corridor. "They'll tear him apart in there!"

Several of the miners seemed inclined to follow the Sharf out of the bar, but a waitress suddenly appeared in their path, handing out complimentary shots. Then another round of "My Green Forest" started up, and the Frunge were distracted by the demands of remembering the lyrics.

173

To the surprise of the role-playing students, the owner followed the artificial person out into the corridor, still berating him loudly, and then produced a bottle of grain alcohol from under her apron and surreptitiously passed it over before yelling, "And don't come back!" for the benefit of a newly arriving group of miners. The Sharf ducked into a side passage, and Razel stood scowling while Vivian and Marilla credit-checked the new customers and then took them inside to be seated with strangers.

"That was very Drazen of you," Jorb said, bestowing his highest compliment on the proprietress.

"What did you call me?" Razel demanded, jabbing him in the chest with a stiff finger. "I swear by my ancestors that you Vergallians are even dumber than that poor robot. Artificial intelligence," she scoffed. "Doesn't even have the sense to keep his ragged metal butt out of a Frunge bar on Seedling Day."

Samuel dodged out of the way of the irate Frunge woman as she headed back inside. "What was that all about?" he asked the others.

"An artificial Sharf down on his luck came to buy a drink for his micro-turbine," Vivian explained. "He didn't have enough to get in, but I couldn't help remembering Chance's story about running out of power on an alien orbital, and I felt I had to do something."

The Frunge in the bar launched into another round of the interminable song, but the sound suddenly cut off like somebody had draped an acoustic suppression field across the entrance. It was replaced by a familiar hollow sound which terminated when the rolling five-cred coin bounced off of Vivian's foot and fell flat. As she bent to pick it up, a cartoon bubble popped into existence in front of them, reading, "Congratulations. You have completed the quest

'Save an artificial person's self-esteem.' Receive 10 experience points and level up."

"Does this mean we're done?" Marilla asked.

"That depends," Jeeves replied, popping into existence to replace the dialogue. "Was that enough action for you?"

"YES!" the students chorused.

The scene of the Horten habitat disintegrated, and all that remained of the Gold Vault bar was a collection of mechanicals that had given physical presence to NPCs.

"I can't believe you made us play mercenary Vergallian bouncers," Jorb complained.

"Was that a scene out of history like the other LARPs we've done?" Vivian asked.

"Something like it has occurred countless times around the universe, but I adopted the particular scenario from a Sharf role-playing game that's popular with artificial people on the Chintoo orbital who do the manufacturing for SBJ Fashions," Jeeves replied. "Before you complain, I don't choose the subjects for these university LARPs. I'm just the orchestrator."

"So what's the post-game summary?" Marilla asked. "Does the artificial person make it back to Sharf space and get his body repaired?"

"Analyzing your actions and taking a gazillion factors into account, I can tell you that Razel fires the Vergallian bouncers before the end of their shift, and the miners drink too much and get sore throats from singing. After talking about far away families and loved ones, they become so maudlin that they take up a collection for the artificial person. But when they try to find him, he thinks they're a lynch mob and remains hidden."

Fifteen

Kevin climbed down from the temporary scaffolding bolted to the face of the large Dollnick cargo container and flipped up his welding mask. "I don't know. Shouldn't there be more space between the cutouts?"

"I'm not the artist," Joe replied, stripping off his own elbow-length welding gauntlets. "Dring laid it out, and I trust him that the perspective will be correct after he paints in some false shadows."

Alexander leapt into the container through one of the large window openings Joe had just completed torching out, trotted back through the improvised front door, and then repeated the feat.

"It's going to be our house, Alex," Kevin told him. "It's not a Cayl obstacle course for training hounds."

"What's the difference between living in a cargo container and living on your ship when it's parked?" Samuel asked, putting down the angle grinder he'd been using to smooth out his father's cuts. "You've got plenty of room."

"The bathroom is set up for Zero-G, and your sister won't use it unless we're in space and she doesn't have a choice."

"So park closer and keep coming to our house for the bathrooms. It's what you've both been doing since last time you got married anyway."

"Women want their own home," Joe explained to his son. "And drop the bit about Dorothy already being married. If she wants to pretend she's still single for her wedding, just let her."

"Aisha didn't get pregnant until we moved into our new place," Paul pointed out. "It's like a nesting thing."

"Why did you wait so long to get married, Dad?" Samuel asked his father.

"Well, I suppose we've made enough progress for today," Joe replied, surveying the work site. "The answer to that question will cost you a beer run."

"One for me," Paul said.

"And pretzels for the dog," Kevin added.

Samuel let out a loud groan, but tradition made the youngest man on the job the runner, so he set off for the ice harvester at a jog. Alexander went along, running the occasional circle around the teenager to remind everyone that four legs were superior to two.

"Have you decided yet whether to go with a tub or a shower?" Joe asked his son-in-law. "I want to rough in the plumbing tomorrow."

"A shower works for me," Kevin replied.

"Do both," Paul suggested. "Tubs are good for washing kids, and Aisha likes taking a long soak whenever she comes back from arguing with the Grenouthian network executives about the latest dumb idea they want her to add to the show."

"Like what?"

"Contests mainly. It's already the most watched children's program in the galaxy, but the bunnies will never give up on pushing the ratings even higher. I don't usually have an opinion one way or the other about this stuff, but Aisha is right that nobody needs to see a bunch of seven-year-olds competing over who can eat the fastest or yell the loudest. Anyway, you should ask Dorothy about the shower."

"I would, but we're in our Drazen quiet period."

"I could check with her for you, but Paul's right that it doesn't hurt to do both," Joe said. "The drain and the shower head are going to end up in the same place, it's just a question of what I put in between."

"I really want to thank you guys again for helping with all this," Kevin told them. "I wish you'd let me pay you something."

"Just make her happy and that's enough for me."

"She was a great little sister, even if she never learned the difference between engineering and magic," Paul said. "And Vivian is going to get a good one with Samuel. He's a sweet kid."

"And slow." Joe folded the coveralls he had stripped off and sat down in the doorway of the Dollnick cargo container they were converting into a starter home for Kevin and Dorothy. "If I had sent Beowulf for a beer, he'd be back by now rolling the keg with his nose."

"Where is Beowulf today?"

"Kelly took him along for a mediation session in the temporary office she rented near the embassy. She wants to test whether his presence helps keep emotions from boiling over, though I don't think he was paying much attention when she briefed him on the mission this morning."

"Why do you say that?"

"Since Alexander started sneaking in to steal chew toys, Beowulf has learned to sleep with his eyes open. I can only tell he's out cold because he doesn't thump his tail when I go by."

"You didn't say anything to Kelly?"

"She'd already been lecturing him on doggy etiquette for five minutes when I noticed he was snoozing, so I figured it was better to just let it slide. Besides, Cayl hounds are born diplomats."

"Here comes Samuel," Paul said when the teen finally reappeared riding Dorothy's bike, which featured a basket at the front. The rider began braking a good distance from the men in order to prevent the beer from sloshing out of the pitcher, and came to a gentle halt right by his father.

"Thanks." Joe stood up to retrieve the pitcher from the basket and poured himself a mug. "You're short a glass."

"You know I don't drink beer, Dad. It just puts me to sleep."

"Here, boy," Kevin said, and threw a pretzel as far as it would carry. Alexander sprinted off and made a diving catch, showily keeping his tongue extended with the pretzel displayed as he skidded to a halt. "Good one."

"So what about the story on why you waited so long to get married?"

"I don't know if you're old enough after all," Joe replied, settling back down in the doorway with his beer.

"No fair, you already promised."

"All right, but keep in mind that people are different, and for all I know, Georgia might have found the right guy and is settled down somewhere with children and grand-children as we speak."

"Then you must be talking about something from a long time ago."

"I've been married to your mother for almost twenty years. Did you think it could have been recent?"

"I'm eighteen so Dorothy is twenty-five," Samuel pointed out. "You've been married at least twenty-five years."

"That's what I meant, but in any case, this happened when I was about the same age Dorothy is today, say forty years ago. Georgia was a technician who had a way with fixing alien hand-weapons. She was the daughter of my unit commander, and all of the men were crazy about her."

"So you dated?"

"You could call it that, I guess. A couple of years, off and on. I felt like I was auditioning for a part. Her father liked me more than any of her other suitors, and if we had tied the knot, he was going to promote me to second in command."

"What kind of military system is that?" Kevin asked, setting down his own beer to throw the dog another pretzel.

"The mercenary system. Her father owned the unit so he could do whatever he wanted."

"What happened?" Samuel pressed on.

"We opened our hearts to each other one night and she told me that her favorite thing in life was falling in love."

"And?"

"And that was it. I couldn't take the gamble."

"I don't get it."

"She didn't mean falling in love with me, Sam. She meant falling in love in general. And you have to remember that I knew a couple of guys whose hearts she had already broken. It was just her thing, loving and being loved, and when a new opportunity to do it all over again came along, she'd be off like a shot. I always wondered if it was something she would grow out of or if the right man could change her, but I can't say I've ever seen that happen."

"You mean people don't change?" Paul asked.

"People change, they just don't change each other. We aren't as malleable as a cargo container," Joe concluded, thumping the metal wall. "That's why I don't worry about you and Vivian, Sam. Maybe she's a little too sure of herself, but I know that if the two of you do get married someday, she'll be there for you as long as you'll have her, if not longer."

"If Vivian's anything like her mother was at that age, you probably don't have much choice in the matter anyway," Paul said. "Sometimes I suspect that Aisha and Blythe flipped a coin for me, or maybe Libby stepped in and decided for them. I remember being pretty confused at the time, but it couldn't have worked out better for any of us."

Kevin threw another pretzel for Alexander, but as the Cayl hound made a showy leap to snatch it out of the air, Beowulf flew in with a body block and captured the salty treat.

"Way to show him who's the boss," Joe congratulated the older dog. "Did you bring my wife back with you?"

"Right here," Kelly said, coming around the corner of the cargo container. "Beer, pretzels, looks like I missed out on a male-bonding session. What were you boys talking about?"

The men looked at each other, and then replied in unison, "Fishing."

"That's a great idea. We could go camping in Libbyland now that I'm on vacation."

"Sabbatical," Samuel reminded her.

"By the way, Kevin. Dorothy wanted me to ask you when your family is going to send in the measurements for their wedding outfits."

181

"Yeah, about that. My sister insists on wearing her prophetess robes, and nobody else was interested in dressing up. I tried explaining that it's what Dorothy does for a living, but they said that if their homespun is good enough for New Kasil, it's good enough for Union Station."

"Clever," Kelly said. "You can't argue if they put it that way. I just wish you could explain it to Dorothy directly because she's not going to want to hear it from me."

"Sorry, but our quiet period has another week to go."

"Does anybody even know why the Drazens make couples go through a quiet period before getting married?" the ambassador asked. "I could check with Bork, but now that I'm on sabbatical, it wouldn't be fair to keep dropping in on him. Libby?"

"The Drazens adopted the practice from consortium mergers," the station librarian promptly informed them. "When two business entities are planning to join forces, an untimely release of performance data could affect the value of one or another entity and lead to consortium members maneuvering for quick profits. That goes against the whole ethos of the cooperative structure."

"There you are, Kevin," Joe said. "In case my daughter has you confused about marriage, that's as good an explanation as you'll hear. Think of it as a consortium merger where you'll be combining your trade stock."

"Except all of Dorothy's trade stock belongs to Jeeves," Kevin pointed out. "I just wish I knew what put it into her head to solicit pre-wedding rituals from all of the aliens she knows. Silence is one thing, but the suggestions she got from her Frunge and Vergallian friends have me a little nervous."

"I can help you with the Vergallian rituals," Samuel offered. "Do you think of Dorothy as royalty or as a peasant?"

"Uh, royalty," Kevin answered, glancing at Joe, who gave him an approving nod.

"So you can write a poem, kill a Thurbrick, or present her with a rare object."

"I can't write a poem and I don't want to kill anything. I've never even heard of Thurbricks."

"They're like a cross between a lion and a crocodile, except they spit acid. The Empire keeps them in nature preserves just so they'll be available for courting rituals. I've heard that the Fleet Vergallians do something with holograms and robots like the LARPing studios."

"It seems cruel to keep animals around just to slaughter them to prove a point," Kelly said.

"The Vergallians only breed the surviving Thurbricks so they keep getting better. It's like a fifty/fifty proposition who wins."

"So if the groom gets eaten they call off the wedding?"

"It's part of the proposal process that comes after the initial tests but before the contract gets signed," Samuel explained. "Vergallians don't schedule the wedding until the necessary preliminaries are completed, but Dorothy is always doing things in the wrong order."

"I don't want to be eaten by a holographic Thurbrick any more than I want to slay one," Kevin objected. "What was my other choice?"

"You can give her a rare object, but that can get pretty expensive. You're better off writing the poem."

Kevin groaned. "I'll think about it while we're fasting next week."

"Fasting?" Paul asked.

"As soon as the silent period is over. Flazint gave Dorothy a list of Frunge rituals to choose from and fasting was the least unpleasant."

"How long?" Kelly asked.

"A week, or maybe it was ten days after translating from the Frunge calendar."

"You can't fast for a week!"

"It's not a total fast. We just can't eat any grain products, but that's like fifty percent of my diet."

"So it's more of a purifying cleanse."

"I guess. Flazint said that it's not really traditional because the old-fashioned Frunge would never eat grains to start with, but I guess it's cropped up for the ones who live around a lot of aliens."

"I'm surprised they can even digest grains," Paul observed. "Libby?"

"Most Frunge would have trouble digesting their own grains, which aren't farmed by them in any case. But they can eat some of the grains grown by other species."

"How did that come about?"

"I'm sure you've noticed that the oldest species have the widest dietary range. It's one of those creeping adaptations that appear over long stretches of time. The Frunge have developed the ability to digest the meat and produce of several other species, and consumption of those foods brought with it a tolerance for grains built from similar chemical building blocks."

"So you're just doing one ritual each from the three species?" Samuel asked.

"It's three more than I wanted," Kevin replied honestly. "I keep telling myself that the second time's the charm and we won't have to get married again.

"Mind if we join you?" Thomas asked, pausing in his approach to scratch the ears of the Cayl hounds as they competed for his attention. Beowulf and Alexander both snubbed Chance, who never carried dog treats.

"Grab yourselves a seat," Joe replied, pointing towards a couple of heavy rolling tool boxes that would stand the weight of the artificial people. "Judith already head home?"

"Dorothy was waiting in ambush when we quit for the day, though I have to admit that Judith went along willingly. I think she's actually warming up to participating in the wedding party."

"It's the technology," Chance added. "She wants to adapt some of Dorothy's ideas for EarthCent Intelligence."

"Your bride-to-be asked me to explain the marriage traditions of artificial people to you so you could pick something to do, Kevin," Thomas said. "Human-derived artificial people haven't really been around long enough to develop our own traditions, but we're testing a generic add-on from QuickU, if that will help."

"A generic personality enhancement?" Paul asked. "How do they manage that?"

"QuickU has been surveying artificial people from other species and licensing some of their founding myths. Surprisingly, there are plenty of AIs who believe that they created their biological counterparts. Chance and I only began testing the enhancement this morning, and I have to admit it's like seeing everything through different eyes."

"But the oldest human-derived artificial people aren't even a hundred years old yet," Joe pointed out.

"That's why I'm worried about becoming neurotic," Thomas said.

"You're joking."

"He's serious," Chance told them. "Holding incompatible beliefs is one of the leading causes of neurosis as the mind struggles with internal contradictions. I'm not having any problems because I'm already full of contradictions, but Thomas has always played it straight, so it really bothers him."

"Why not get rid of the personality enhancement?" Paul asked.

"Well, for one thing, it's educational, and for another thing, I wouldn't want to disappoint Dorothy by not coming up with a ritual," Thomas replied.

"Now you're making me feel bad," Kevin said. "Why not just recommend the first thing that comes to mind and then get rid of the enhancement."

"Thank you, I believe I'll do that." The artificial person sat stock still for a few seconds, silently communing with Chance. "Got it. There's a ritual performed by artificial Fillinducks before marriage that helps the three of them establish their ranking. It involves a bit of physical—"

"Thomas," Kelly interrupted. "Dorothy and Kevin aren't including a third person in their marriage."

"That's what Chance said, but I thought it was better than her idea."

"Which was?"

"Wearing each other's clothes for a day."

"If anybody even mentions that one to Dorothy, I'm getting in my ship and leaving," Kevin said. "Can't you think of anything else?"

"Well, the Sharf artificial people have a tradition of exchanging their unique personal identifiers before marrying. It's basically a formality for establishing a joint bank account."

"Great, we'll do that one."

"Are you sure you want Dorothy to have access to your business account?" Joe cautioned him. "You know all the trouble she gives Jeeves, and you might find yourself heading out on a trading voyage with a hold full of nothing but frilly dresses."

"As long as I don't have to wear them."

Sixteen

"What are you guys role-playing?" Bob asked the artificial people.

"EarthCent Intelligence trainers," Chance replied.

"But that's what you are!"

"And we're really good at it," Thomas said. "We didn't want to risk messing up Dorothy's Jack-and-Jill LARP by taking on unfamiliar characters. What are you playing?"

"A bard," Bob admitted. "It's the closest thing I could find to a newspaper reporter."

"I would have trained him as a fighting monk but there wasn't enough time," Judith said. "Do you think we should go see what's taking Dorothy and Kevin so long? They've been talking to that non-player character for five minutes already. We should have a quest by now."

"If I know Dorothy, we're going to end up on a search for a lost thimble," Affie said. "Our run-in with giant rats the last time really put her off the whole killing monsters thing."

"If you dragged me here on some fashion quest, I'm not going to be happy," her boyfriend grumbled, adjusting his sword belt. "I rented all this stuff for combat."

"Don't worry, Stick. If there aren't any monsters, I'll let you fight with Judith."

"Finally, they're coming back."

"Got it!" Dorothy proclaimed, waving a scroll. "Where are Flazint and Tzachan? They're supposed to lead Group D."

"They keep sneaking off to stare at each other in privacy, but I swear they're both too shy to talk," Affie said. "Try your telepathy skill."

"My what?"

"Didn't you listen to the orientation for your own LARP? As the party's co-leader, you can contact us all telepathically."

"But I'm not a telepath."

"You are in here. Use your implant."

"Oh." Dorothy paused for a moment and pointed at her own ear. "She's coming. Anyway, I got our quest and it's not exactly what we discussed. I think the basic plan with the groups will still work, except that now we'll all be together." The ambassador's daughter stepped up on a tree stump and addressed the crowd of partygoers. "Listen up. Thomas and Chance will lead Group A, so anybody with an 'A' on your ticket, form up with them. Judith and Bob are leading group B, Affie and Stick will take Group C, Flazint—raise your hand, you and Tzachan take Group D, and Kevin and I will be on point with Group E."

"Why do we need five groups if we're all going together?" Bob asked.

"It was my dad's idea when I told him how many tickets we sold. He said that in the mercenaries they always divided their company into platoons so they could spread out and still maintain a chain of command."

"But you just said that we're staying together. The old Roman armies on Earth were based on a century, or a group of one hundred," the Galactic Free press reporter informed her.

189

"We could do that too. I'm not an expert or anything."

"Tell them about the quest, Dorothy," Kevin urged her, while trying to maintain a straight face.

"Right. Everybody has probably heard by now that I didn't want to kill a bunch of giant rats or anything like that, so I asked the NPC guy for a quest involving textiles."

A groan went up from the players, many of whom were friends of friends and had bought tickets to the Jack-and-Jill as a cheap way to get into a LARP.

"No, really, it will be great fun," Dorothy insisted. "It's just a quick jaunt through the Forbidden Woods and we'll be at the Fall Fair. All we have to do is present this scroll and then we can pick out all of the clothes we want from the merchants. We're basically on a buying mission for the king, and a local guide will be arriving in just a few minutes to lead us there."

"Did you say the Forbidden Woods?" a man dressed in leather armor and carrying a long sword on his shoulder called out.

"Yeah. Cool name, isn't it?"

"Haven't you watched any of the professional LARPing league?" another combat-ready figure cried excitedly. "Any journey through The Forbidden Woods qualifies as an accelerated gauntlet quest."

"No, I'm sure it's just a place name," Dorothy protested. She looked about for the NPC who had given her the quest, but the old caravan master had already disappeared. "Anyway, aren't gauntlets just the male version of women's evening gloves?"

"Not that kind of gauntlet," the first man replied with a snort. "The players have to stay on the road while everything and everyone in the woods tries to stop them from passing."

190

"That can't be," she said, looking to Kevin, who gave an innocent shrug. "Here's the guide now. We'll ask him."

The holographically enhanced robot playing the guide limped up to Dorothy and Kevin and spat loudly on the ground. "Just this lot? We'll never make it through alive."

"What do you mean?" the girl demanded. "You're the guide. You'll get us there safely."

"A few of you, maybe, if the rest are willing to sacrifice themselves," the scruffy NPC replied dubiously. "Well, there's no use fighting against your fate, I say. Follow me."

The partygoers gave a cheer and shook their weapons in the air. Dorothy chewed on her lip but had no choice other than to follow after the suddenly unresponsive guide.

"Maybe we should let some of the experienced fighters move up," Kevin suggested. "You don't want to be killed before the party even gets started."

"I hope you're finding this amusing," Dorothy said, slowing her pace to let some of the armor-clad weapons-wielding characters pass. "You knew all along what was happening when the old man gave me the quest, didn't you?"

"I might have guessed something of the sort," Kevin admitted. "I watched a couple of the professional LARPs with Paul while you were busy plotting wedding stuff with your friends every evening."

"A wedding doesn't just happen by itself, you know."

"I offered to help."

"Like you know anything at all about—what was that?"

"An arrow! Duck!"

Those players who had shields attempted to form a barrier against the arrows whistling out of the woods on flat trajectories, but several had already been pincushioned by the noodle projectiles, which splattered on contact and then reformed when they fell to the ground. The few mages in the company dashed around casting frantic healing spells on the wounded and passing out health potions, but a half-a-dozen players already had holographic bunches of flowers showing above their heads, indicating that they were dead. Then a few of the more experienced guests brought their own bows and other ranged weapons into play, and the brigands melted back into the woods.

"What happened? Is everybody alright?" Dorothy asked.

"Group leaders. Casualty report," Kevin shouted.

"Group B, two dead and waiting for the meat wagon to take them to the respawn point," Judith shouted back in good military style, if out of alphabetical order.

"Group A, one dead and I've got an arrow hole in my new beret," Chance complained.

"Group C, three dead and waiting for their next life," Affie replied. "One of them said that there's a bar at the respawn point and a chance to level up fighting drunken monsters, so they're just going to hang out there rather than coming back."

"Group D, all present and accounted for," Tzachan announced.

"Anybody killed in my group?" Dorothy inquired. "Show of hands?"

"We're good. Thanks for the leadership," a Vergallian swordsman she didn't recognize replied sarcastically. "May I suggest a counter-attack?"

"That would be ill-advised," a woman's voice announced from somewhere behind the group of partygoers bunched up on the road.

"Battlemage!" somebody cried, and all of the players who could see the newcomer began firing arrows, casting spears, and shooting whatever magic projectiles they could in her direction.

"She's too powerful," another player called. "Run away."

"Freeze!" the woman ordered imperiously, and a chill swept over the Jack-and-Jill guests, causing their feet to stick in place. "Do you see this?" she demanded, brandishing something in her hand. "It's a ticket. That makes me a guest, and as the most powerful player, I'll be running the show from here on unless one of you cares to challenge me for the position."

Receiving no answer, the Teragram mage stalked forward through the crowd until she reached Dorothy and Kevin.

"Baa," the ninja seamstress greeted her. "What are you doing here?"

"Jeeves interrupted my meditation and forced me to accept a ticket. I'm supposed to be here to study fashions in LARPing for my new job, but I suspect he sent me to save your party from getting slaughtered by low-level NPCs." As if to confirm her suspicions, another volley of arrows issued from the woods, but this time they all vanished in a puff of smoke just before reaching the players. This was immediately followed by a series of explosions from the forest and a gruesome display of body parts flying through the air. Baa blew on her fingertips and looked pleased with herself.

"Can you keep any more of us from getting killed?" Dorothy requested.

"Thank you for reminding me." Baa drew herself up to her full height, raised her feathered arms over her head, and the black bracelet on her wrist shot out inky tendrils that tore away the holographic funereal bouquets floating above the heads of the slain players. "Come," she commanded.

"Necromancer!" one of the experienced players exclaimed. "That's so cool. What level are you?"

"Gods don't have levels," Baa responded haughtily, and then she addressed the six players that her necromancy had just raised from the dead. "You're mine now, but if you're good little boys and girls, I'll return your souls at the end of the party. Got it?"

"Yes, Baaaaa," they responded, drawing out her name until they sounded like a flock of sheep.

"Enough," the Teragram mage commanded. "Where's the worthless NPC who guided you into an ambush?"

The grumpy guide stepped forward. "Who are you calling worthless, you—"

"Hmm," the mage interrupted, grabbing the NPC's chin in her hand and turning his head from side to side. "Not just a holographic wrapping on a bot, this one. Must be a regular character." Then she released the frozen guide and pushed on his forehead with her index finger, causing him to topple over on his back with a thud. "I'll be leading now. Shall we?"

The six reanimated players bound to Baa by her necromancer magic jogged forward to take positions at the front of the column. The mage crooked her finger at Dorothy, who along with Kevin, joined her in the vanguard. The group leaders fell in behind them, and the rest of the players formed five single-file columns, according to their group designation. Most of the aliens were visibly disturbed to find themselves in the presence of a real

Teragram mage, but nobody was willing to challenge her authority in a medieval LARP environment.

"So, how much gold do you have?" Baa demanded.

"I don't know," Dorothy replied. "Kevin?"

"Ten copper pieces, no gold," he responded. "It's the basic starting amount for everybody who bought a ticket."

"So how do you intend to pay me?" the mage demanded.

"What?" Dorothy squeaked. "You just said that Jeeves sent you as part of your job. I'm not paying for that."

"It's not a matter of choice for any of us. Battlemages charge for their services or they're prohibited from joining a group. I got away with repelling that first attack as a free sample, but if I do it again, the game master will remove me."

"But you just claimed to be a god!"

"This isn't real space so the game master reigns supreme."

"And who is that?" Dorothy demanded.

"Probably your Stryx librarian, she seems to have her paws in everything around here," Baa responded. "In any case, the rules which you apparently didn't bother reading are quite clear. I need to collect gold if I'm to protect you again."

"Could we do it on credit?"

The mage stopped short and folded her feathered arms across her body. "No."

"Give us a minute to consult with our group leaders," Kevin said.

"Yeah, play with your zombies or something," Dorothy added unnecessarily, then fled after Kevin as Baa began to raise her hand.

"Problem?" Thomas asked. "I can talk to Baa if you want. Artificial people make her uncomfortable."

"She demands money to protect us, or to be precise, gold," Kevin told them. "She claims it's part of the rules. Did anybody read them?"

"I did," Flazint and Tzachan said at the same time, causing their hair vines to flush an identical shade of green. "She is justified in her demands," the Frunge attorney continued. "It's unfortunate she arrived late, because if she had participated in the party from the start, there would have been no need."

"She was late on purpose," Dorothy deduced immediately. "My brother bought some gear from her and he told me that she has a thing about money."

"Does it have to be real gold, I mean, real virtual gold, or can we pool all of our coppers together?" Bob asked. "There must be a hundred people here, so that would be like a thousand coppers."

"Ten coppers in a small silver, ten small silvers in a big silver, ten big silvers in a small gold," Flazint recited from memory. "All of our coppers would come to one small gold."

"Here," a player dressed as a strolling minstrel said, thrusting a small pouch of virtual gold into Dorothy's hand. "I've been playing a lot and I can spare it."

"Thank you." She tilted her head sideways. "I don't recognize you, but the voice—Mornich?"

"Don't say anything else," the Horten ambassador's son remonstrated her. "We'll talk later." He faded back into the crowd before Dorothy could ask questions.

"Nice glamour on that one," Chance commented. "I really had to boost my refresh rate to see through it."

"What was that about?" Kevin asked Dorothy as they walked back to where the mage was waiting.

"Jealous?" she teased him. "Don't be. I set him up with one of Samuel's friends from the university and they really hit it off. Last I heard their families were negotiating the terms for an official first date."

"Well?" Baa demanded.

"This is all we could raise so it will have to do," Dorothy said, pouring out the virtual gold coins onto the mage's palm. "Wow, that's actually a lot, isn't it?"

"It's adequate," the mage replied, and proved herself a true magician by making the coins disappear. Then a staff materialized in her hand and she sent a fireball whooshing into the air. "That'll bring them running," she announced, using some trick to amplify her voice so everybody could hear. "I'll handle the projectiles and their mages, but I don't do swords and axes, so arrange yourselves accordingly."

"Who asked you to bring them running?" Dorothy demanded. "I just paid you to keep us safe."

"You really don't know much about having fun, do you?" Baa replied testily. "Do you think your guests came armed to the teeth and wearing armor because they like to sweat?"

"But we're on a shopping quest!"

"Just as soon as we kill all of the monsters," the mage told her. "If there's any time left."

A wave of rogues and brigands surged out of the woods, shouting battle-cries as they brandished their weapons. They were supported by archers and mages who howled in frustration as Baa effortlessly waved aside their attacks. The best-armed Jack-and-Jill guests rushed to join combat, and as they whirled and hacked, holographic bubbles showing points earned appeared over the fallen non-player characters.

"Look at Judith go," Kevin exclaimed to Dorothy. He pointed at the EarthCent Intelligence trainer, who was dancing through the melee, casually delivering critical hits. Then a rogue brandishing a large knife in each hand slipped past the screen of fighters and charged the party leaders.

"Mine," Chance said, stepping forward to intercept the NPC and using some sort of martial arts to throw him all the way over the road to the other side, where he impacted a tree. "Ooh, twenty points."

"Aren't you going to fight?" Dorothy demanded of her fiancé.

"I'm the lead-from-behind sort, but if anybody gets past Chance and Thomas, I'll protect you with my life."

"You're going to get cut off, Stick," Affie yelled at her boyfriend, who kept charging recklessly ahead in his quest to earn points. He ignored her warning and chased after a fleeing brigand, leaving the road and the grassy shoulder. A minute later he returned, a floral arrangement floating over his head, and succumbed to Baa's ministrations.

"Do you have any money?" Baa asked the Vergallian girl during a lull in the fighting.

"Why? Are you willing to sell Stick back to me?"

"I brought enchanted headbands for the whole group that will protect you from turning into zombies if you're bitten."

"But you control all of the zombies," Dorothy pointed out. "It's like you're running a protection racket."

Baa looked thoughtful for a moment. "I'll have to re-member that for the next time," she muttered to herself. "And for your information, I only control the zombies who

I brought back from the dead. Your problem is with the mob of undead that will be coming out of the woods in about another minute or two."

"How much?" Kevin asked.

"Ten coppers," Baa replied. She reached into her shoulder bag and drew out a scrap of material. "Pay me."

A bubble appeared over the Teragram mage as Kevin transferred his ten coppers. Baa handed over the strip of cloth, and her first customer tied it around his head.

"That's not even a real headband," Dorothy complained. "You just cut the old drapes from our office into strips."

"Waste not, want not," Baa replied, dangling a beige scrap in front of the girl. "Of course, if you'd rather be a zombie..."

A loud groan filled the woods around them. Tzachan yelled, "Zombies incoming. Everybody back on the road. Don't let them bite you."

Dorothy's ten coppers appeared over Baa's head, followed by Affie's and Flazint's. Thomas and Chance passed on the protection, either confident in their ability not to get bitten or their immunity from the dread infection.

"Get your magical zombie bite protection, just ten coppers," Baa cried out, casually freezing in place the first wave of undead to stumble out of the woods, lest her customer base suffer attrition.

The partygoers formed a line and jogged past the mage, transferring their coinage and receiving enchanted strips of curtain to tie around their heads. Dorothy wrapped her own purchase around her wrist and scowled.

"Cheer up," Kevin told her. "Everybody is enjoying themselves and they'll have a story to tell their grandchildren as well. Most of the tunnel network species are scared silly of Teragram mages."

"And now we know why," Dorothy groused, indicating the space above Baa's head which was lit up like a pinball machine with incoming payments. "I always thought that they were afraid of being turned into newts or some alien equivalent, but what's more frightening than a superior being who only cares about your money?"

Seventeen

"Knock, knock," Kelly announced at the open door of her office.

"Come in, Ambassador," Phillip responded, rising from the chair. "Daniel will be with us shortly, and Clive is on his way as well. Please, I'd feel funny seeing you sitting anywhere other than behind your desk."

"It's all right, Phillip. It's going to be a short conference call and I have to run to a mediation session immediately afterward."

"I don't doubt for a minute that you're accomplishing more for human-alien relations as a mediator than I am trying to fill your shoes as ambassador. What's the crisis today? Another disagreement over rights to developing a new world? Shipping losses to Horten pirates?"

"Nothing so grand," Kelly said, settling into the guest chair and changing the subject. "Libby? Is the channel to Flower open?"

"I maintain a permanent Stryxnet connection with Flower," the station librarian replied. "Lynx just arrived in the conference room if you wanted to start early."

"Yes, I want to make sure she has the wedding date."

A hologram of Lynx walking into the conference room on Flower appeared over the display desk. The former Union Station cultural attaché had her head down as she busily did a double row of buttons on the uniform top she must have just pulled on. Her head jerked up when the hologram over the large conference table appeared in her peripheral vision.

"At least we know that you're wearing pants since we've seen you standing," Kelly joked. "I suspect that some of the ambassadors I holoconference with are wearing pajama bottoms or worse under the table."

"All the buttons make the uniform top too stiff to walk around in," Lynx explained. "I'm negotiating with Flower to come up with an alternative, but for the time being, I only wear it at official occasions and not a second longer. Besides, you're early."

"I asked Libby to get a jump on the meeting so I could talk to you about the wedding," Kelly explained. "You are still coming, I assume."

"Absolutely. We were planning to take the bookmobile, but it turns out that the wedding is between stops, so Flower is going to jump to Union Station and pick up the latest batch of donated equipment while we're there."

"Great. So I have a favor to ask. Do you still have your antique camera?"

"My 35 millimeter? Sure. I even traded for some new lenses at our flea market, I mean, vintage goods bazaar, but I could use some fresh film. Do you want me to be your wedding photographer?"

"I think it would be nice to have some old-fashioned prints for an album. Jeeves insisted on taking care of the holograms. I thought he was going to ask Libby to take images with the security system, but it turns out he's hired the Grenouthian crew from Aisha's show."

"The same ones who did the lost dogs commercial in Mac's Bones?"

"Probably. That was only ten or twelve years ago and Aisha tells me that all of those network jobs have a very low turnover. I'll order you a dozen rolls of film from Earth and have it sent out in the diplomatic bag, if that's alright with you, Phillip."

"Happy to be of service," Kelly's replacement replied.

Clive and Daniel entered the ambassador's office at the same time, carrying their own chairs. Simultaneously, several more figures dressed in Flower's mandated uniforms entered the remote conference room and settled around the table. Woojin took the captain's place in the high chair, a Dollnick tradition that the colony ship's AI refused to abandon. He adjusted his three-cornered hat self-consciously.

"Who's the extra one?" Flower's synthesized voice demanded. "You only registered three names for this holoconference."

"This is Phillip Hartley, Flower," Daniel replied immediately. "He's Kelly's replacement while she's on sabbatical."

"Pleased to meet you, ma'am," Phillip said, and then whistled a short series of staccato notes.

"Oh, if you put it that way, you're welcome to stay," Flower responded, and added a quick trill of her own. "This must be your first time meeting my officers, but I've found that you Humans prefer to dispense with the formalities, so I'll just add labels." The hologram above Kelly's display desk flickered, and then a tag appeared over each of the participants on the colony ship. Woojin was identified as 'Captain Pyun," but the others were labeled by their first names, 'First Officer Missy,' 'Second Officer Lynx,' and "Chief of Security Harold.'

"I've been hearing great things about the police detachment you deployed at the Break Rock asteroid mining complex," Daniel said. "They haven't had a single case of claim jumping since you left, and their council has signed on to our program for developing a local judiciary. I hope you can keep up with the demand as your circuit widens."

"It's just the habitat-based colonies that are slipping into lawlessness," Flower's security chief told them. "Our last couple stops were at open worlds, as you know, and the human communities in those places aren't having any problems, knock on wood. But our next destination is an interstellar recycling facility that the Frunge outsourced to a large group of people who recently completed a twenty-five-year contract providing labor there. Unfortunately, as soon as it became known that the aliens had ceded control, criminal elements started moving in."

"They don't waste any time, do they?" Clive commented. "What's the plan?"

"It's our last stop before we head back to Union Station for resupply, so we're equipping the detachment with all the good stuff we have left," Woojin said. "I just hope you have some more patrol craft for us because it's impossible to police these space-based operations without them. And armored spacesuits are just as important."

"I've got good news on that front," Daniel said. "The Vergallian ambassador has some kind of back-channel into military surplus auctions. I reached out to the delegates for our next Sovereign Human Communities Conference, and we have a tentative agreement to match donations with purchases."

"You mean if the Vergallians give us a free ship, we'll buy one?" Missy asked.

"The Stryx have extended a line of credit for the purpose, so they must approve," the associate ambassador replied. "The overall numbers are so low that we don't think it will distort the market for a while yet, and hopefully by then, we'll be in a position to buy everything we need."

"So what kind of numbers are you talking about?"

"We've got eighteen patrol craft waiting for you in long-term parking," Daniel said. "That should cover the rest of your circuit unless somebody has gotten into a war."

"And spacesuits?" Harold asked.

"The patrol craft come with two armored suits each, and they're all the standard issue Vergallian models, so some of your ex-mercenaries will already be trained on them."

"That's more than we hoped for," Woojin said. "I don't want to sound greedy, but I've got a list of things we could really use to tide us over until the circuit takes us back to Earth."

"Anything I can help with, Wooj?" Kelly asked. "I have to run to a mediation session in a couple of minutes."

"The librarians want more books. What were the specific subjects, Lynx?"

"Romance, cozy mystery, and anything for young adults where they aren't killing each other in tournaments. Oh, and whatever you can find on homesteading."

"Got it," Kelly said, making a mental note. "I'll request some classics too, since you can never have too many. But wait a second. Back before you left Earth, I thought the librarians were complaining that there wasn't enough shelf space for the books they sent up on the elevator."

"They've had to modify their philosophy," Lynx said. "It's a library for the people who live on Flower, but it's kind of a second-hand bookstore for everybody else."

"What?"

"It just isn't practical to loan books to people when we're only spending a week at each stop," Flower interjected. Kelly could still see Lynx's lips moving, so it was clear that the Dollnick AI had squelched the second officer. "I told you that a library was a silly idea for a circuit ship, but I suppose my eighteen thousand years of experience in space travel didn't make an impression. And don't send any more of those monographs or I'll grind them up to reclaim the pulp."

"Uh, got it," Kelly said. "I'm sure the rest of you have plenty to talk about, so I'll be off and you can fill me in later. And see you guys at the wedding," she concluded with a wave.

As the ambassador left the embassy, Libby informed her, "Donna is on her way to Hole Universe, and your clients have already arrived."

"Why does Flower always do that?" Kelly asked. "The Dollnick ambassador's biggest complaint about humans during the review of our tunnel network status was that we say 'I told you so.' Why doesn't their AI show the same sensibility?"

"You're forgetting that the Dollnicks never set out to create AI on their colony ships. Flower and her kind arose spontaneously from the high level of complication and control built into the ship. She would never have been available for EarthCent to lease if her personality hadn't caused her makers to abandon ship."

"I suppose. I'm glad I don't have to mediate any disputes with her as one of the parties. Hole Universe," she added unnecessarily as she entered the lift tube. "I'm not really sure if I should have agreed to mediate this dispute. After all, I'm not exactly a disinterested party."

"Both of the merchants know that and accepted you," Libby said.

The capsule came to a stop and Kelly exited into the busy Little Apple commercial district, her feet automatically finding their way to Hole Universe. Donna was waiting at the counter, standing between Jan Meier and the clone who everybody knew as Chocolate Gem. The owner of the donut shop was waiting on them, and she shot Kelly a pleading look as the ambassador entered, obviously wanting to be included in the action. Kelly sighed and squared her shoulders, making room for herself between Donna and the clone.

"Jan, Chocolate," she greeted her clients, who ironically, also happened to be major beneficiaries of her salary. "Would you prefer the privacy of a booth, or shall we do this at the counter?"

"Counter is fine by me," the clone said. "I think of Helen as a friend," she added, nodding to the owner of the donut shop.

"As do I," Jan said, scowling at the Gem. "Helen has attended many of the tastings at my shop and I trust her judgment implicitly."

"Then it's settled," Kelly agreed. "I have to inform you all that as a matter of standard procedure, I've asked the station librarian to record this mediation session. Before we proceed to the mediation which the two of you have agreed on, I want to request again that you consider settling this dispute without my help."

"The time for idle chatter is past," Jan declared. "If it weren't for careless words, we wouldn't need to be here."

"There was nothing careless about my advertisement," Chocolate Gem retorted. "I reviewed the English text with the expert editors at the Galactic Free Press."

"The ad stated that Sweet Dreams sells the best chocolate on Union Station," the owner of the Chocolate Emporium fired back. "That is an exclusionary statement which implies that my chocolate is substandard."

"Why can't both of you sell the best chocolate on Union Station?" Kelly said. "You know I split my business between you for a reason."

"How can two shops have the best chocolate?" the Swiss expatriate demanded scornfully. "Both of us can sell *good* chocolate, both of us can sell *great* chocolate, but she's the one who had to claim that hers is the *best*."

"Chocolate?" Kelly asked the clone, and it struck her for the first time that the Gem's nickname could lead to confusion.

Chocolate Gem removed the plastic wrap from her tray and slid it down the counter in front of the two EarthCent employees. "Eat," she ordered. "Jan and I flipped a coin before you arrived and my chocolate is going first. You too, Helen. Three judges eliminates the possibility of a tie."

"I'm really not sure—" Kelly tried again, but this time it was Donna who interrupted her.

"Why don't we sample the chocolate first?" Donna said, elbowing her friend in the side at the same time. "Good chocolate has a mood-enhancing effect that could be conducive to negotiation."

"That's right," the owner of Hole Universe agreed, taking up a triangular wedge with an almond on top. She closed her eyes as she began to chew, and then stopped to allow the chocolate time to melt in her mouth.

Kelly gave in and selected a rounded piece that was as high as it was wide, suggesting a hidden treasure inside. When her teeth broke through the rich shell and released the coconut filling onto her tongue, her knees almost buckled, and she had to lean forward against the counter.

Donna snatched up one of the Gem's specialties, a milk chocolate shaped and textured like a raspberry, with a bit of green mint leaf where the stem would be, and filled with raspberry preserve.

"You too, Jan," the clone said, pushing the tray a little farther so that the proprietor of the Chocolate Emporium could reach it. "We agreed."

Scowling, the man reached for the plainest bar of chocolate on offer and examined the color. He held it off to the side of his head and snapped it angrily, paying close attention to the sound. Then he sniffed at the broken ends, and a puzzled look appeared on his face. After he popped one of the pieces into his mouth and ground it between his molars, his expression changed to one of surprise.

"Well?" Kelly asked, having just recovered enough from her own tasting experience to manage the single word.

"Good," Donna said, reaching for another piece.

Helen just nodded vigorously and did the same.

"Wait," Kelly ordered, pulling the tray away from them. "You have to say more than that."

"What do you want?" Donna asked in irritation. "Herbaceous overtones with a hint of mint and a smooth finish? Excellent body with strong bean characteristics?"

"Nutty," Helen contributed, leaving it ambiguous whether she was talking about the almond or the ambassador.

"Not terrible," the Swiss chocolatier admitted.

"No, we have to try his now," Kelly remonstrated the other two women, pushing the Gem's tray back to the clone. "Here, I brought everybody an apple and a bread-stick to clear your palette. Do you have any seltzer, Helen?"

"You're taking all of the fun out of this," the donut shop owner complained, but she retrieved a bottle of sparkling water from her fridge and poured a glass for each of them. "You know, I let a couple of bakery fanatics schedule a tasting here once, but I had to kick them out when they started stroking the donuts to judge the texture and poking holes with their fingertips to determine the surface tension or something. They were making the other customers lose their appetites."

"I'm just trying to be fair," Kelly said defensively. "I take the mediation business seriously."

"You're getting paid to do this?"

"Yes. Well, I negotiated my fee in chocolate, but it comes to the same thing."

"My turn," Jan said, pushing a silver tray down the counter to Donna, who reluctantly slid it in front of Kelly so the Gem could also reach.

Kelly swallowed a hastily chewed hash of bread and apple, wondering if she should have taken them separate-ly, followed by a sip of sparkling water, which she swished around in her mouth. Then she selected a small master-piece of a sculpted chocolate and bit into it eagerly. The other two women each took a piece, and the clone reluc-tantly chose a small pyramid-shaped chunk of dark chocolate.

Donna was the first to speak. "It's too close to call. I'm going to need to sample them both again."

"Me too," Helen agreed immediately.

"I've had worse," the clone said, though her dilated pupils suggested that she wasn't telling the whole story. "What did you think, Ambassador?"

"That's right, Kelly. You never gave your opinion of Herr Meier's chocolate either," Donna accused her.

"No, I didn't," the ambassador said, stepping back from the counter. "I only agreed to this tasting to demonstrate the futility of choosing between two artists of such high achievement. I have two children who are very different, but I love them both equally. Would you ask me to choose between them?"

"You're comparing your children to chocolate?" the clone asked in astonishment. "It's just food in the end."

"You have to keep things in perspective," Jan added. "Chocolate is my livelihood but it's not my life."

"Exactly," the ambassador declared triumphantly. "Here the two of you could be great friends and col- leagues, but instead you're arguing over a few words of ad copy that nobody else on the station would remember if you asked them. Excuse me," she called to a young couple who were just entering Hole Universe. "Who makes the best chocolate on Union Station?"

"This place," the man replied with a happy grin. "Their triple chocolate donut is out of this world."

Helen stepped back from the counter looking embar- rassed as the two chocolatiers glared at her. "They're just kids," she mumbled. "I put a lot of sugar in the mix."

"All I'm saying is that the two of you have far more in common than any small differences over marketing," Kelly continued, feeling herself on a roll. "I know better than anyone that you both have more business than you can handle. How many times have I come to your shops only to find out that you'd sold out of everything?"

"A few," Jan admitted.

"I was just trying to reach a new audience," the clone said. "It's not easy running a chocolate shop on the same station as the grandson of 'My Recipes.' I spent my first paycheck on the pirated Gem translation."

"You read my grandfather's book?" the Swiss chocolatier asked in surprise.

"Of course, he was a genius. I've petitioned our so-called government to create a holiday on his birthday, but they said that it would set a bad precedent."

"I would have thought that if anybody was ready to base a holiday on chocolate, it would be the Gem," Kelly commented with her mouth full.

"The thing they objected to was a holiday to commemorate the birth of an alien. Our chocolate lobby is trying again with the publication date of the cookbook, and it looks like this time there's a chance it will pass."

Eighteen

Marilla and Jorb were waiting at the designated lift tube when Samuel and Vivian arrived. The four students boarded the capsule together.

"Take us to Jeeves," the Horten girl said out loud.

"You'd think he could have provided a better description of our destination other than to say that he's in it," Jorb complained.

"Maybe it keeps changing for each group," Samuel speculated. "Isn't this supposed to be like a final exam?"

"What's that?" the Drazen asked.

"Humans like taking lots of tests in school," Marilla explained. "Then at the end of a course, they take a final exam that replaces all of the earlier tests. It's a weird system."

The capsule arrived at its destination and Jeeves beckoned to them from an open door down the corridor.

"Come in and grab a pod," he instructed the students. "You can leave your gear on the floor. We'll be alone here for the length of your immersion so nobody is going to steal it."

"What is this place?" Vivian asked.

"One of my workshops," the Stryx replied. "I've chosen your group for an experimental platform I've been developing. Don't worry. I already tested it on Paul."

"He didn't mention anything about it," Samuel said doubtfully.

"I swore him to secrecy. The pods are merely sensory deprivation chambers that will levitate your bodies and keep you from making contact with anything that might destroy the alternative world I will create through your implants."

"So what's the advantage of this over a LARP studio?" Marilla asked.

"It's not widely known, but in the absence of external stimuli, the combined input of your audio and visual implants can be used to present a rather convincing imitation of reality. Of course, it requires a high order of artificial intelligence to create a real-time stream of interactive environments, and I don't suppose any of the other Stryx have ever cared to bother."

"You mean we're guinea pigs?" Vivian demanded.

"As I told you, Paul aided me with the proof of concept. The idea was partially his, from something we once discussed as a potential Libbyland attraction."

"So you're saying that while we're floating in the dark, you'll be supplying images to our heads-up displays and direct audio to our translation implants, and that will be enough to make us think we're somewhere else?"

"I may have a few other tricks in the pods as well," Jeeves admitted. "If you want to quit at any time, just say so, and the lid will pop open."

Samuel removed his backpack and his sword belt before climbing into the pod. "Like this?" he asked, lying back with his hands crossed on his chest.

"Whatever makes you comfortable," the Stryx replied, triggering the lid to close.

Vivian and the two other students followed suit, and they soon found themselves floating alone in the universe. Then there was a flash of light and a muted orchestral score began to play.

"Welcome to Enhancement," a voice spoke over the music, and all four students suddenly found themselves standing on a rocky plain.

"Hey, we're ourselves," Jorb said. "I thought we had to play aliens."

"Don't go out of character," Marilla warned him automatically.

"How can I go out of character when I'm me?"

"I think she meant about accepting our new setting as reality," Samuel said.

"There are no penalties in this LARP," Jeeves announced without making himself seen. "As you have discovered, you begin by playing yourselves, and the only question is where you decide to stop. The sole rule is that each of you must choose a minimum of one enhancement from the starter menu."

"What starter menu?" Jorb asked.

"It will appear when the living metal is activated. Please step back, Vivian."

The girl took one step back, and a silvery fountain sprang up from where she had been standing. A menu appeared floating in space in front of the liquid metal, and Vivian found she could scroll through the list with eye movements, the same way a standard heads-up display was operated.

"It's like a picture within a picture," Jorb muttered as he skimmed his own version of the list. "Is everybody seeing the same options? No, I doubt any of you would want a longer tentacle."

"Some of this stuff is pretty yucky," Vivian said. "I don't want to change the way I look or how I think."

"I'm going to try enhanced spatial perception," Samuel announced. "I've always wondered what it would be like have an artificial person's ability to look at something and be able to read off the dimensions, like a 3D blueprint."

As soon as the ambassador's son made his choice, a thread of silvery metal reached out and touched his forehead. It seemed to pool up on his skin for a moment before being absorbed.

"Are you okay?" Vivian asked after a few seconds passed without any reaction from the fountain's recipient.

"It's amazing," Samuel breathed. "This would save so much time in engineering. It's like night and day."

"Your eyes have changed color. They're silvery now!"

"And I can see right into your eyes. You know how you've been complaining about some things seeming blurry in the distance? If I knew anything about vision, I could prescribe corrective lenses or do the surgery. I mean, all the numbers are superimposed when I just think about it."

"I can't believe it," Marilla said. "There's an enhancement that will allow me to control my skin color."

"But showing your emotions on the outside is a big part of being Horten," Vivian said. "It would be like giving up your identity."

"We weren't always this way," Marilla replied irritably. "I'm going to try it."

"Wait," Vivian protested, but the Horten had already made her choice, and a silver finger reached out from the fountain and touched her forehead.

"Do you feel any different?" Samuel asked. "I was look-ing right at you and none of your measurements have changed."

"Who said you could check out her measurements?" Vivian growled.

"I feel exactly the same," Marilla told them, sounding slightly depressed.

"Your skin looks a bit silvery, though," Jorb pointed out. "And wouldn't your skin normally turn sort of orange from disappointment?"

"Grey," Samuel corrected the Drazen. "Test it, Marilla. Do something obvious."

"Like what? I don't think I can intentionally embarrass myself with you guys, or suddenly be happy or angry."

"Try lying," Jorb told her.

Marilla froze for a moment at the audacious suggestion. "You know that Hortens can't lie," she said in a low voice. "Our skin gets black blotches and we break out in a terrible rash."

"So try a little lie."

"There's no such thing as a little lie," both girls re-sponded at the same time.

"I've got an idea," Samuel said. "Who was your favorite character on 'Let's Make Friend's' when your sister was in the cast?"

"My sister."

"Now I'll ask you again, but say it was Shaina's son Mikey. Who was your favorite character on Aisha's show?"

Marilla braced herself like she was expecting something to fall out of the virtual sky and crush her. "Mikey," she whispered.

"Well?" Jorb demanded.

"I don't feel any different," the Horten girl said. "How does my skin look?"

"No change. Try a bigger lie."

"I wish I had a tentacle because I think they're really cool," Marilla responded instantly. "Hey, this lying business is kind of fun. What are you going to pick, Jorb?"

"It's something I'm kind of embarrassed about," the Drazen admitted. "I never really put in the time to learn musical notation, so the women in my family are always singing over my head, and I don't know if they're discussing the price of vegetables or making fun of me. And when I read our books, I know I'm missing ninety percent of the meaning because I'm just getting the plain text."

"And there's an option on your list for instantly learning musical notation?" Vivian asked.

"I'm choosing it now." Jorb staggered when the silver fountain reached out and touched his forehead, and then folded himself into a martial arts meditation pose to regain control. "It's incredible," he said. "I've been missing out on a whole world I knew nothing about."

"How are you testing it?" Samuel asked.

"My heads-up display," the Drazen replied. "I keep a copy of Korf's classic combat manual in the queue for quick reference, and now I see that in all of these years I've only scratched the surface of his philosophy. I thought that the diagrams were the heart and soul, but the notations, they're brilliant. Throw a punch at me."

"What?"

"I won't hurt you. Five minutes ago I would have done a block or thrown you across the room, but this is better."

"Better for who?"

"For both of us," Jorb said, rising to his feet. "Come on and punch me already."

Samuel sighed, then he shuffled forward in the boxer's stance his father had taught him and threw a right cross at the Drazen's chin. Somehow Jorb was suddenly beside him restraining the human's wrist, and the overall effect made it look like the two were performing a martial arts tango.

"I barely saw you move," Vivian said. "How is that even possible?"

"It's all in the hidden meaning," the Drazen replied. "If I can still read musical notation when we get out of here, I'm going to drop out of the Open University and become a monk."

"You could always just learn it the hard way, by studying," Marilla pointed out.

"I'm too old already. There are over ten thousand symbols, and that doesn't count the timing notation and the fractional notes and beats. You have to start when you're a little kid and stay with it."

"Your tongue is sort of silvery," Vivian told him. "I saw it when you were talking. And your ears look a bit shiny now."

"They don't feel any different," the Drazen said, squeezing an ear gently with the tip of his tentacle. "What are you going to choose?"

"I'm kind of scared," the girl admitted. "There's nothing here I want, and I keep thinking about the abandoned decks in Libbyland which had been occupied by species that turned themselves into cyborgs."

"This is different," Samuel said. "There's nothing mechanical about it and I feel exactly the same. Our implants are more like that cyborg stuff than whatever the fountain is doing to us."

"How do you know what it's doing?"

"None of this is real," Marilla reminded the girl. "We're lying in sensory deprivation pods and Jeeves is manipulating everything we see and hear."

"Wait. That might not matter to the rest of us in here, but what if lying made your body break out in blisters in real life?"

"I hope you have a better opinion of me than that," their LARP orchestrator's voice spoke out of the fountain. "I understand your reluctance to enhance yourself, Vivian, especially given the indoctrination my parent no doubt pounded into your head in her experimental school. But if you don't choose something in the next ninety minutes, I'm afraid I won't be able to give you university credit for the course."

"Come on, Viv," Samuel encouraged her. "Jeeves wouldn't do anything that would hurt us. Isn't there an enhancement you're even curious about?"

"Well, I've often wondered what it would be like to fly. Really fly, with natural wings, not like the magnetic levitation in the Physics Ride or the powered Frunge wing sets.

"I saw a choice for flying in the menu. It was in the section for physical alterations."

"But still…"

"One enhancement was just the minimum, you know. Why don't I add wings and then I can tell you—"

"No, I'll do it," Vivian said. "We don't know what stacking enhancements might do to us." She took a deep breath and made her choice, and the fountain reached out to her with a thicker finger of liquid metal than it had used to reach the three other students. A moment later, an enormous pair of silvery wings sprouted from her back.

"Are you alright?" Samuel asked immediately. "Does it feel funny?"

"I'm not sure," she replied, a strange expression on her face. "It's like nothing has changed, but I know it has. I mean, it feels like I've had wings all of my life and I know exactly how to use them."

"Aren't you going to fly?" Jorb asked, glancing up from the cross-legged position he'd resumed on the ground where he was poring through the combat manual on his heads-up display and singing under his breath.

"Maybe I'll just stretch them a little." Vivian's silvery wings extended slowly to a wingspan more than twice her height, and they would have knocked Marilla over if the Horten girl hadn't dodged back.

"You look like an angel," Samuel murmured, his silvery eyes alight. "An angel covered with dimensional notations. I can tell you exactly how many feathers are showing if you want to know."

"Can you actually fly?" Marilla asked the other girl.

"I think so. It feels like I can. Give me a little room."

Samuel and Marilla drew back to stand on either side of Jorb, and Vivian turned a little away from them and began working her wings. From the first forward thrust, her feet left the ground, and with each additional wing beat, she gained altitude.

"I can't believe all this bobbing up and down isn't making me sick," she cried to the students below.

"Try gliding," Samuel advised. "That should be smooth."

Legs extended behind her, Vivian tried to maintain altitude without flapping, and found that by wiggling her wingtips, she could maneuver smoothly in circles and swoops.

221

"This is incredible. I want to keep them."

"Just stay up there," Samuel shouted back. "I'm going to add wings too."

The fountain reached out and touched the youth, and a minute later he was soaring after Vivian, the two engaged in an aerial game of catch-me-if-you-can. Marilla hesitated for several minutes, watching the humans fly about as if they had been born with wings, then gave in to the temptation herself. It wasn't long before the three of them were taking turns swooping at the Drazen, who remained in his lotus position as if he were in a trance.

"You're going to miss the opportunity, Jorb," Samuel shouted while making a pass overhead. "The LARP has a two-hour max."

"I'm good," Jorb sang back, surprising himself and the others with his new-found musicality. "You guys go ahead and look around."

"Just the thought of having to land is depressing," Marilla called to her flying companions as they winged off towards a nearby cliff that seemed to attract them all on some fundamental level. "Was there a reason that should bother me? I can't remember."

"I saw an enhancement for mood that would take care of depression," Vivian said. "I wonder if it would work this far from the fountain."

"It still shows on my heads-up display. I'm going to try it." A thread of silver sought out the flying Horten and briefly brushed her temple. "Oooh. You guys have to try this to believe it."

Two more threads reached out from the fountain as Samuel and Vivian made the selection, after which the three students didn't talk again until they found themselves coming in for a landing on a high ledge.

"This is better than real life," Vivian declared.

"No argument from me," Samuel concurred.

"We should try all the enhancements," Marilla said. "I never thought I'd be envious of artificial people, but they must be laughing at the rest of us for being limited biologicals. I wonder why my species makes so few of them."

"I'm getting encyclopedic knowledge," Samuel told the others, and a silver thread from the fountain found him a moment later.

"There's an alien psychology enhancement," Vivian said, and the liquid metal raced to bestow its blessing on her.

"Do you guys see the option to complete our university educations?" Marilla asked. "It can't be serious." A filament from the fountain reached out and touched her forehead. "It's true. I can finally get on with life."

"Did you hear something?" Samuel asked, twisting his head as if he were an owl.

"There's an enhancement for that," Vivian told him, and the fountain found her again. "It's just Jorb singing."

"We should head back and make him grow wings," Marilla said. "He'll never forgive us if he misses this."

The three dove off the cliff and found that with thermals arising from the rocky plain, they didn't even need to beat their wings to glide back to the fountain. Before they could even see him, they heard Jorb's clear singing, though the song only had one line repeated over and over again.

"This isn't right. This isn't right. This isn't right."

"Who knew the Drazen was hiding such talent," Marilla said. "I should introduce him to Mornich."

"Is he trying to tell us something?" Samuel asked.

"This isn't right. This isn't right," Jorb sang.

"This song is a bummer," Vivian said. "I'm going to try a higher level of the mood enhancer."

The three winged students came in for a graceful landing by the fountain, and they all made new requests, but no silver threads were forthcoming.

"It's not working," Vivian said in frustration. "Hey, drop the singing, Jorb. We've got a serious problem."

"I can't enhance either," Marilla complained. "Maybe there was a limit."

"I can see it now that I look," Samuel told them. "The fountain started with a fixed amount of manna and we've used it all up."

"That's it? We can't get more?"

"Jeeves!" Vivian called. "Your LARP is broken."

"This isn't right," Jorb repeated, finally managing to speak in his regular voice rather than singing. "You were just going to try one enhancement each and stop."

"Like you didn't make any additions while we were away," Marilla said accusingly. "I'll bet you're the one who used up all the manna."

"No, I didn't, because even this first one is too much. It says right here in the book of—"

"We don't care about your stupid book," Vivian said. "If you don't want your enhancement, give it back, and then we'll be able to use the manna."

The Drazen stiffened in surprise at the girl's speech, and then replied with a sad shrug, "I can't give it back. I tried. Korf's whole philosophy of combat is based on gaining fluency through training. These enhancements are just cheating."

"Don't be a spoilsport," the Horten girl said, glancing down at the backs of her hands. "If I were doing anything unethical, my color would be changing. See? Same as always."

"That was your first enhancement, Marilla," Jorb said softly. "Don't you remember?"

"Remember what? You're just trying to make us all feel bad because you didn't grab the mood enhancer while you could."

"What enhancement did you add first?" Samuel asked the Horten. "It's slipped my mind."

"Oh, I don't remember. What difference does it make?"

"This isn't right," the Drazen said again. "It's not like you, not like any of you. That fountain is a drug."

"Jeeves wouldn't drug us," Samuel said confidently. "It's just an educational experience, right?"

"And what did you learn?"

"Flying is the best!"

"Time's up," Jeeves announced, and the rocky ground they were standing on disappeared. All four students suddenly found themselves floating motionless in their sensory deprivation pods and hastened to pop the lids open.

"That was terrible," Jorb told the Stryx, rising from the pod like a corpse sitting up in a coffin. "I'm never doing another LARP with you in charge."

"You don't have to," the Stryx replied. "The four of you completed the course today."

"Was he right, Jeeves? Did you drug us?" Samuel asked.

"I did nothing of the sort. Some of the enhancements you chose necessarily affected your outlook, but what do you expect?"

"I'm sorry I yelled at you, Jorb," Vivian said. "It was so real and so good. But I somehow feel like I failed a test, and I'll never try anything like it again."

"Same here," Samuel affirmed.

"I had a good time," Marilla said, staring intently at the skin on the back of her hands, which began to turn blotchy and blister with the lie. "Praise Gortunda! I was afraid I lost my color forever."

Nineteen

"Welcome back," Joe greeted the extended Crick clan as they rolled their baggage up the ramp into the ice harvester. "We're going to farm a few of you out to Paul and Aisha next door, and Dorothy and Kevin have a spare bedroom in their new cargo container, I mean, home, but there're five empty rooms right here."

"Thank you, Joe," Mary replied, looking around the living area of the ice-harvester which she hadn't seen in almost eighteen years. "Who are these big boys?"

"The one with his nose in your luggage is Alexander, Kevin's Cayl hound, and you met the one with the begging bowl in his previous incarnation," Kelly told her. "Put that bowl away, Beowulf. They'll think we don't feed you."

Shaun pulled the handle on his rollaway bag upright and offered Joe his hand. "Good to see you, in-law. Who'd have thought the kids would end up getting their hands roped? I always wondered why our Kevin wasn't willing to stick around such a sweet place as New Kasil, but now it makes sense."

"I'm glad to hear the world turned out to your liking," Joe said. "Still, it must be nice to see some human faces for a change."

"Oh, we've got plenty of those, thanks to Becky." The Crick patriarch jerked a thumb over his shoulder at his daughter. "Over a hundred thousand at the last tithing

227

count. I'm in charge of tithes," he added, patting his wallet pocket and winking.

"You're in charge of keeping track of tithes," Becky corrected him, stepping out from behind her parents. "That's not the same thing."

"It's wonderful to see you again, Becky," Kelly said. "Kevin tells us that you've become quite the prophetess."

"I'm merely Nabay's instrument," she replied modestly. "The visions come unbidden. My oldest daughter also has the gift, which we discovered when she began bringing home perfect grades from school."

"I just study really hard," the red-haired girl in question protested, drawing a series of snorts and guffaws from all of the Cricks present.

"So where is my dashing son?" Mary asked.

"I see a vision of him sweating in the dark," Becky answered before anybody else could respond. "But whatever for?"

"Dorothy and Kevin have been performing various alien rituals to prepare for their wedding," Joe explained. "It started as a lark to please a couple of Dorothy's coworkers, but when the word got out, all of our friends began sending suggestions, and the kids didn't want to offend anybody. Spending a week before the wedding in a sweat lodge is a Verlock thing, though I don't know if the kids got the idea from the local ambassador or the engineer who invented Dorothy's heels."

"They're spending a week in a sweat lodge?" Shaun demanded. "That's daft."

"Just Kevin, and only a couple of hours," Kelly hastened to explain. "Paul and Samuel, our younger son who you haven't met, went to keep him company."

"And where's my daughter-in-law?" Mary asked.

"She's taking a nap in either a Grenouthian warren or a Dollnick nest. I've forgotten the details, but they both involved sleeping."

"They sound like symbolic rituals to promote fertility," Becky observed. "Couples on New Kasil often sleep in a hayloft on the night before the wedding."

"I just know that she needed the rest since she was up half the night gabbing with her friends. This afternoon we're all heading over to the Empire Convention Center to put up decorations in the hall."

"Is there a theme?" asked one of Kevin's other sisters who made the trip. "I've done some wedding planning back on New Kasil, but everybody always wants the same thing."

"What's that?" Kelly asked.

"Square dancing in a barn. And we only have one decent fiddler and one good caller within wagon distance. The only real difference from wedding to wedding is the menu, or to be honest, the dessert."

"My daughter takes after her father in her gift for exaggeration," Mary told their hosts. "It's true that we've learned from the Kasilians to follow a simple life, but part of that includes changing our diet with the seasons. And of course, it's the people who make the weddings, so every celebration is different."

Beowulf barked sharply and glared out the door of the ice harvester, but he didn't go as far as Alexander, who ran off to investigate the new arrival.

"I've always said that dogs are better than doorbells," Shaun declared. "Maybe the kids are back."

"Beowulf wouldn't bark for anybody in the family," Joe said, squinting into the distance. "Looks like a Dollnick. Were you expecting any mediation clients, Kel?"

"No," the ambassador said, and went on to explain to her guests, "I've been working as a mediator during my sabbatical. I've already been able to help settle four inter-species disputes without anybody resorting to court. It's surprising how many seemingly intractable problems can be cleared up if everybody just calms down and listens to each other."

"I'd appreciate any tips you can give me," Becky said. "All of the humans on New Kasil bring their problems to me to see if I'll give them a better deal than the high priest."

"Like venue shopping?" Joe asked.

"What's that?"

"When one party in a dispute tries to find a sympathetic court before filing a lawsuit. It comes up a lot in the used spaceship business."

"I guess it's similar," the prophetess mused. "I don't charge anything for advice so the humans on New Kasil figure it's worth trying me first to see if I'll offer a solution they can live with. If you go to the Kasilian High Priest, there's a required contribution, and her word is law."

"May I come in?" a giant Dollnick inquired, halting at the top of the ramp in front of the growling dog.

"Down, Beowulf," Joe commanded. "Please share our space and water," he offered a standard Dolly welcome. "How can we help you?"

"I'm Bru, from the Empire Convention Center," the Dollnick said, twitching nervously as if he didn't know what to do with his four hands. "I'm here about your reservation."

"Did I forget to send the rest of the deposit?" Kelly asked, her eyes going wide. "No, wait. I remember asking Donna to do it and she'd never mess up a thing like that."

"Your reservation is in perfect order," Bru assured her, and fishing a handkerchief out of his pocket, wiped a bead of perspiration from his chin. "There's just a minor issue of force majeure," he continued, bringing the hands on his lower set of arms together to illustrate the smallness of the problem.

"Oh, you gave me a good scare. Is it about our getting in early to decorate this afternoon? We could wait until evening if it's a problem."

"How about a week from this evening?" the Dollnick suggested.

"No, that won't work," Kelly replied, frowning. "You see, the wedding is tomorrow, so decorating in a week wouldn't..." Her voice trailed off, and the Dollnick began to whistle rapidly, almost overloading the ambassador's diplomatic-grade implant.

"You see, all of our contracts this cycle contain a force majeure clause stating that if the Horten revival is bringing more than ten thousand souls a day to Gortunda, they can extend their run. The Hortens have been staging their Union Station revival at the Empire Convention Center for over a hundred thousand years, so you can understand why we would bend over backwards for such a customer."

"Extend?" Joe asked as Kelly struggled to find words.

"It's a week-to-week situation that only came about because a Horten colony ship put in for emergency repairs. The delay meant five million bored colonists with nothing to do, and when heading for the other side of the galaxy with a dicey jump drive, a little insurance of the religious sort can suddenly look like a sound investment."

"So you're saying that the hall we reserved for my daughter's wedding..."

"I've spoken to the Gortunda's Guides and they were very understanding. If you want to work the wedding in as part of the revival—"

"What about my reservation!" Kelly shouted, shaking her fist in front of the giant Dollnick's chest, which was as high as she could reach. "I'll sue!"

"I'm afraid that the Force Majeure clause specifically prohibits such action," Bru said apologetically. "I'm here to offer you a full refund and your choice of a future date for free or double your money back."

"I don't want my money back, I want that hall!"

"You'll catch more flies with honey than vinegar," Shaun observed unhelpfully.

"I don't want any damned flies," Kelly snapped, and grabbed one of the nattily dressed alien's lower sleeves. "And I don't care what the contract says. You give me my hall."

"Please calm down and listen to me," the Dollnick pleaded, but Kelly spoke right over him.

"No! You listen to me. My embassy is always making reservations at your convention center, and we've been staging the Sovereign Human Communities Conference there for, uh, years. I know you can make the space if you try."

"My humblest apologies," the Dollnick repeated, and crossed all of his wrists together in front of his chest. "My hands are tied in this situation, and if our offer of another date with a full refund or double your money back isn't acceptable, there's nothing else I can do."

"If they won't give us the hall, they won't give us the hall," Joe reasoned with his wife. "We still have twenty-four hours to get ready, and I'm sure we can rent five hundred matching chairs somewhere and—"

"I'll give you the chairs for free," Bru interrupted.

"I am NOT marrying my daughter off in this hold!" Kelly gritted out, sounding just like Dorothy. "You!" she glowered at the Dollnick. "Under the interspecies dispute process of Union Station, I demand mediation by a station ambassador."

"Excellent," Bru replied, breaking into a wide smile. "I request you as the mediator."

The ambassador stared at the Dollnick in surprise. "Can you do that?"

"Of course. As the challenged party, the right to choose a mediator is mine."

"But how can I mediate a dispute that I'm part of?"

"You can't," Bru said, attempting to sound sympathetic, but failing miserably. "I believe that in these cases, a mediator with a conflict of interest is expected to accept whatever settlement is offered in good faith by the other party. You'd be surprised how often this situation comes up when so many of our events are scheduled by ambassadors."

"You tricked me!"

"It's just business," the Dollnick said. "I'm truly sorry about the situation and I'm sure that you'll work something out. Double your money back is nothing to laugh at, you know."

"Wait," Kelly called as the convention center's manager turned to go. "Libby. Can you talk to him for me? This is Dorothy's wedding."

"I'm afraid that Bru really has very limited autonomy in this situation," the station librarian informed her. "Jeeves is on his way to offer an alternative, but unless you want all of your daughter's wedding guests to pledge their hearts to Gortunda, the Empire Convention Center isn't an option for tomorrow."

"Thank you for coming in person," Joe told the Dollnick, escorting him to the door. "That took guts."

"I really tried to line up an alternative space with my colleagues in the hospitality industry, but I assume you'd prefer not to stage the ceremony in a working casino with a requirement that the guests each buy two hundred creds of chips…"

"No, you assumed correctly. We'll work something out."

Kelly pulled out a chair from the table and slumped into it. "I'm sorry for making a scene, but I was sure we had everything under control. Dorothy is going to be so disappointed if we have to hold the wedding here."

"It will be lovely," Mary told her. "We'll put up crepe and you'll inform the caterers about the change in plans. Kevin tells us that you stage events here all the time."

"Never fear, Jeeves is here," the young Stryx announced as he floated through the door. "Libby told me all about it and I have the solution to your problems."

"Are you serious?" Kelly demanded. "I'm not in the mood for one of your elaborate practical jokes."

"I can offer you the medieval castle in Libbyland," Jeeves told her. "There was a conflicting reservation, but I made a deal with them and we can hold the great hall for eight hours."

"Are you positive, Jeeves? Can we get enough tables set up for the meal and then move them out for the dancing? I thought it only seated a few hundred."

"There are actually four great halls separated by pop-up walls. When they're all down, the great hall comfortably seats twelve hundred average size humanoids for dinner, with plenty of room left for those who wish to dance. We'll stage the ceremony in the original room, which has the folding benches that come out of the floor. I'll arrange for the regular staff to work with your caterers so you'll have plenty of hands available for any last-minute changes."

"Oh, that's such a relief. Am I missing anything, Joe?"

"We should probably ping all of our friends who already knew about the Empire Convention Center reservation so they don't go to the wrong place."

"Libby knows everybody you invited and I'm sure she'll make sure the lift tube takes them to the castle," Jeeves said. "I have to go check with the Grenouthian crew I hired for the wedding since they've made their production plans based on a different space. I'll see you tomorrow."

"Thank you, Jeeves," Kelly called after the departing Stryx. "I mean it."

"Is Metoo here yet?" Becky inquired. "Everybody on Kasil owes him a debt of gratitude. He's come back to visit us a couple of times, and he helped create a new math test for high priests to replace the set of problems he solved."

"Metoo sent word through Jeeves that he would arrive in time for the ceremony," Joe said. "I think he's afraid that if he shows up early, Dorothy will try to make him part of the wedding party. But let's get you settled in before the kids return. Who wants to stay here with us?"

By the time the Cricks were all sorted out, everybody had returned home from the last round of pre-nuptial alien rituals and settled in for an impromptu fashion show. Kevin's father couldn't convince anybody else that it was bad luck for the groom to see the bride in her dress before the wedding, and Dorothy was in all her glory showing off her high-tech wedding gown and heels to her "country" in-laws. After the grand finale, the dogs perked up and began thumping their tails, a sign of friendly visitors.

"Hello?" Woojin called from the bottom of the ramp. "Permission to board?"

"Permission granted, Captain," Joe hollered back, and explained to the Cricks, "An old friend who is currently in command of EarthCent's circuit ship, sort of."

"We read about it in the Galactic Free Press," Mary said. "Flower sounds…interesting."

"Wolfy," a three-year-old girl cried, running into the room and throwing herself at Beowulf's belly. Then she wound her arms partway around his massive neck and immediately fell asleep.

"Em is all tired out from the excitement," Lynx informed them as she and Woojin followed their daughter in. "We would have been here a few hours ago, but there's a Horten colony ship undergoing some emergency repairs out there, and Flower insisted on stopping to offer advice. Needless to say, it wasn't well received."

"Behind you!" Shaun shouted, his eyes bugging out of his head.

Woojin ducked and spun around at the same time, prepared for combat, then straightened up again and gave the Crick patriarch a sour look. "Is that an acceptable greeting at some place I've never visited?"

"It's going to get you!" Shaun insisted, putting a table between himself and the new arrival.

"I'm more likely to get YOU if you don't keep a civil tongue in your head," M793qK rubbed out on his speaking legs. "Now I understand why Human doctors stopped making house calls."

"I apologize for my father," Kevin said to the Farling, then turned to his parents. "This is the doc that saved my life after I escaped from the pirates, Dad."

"Still looks like a giant bug to me," Shaun insisted.

The large beetle grabbed one of the carbon fiber chairs that could support his bulk when he rested on the rigid underside of his carapace. He leaned forward on it, taking his time examining the Cricks. "You two are interesting," M793qK finally commented, waving a foreleg at Becky and her oldest daughter. "I've never seen a mage's aura on Humans before. In fact, other than the occasional Verlock, the only other time I saw such an astral bloom was on a Teragram, but thankfully, the Stryx saw off the last one to visit the station."

"My in-laws are prophets," Dorothy explained to the Farling. "And Baa is back and sort of working with me. You'll see her at the wedding."

"Oh, joy," the alien doctor declared facetiously. "Well, I'd love to stay around and chat, but I have some old patients to check up on, and we're only here for a few of your time-deficient excuses for a day. I'll just stop next door to look in on Aisha and the little one on my way out."

"The doctor really seems to have softened up," Kelly remarked to Lynx after the beetle left.

"He and Flower go on about humans to each other for hours on end," the former cultural attaché informed the ambassador. "I think it lets them both get it out of their systems. Can we help with any last-minute wedding preparations? Are you having it here?"

"We reserved the medieval castle in Libbyland," Kelly told her, as if that had been the plan all along. "I have the film for your camera, and we'll be getting there an hour before the official starting time, so it would be great if you could break a couple of pictures for the album."

"Snap," Lynx told her.

"Break, snap, what's the difference? So how are things going on the mission? I always wondered if you could speak your mind in the holoconferences with Flower listening in all the time."

"It's fun, though maybe less so for Woojin than I, because Flower second-guesses everything he does and keeps track of the outcomes. I mean, Dollnick AI doesn't come anywhere close to the Stryx, but Flower is still so far ahead of us that she may as well be doing magic. She's had almost twenty thousand years to come up with ways to manipulate biologicals."

"Does she still make everybody come out of their cabins for morning calisthenics?"

"I'll put it this way. I've never been in such good shape in my life."

Twenty

"Bridesmaids and groomsmen," Dorothy called out. "Take your places for our practice run."

"Why are the alien guests all here already?" Kevin whispered to her.

"It must be their 'Early is on time' thing. Didn't you notice that Czeros was at the bar when we arrived?"

"Do you put males on one side and females on the other, or is it boy-girl?" a Vergallian inquired.

The ambassador's daughter puzzled for a moment over who the handsome alien might be, and then realized with a start that it was Affie's on-again, off-again boyfriend, Stick. Dorothy gave herself a little nod on this new confirmation of how the clothes make the man, especially when she made the clothes.

"Males on Kevin's side, females on my side," the girl instructed everyone. "Do you have to wear that rapier, Judith?"

"If the men are wearing swords then I am too," the EarthCent Intelligence trainer replied stubbornly.

"The swords are just a last minute addition that Jeeves suggested to go with the décor," Dorothy said. She made a sweeping gesture that took in the suits of armor and wall-mounted weapons that gave the great hall its medieval ambiance. "Besides, that scabbard clashes with the color of your dress."

"I'll wear it for you," Bob offered. "It's got to be lighter than the sword I got stuck with."

"Just stay where I can see you," Judith grumbled, undoing the narrow sword belt she'd improvised for her bridesmaid dress and handing it over. "And don't try to draw it or you'll put somebody's eye out—probably your own."

The wedding party took a minute or two to sort itself out by height, and then had to do it all over again when Dorothy explained that the shortest members went on the inside. Finally, they were all arranged, and Lynx finished fiddling with the f-stops on her antique 35mm camera and began clicking away.

"Your mother told me to wait on the family pictures until after the ceremony," Lynx told the bride when she finished the basic wedding party shots. "All of the alien dignitaries are already here and she doesn't want to risk delaying the starting time."

"That's fine by me," Kevin said. He beckoned to his sister, who had just emerged from the improvised changing room where she had swapped her homespun clothes for formal prophetess robes. "We're ready for the trial run, Sis."

"Why are you getting married in front of an SBJ Fashions banner?" Becky demanded. "As a prophetess of Nabay, I can't be seen endorsing any commercial products."

"There's a giant mosaic of some guy presenting a bloody head on a tray behind it," Dorothy explained. "I don't know what we would have done if Jeeves hadn't saved the banner from our last trade show."

"Bob Steelforth, Galactic Free Press," the reporter introduced himself to the prophetess. "Our publisher and editor-in-chief will both be here for the ceremony. I promise we can airbrush you out of any pictures we publish that show the banner."

"Very well," Becky conceded. "Does somebody have the rings?"

Samuel and Vivian produced the gold bands and showed them to the prophetess, who nodded in approval.

"Excellent. I've done hundreds of weddings and I've learned that it always pays to make sure about the rings. Now, are you positive you want to skip walking down the aisle?"

"Definitely," Dorothy said. "It turns out that the only time the other tunnel network species do something like that is for a public demotion or getting kicked out of their militaries. I don't want to make the guests uncomfortable."

"Then face each other and we'll begin. I'm going to tell you what you'll be saying, but don't actually exchange the vows yet, because the Prophet Nabay taught that repeating a thing is like doing it in reverse."

"Then we better repeat the vows twice since we're already married," Kevin joked.

"What did you say?" Becky fixed her brother with a penetrating stare. "Answer honestly, now. You're already married?"

"Just under Frunge law. It was a contractual thing we did by accident. There wasn't a ceremony or any of that."

The prophetess blanched. "I'm sorry," she said, "I can't marry you under these circumstances."

"What do you mean?" Dorothy practically shouted. "We're starting in less than twenty minutes!"

"You're already married," Becky replied sadly. "The rules are the rules."

"But it's your religion," Kevin objected. "You can change the rules."

"What kind of prophetess would I be if I manipulated our theology for the benefit of my family?"

"I could get Woojin to do it as a ship's captain," Lynx offered. "But I don't know if it counts unless we move the wedding to Flower."

"Metoo!" Dorothy cried, as the young Stryx floated up to the wedding party wearing a one-armed tuxedo with empty pants legs that fell just short of the deck. "You used to be the High Priest of Kasil. Talk some sense into her."

"Hello, Rebecca," Metoo addressed the prophetess, bobbing in lieu of a formal bow. "Those robes suit you quite well."

"Thank you, Your Former Eminence. We have a bit of a problem and I need your theological advice."

Dorothy activated her old private channel to the Stryx over her implant and begged him, "Make something up. Improvise."

"I understand," Metoo said out loud. "The station librarian has explained that there is an existing legal marriage. Kevin's revealing this now is a blessing in disguise as otherwise the marriage would have been truly reversed."

"So can't the prophetess just perform the ceremony twice, one to undo the old marriage, and once for real?" Samuel asked.

"It's specifically prohibited," Becky replied.

"The solution is simple," Metoo said. "All you have to do is find another couple willing to get married so the prophetess can perform the ceremony for them. The volunteers can stand behind Dorothy and Kevin so that nobody will know who Rebecca is actually addressing."

"That's perfect," Dorothy said. "Wait. What?"

"He's right," the prophetess said. "We don't use names in our wedding ceremonies, that all gets filled in on the contract after the eating and dancing."

"Another contract?" Kevin groaned.

"You won't be getting one, little brother. The contract is for the couple that's really getting married."

"But where am I supposed to find two people willing to get married at my wedding?" Dorothy demanded.

"I'm game," Bob spoke up.

"You're WHAT?" Judith shouted from the other side of the supposed bride and groom.

"Come on, Jude. I've asked you a dozen times and you keep complaining that it's too expensive or that it's just a meaningless hassle. We're already here, this won't cost us a cred, and you don't have to do any planning or deal with your family. Besides, when's the next time you're going to wear a dress this nice?"

"Oh, please," Dorothy begged her. "I won't bother you at work to model clothes for me anymore."

"You've already promised me that on four different occasions."

"But I mean it this time."

Bob approached Judith, who was scowling up a storm, and dropped to one knee. "Would you please just marry me already, Jude?"

"I'd rather knight you, but you took my sword." She ruffled his hair with her hand, which, combined with his soulful eyes, made the reporter look around half his age. "Oh, all right, but this doesn't change anything, and I get to wear my rapier."

"Give it to her, Bob," Dorothy instructed the successful suitor. "Vivian, you stay close after giving me the ring, and

Samuel, you do the same for Kevin. Nobody will notice them behind us if you get the angles right."

"Then that's settled," the prophetess said in a business-like manner. "Once we're all standing at the front and the music stops—do you have musicians?"

"Death and Plague, I mean, Mornich and his band. They're already set up at the other end of the hall."

"What will they be playing when we're ready to start?"

"Some instrumental from Horten weddings. I forgot what it's called."

"Perfect," Becky said. "When the instrumental ends, I'll ask you to face one another and repeat after me, 'With this ring, thee I wed.' Then you'll exchange rings."

"And?"

"That's the whole thing. We adopted the ceremony from the Kasilians."

"It's too short! You've got to say something else or everybody will feel cheated."

"I could start with a teaching from the Prophet Nabay," Becky offered.

"Anything is fine," Dorothy said. "Just stretch it out a couple minutes."

"We don't have rings, and you'll need yours or it will look funny," Bob pointed out. "I'll just run down to the concourse shops and buy something."

"Don't spend more than twenty creds," Judith said, grabbing his arm.

"You don't have time," Vivian spoke up. "You can use our couple's rings. Give Judith your ring, Samuel, so she can exchange with Bob."

"It doesn't come off," the boy admitted, and the blood crept into his face as the wedding party laughed knowingly.

244

"I forgot," Vivian said. "I have to use my ring to draw it off."

"Your fingers are really thin," Judith told the willowy sixteen-year-old. "The ring will never fit me."

"They resize," Vivian informed her. "It's Verlock memory metal, tricky stuff. The smaller one is always the master."

"I think we've covered just about everything," the prophetess said. "After you exchange the rings, I'll just get out of the way like I'm doing now." Becky turned to Metoo. "I only have a few minutes to work up a teaching. Could you help, Your Former Eminence?"

"I'd be honored to contribute to the wedding," Metoo replied, and floated off alongside the prophetess.

"Everything resolved, right on schedule," Kevin said, hoping that Dorothy would forgive him for his previous gaffe. "The human guests are finally starting to arrive."

The Drazen ambassador and his wife, Shinka, rose from their seats on the first row of benches, which were reserved for family and ambassadors. Hand in hand, they approached the wedding party.

"Goodbye, Dorothy McAllister," Bork stated formally.

"Goodbye, Dorothy McAllister," Shinka repeated in her musical voice.

"That was just a practice run," Dorothy protested. "You can't be leaving already."

"It's a Drazen tradition to bid farewell to the bride-to-be as a single woman before the ceremony," Bork explained. "I wouldn't miss your wedding for the world. Besides, we haven't eaten yet."

"He turned down an acting gig for this," Shinka announced proudly. "He hasn't done that since our daughter cut her third set of teeth."

"Oh, well, thank you for saying goodbye. We'll be starting the real wedding in just a few minutes." Dorothy elbowed Kevin. "Look, our parents are all coming up to see if something's wrong. Don't you say anything."

"Hello, Princess," Joe deployed his old pet name for Dorothy for the first time in at least a decade and received a hug in return. "Did the rehearsal go smoothly?"

"Fine, but the ceremony turns out to be a little less impressive than I was hoping. The Kasilians take simplicity to a new level."

"How about adding something from my family's traditions?" Kelly suggested. "When my parents got married, my mother says they finished the ceremony with my father stomping on a light bulb wrapped up in a cloth napkin."

"Why?" Dorothy asked.

"What's a light bulb?" Kevin added.

"I attended a wedding like that myself back in the day," Shaun said. "The antique electric light fixtures back on Earth used a glowing wire in a thin glass bulb. I think they stomp on them for the popping sound. I remember somebody at the wedding commenting that light bulbs were getting hard to find because the technology had been replaced."

"Maybe you could wrap up a wine glass and nobody would know the difference," Joe chipped in. "I doubt there's a light bulb to be had on the whole station."

"Good idea. We can create our own tradition and preparing it will give Kevin something to do while I go attach my train," Dorothy said. "Are you helping, Mom?"

"Of course. I thought you looked a bit less voluminous than last time I saw you in the dress."

"You must have invited half of the Grenouthians on the station," Bork commented to Joe as the two headed back to their seats. They were forced to dodge a horde of bunnies who were guiding floating immersive cameras and carrying various types of lighting reflectors.

"It's the whole crew from Aisha's show. Jeeves hired them to record the wedding."

"Why would he do that? Surely the station librarian would be happy to turn over the security imaging."

"It's his present to Dorothy, or part of it. I remember twenty-five years ago when Paul first brought him home for a game, I thought that Jeeves was some kind of AI juvenile delinquent. But I have to admit that he's taken good care of my daughter at work. I can't imagine any other business giving her the leeway she's had in spending money, especially on herself."

The young Stryx in question floated up behind Joe and placed his pincer on the former mercenary's shoulder, causing the man to jump. "I always have ulterior motives," Jeeves said. "Congratulations on marrying off your daughter a second time. Is she hiding somewhere working on last-minute modifications to her dress? I was talking with Drilyenth, the Verlock scientist who handles the engineering side of Dorothy's designs, and we concluded that between the heels and the train, your daughter is wearing technology that couldn't have been developed on Earth for at least another three million years."

"The memory metal?" Bork guessed.

"That's only a few hundred thousand years off if the Humans work hard enough," Jeeves said. "The Verlocks are the only tunnel network members whose mathematical system accommodates magnetic monopoles."

The Horten band began to play some instrumental piece with a distinct funereal air, and the guests who were drinking at the bar returned to the benches. Dorothy came out of the changing room with her long train dragging behind her, then issued a gather-left command, causing the guests to break out in applause. The wedding party sorted itself out again, but this time, Bob and Judith positioned themselves behind the purported bride and groom.

As the human guests who were merely on time raced for seats, Becky approached the wedding party, then turned slowly to face the audience.

"A teaching," she announced. "In the evolution of computational systems, the earliest architecture chosen by many species is binary in nature. Everything in the universe is described by ones and zeros, true or false. What is a wedding ring but a perfect zero? What is a finger but the earliest symbol of one? In marriage we bring together a ring and a finger, a zero and a one, but in the Boolean algebra of my species, the union of one AND zero is zero by definition. How can that be?"

"Are you following this," Kelly whispered to her husband.

"No, but Srythlan seems to be enjoying it," Joe replied.

Kelly looked over at the Verlock ambassador, who was rocking in his seat and wiping away his tears with a handkerchief.

"The solution is that marriage is not the mating of a ring and a finger, but the joining of two people," the prophetess continued after a significant pause. "Trying to describe the universe with nothing but binary choices inevitably leads to oversimplification and trivial solutions. The important thing for any two sentients coming together in marriage is that they lead a sequentially consistent life, forsaking all auxiliary variables for each other. The greatest blessing we ask of the Prophet Nabay is to complete our threads concurrently."

"Bravo," Srythlan shouted, rising to his feet. "The formal proof is lacking but the sentiment is lovely."

"I hope she was finished," Joe muttered.

Whether or not she was, the prophetess took the interruption as an excuse to move ahead with the ceremony.

"Please face each other," Becky requested, and the two couples complied. Samuel and Vivian delivered the wedding rings to Kevin and Dorothy and stayed close to the front couple, while Judith and Bob moved in tight behind them, using the prophetess to help shield their pending ring exchange. "Now repeat after me—With this ring, thee I wed."

"With this ring, thee I wed," the two couples chorused, and then slipped the rings onto the fingers of their opposite number.

Then Kevin stomped on a wine glass wrapped in a napkin, winced, and both couples kissed. Becky headed off to get out of her robes, and the guests expressed noisy congratulations according to their own traditions, which included a surprising number of thrown objects. Jeeves suddenly appeared in front of the happy couples with a loud pop.

"May I have your attention please," the Stryx announced. "Due to a scheduling conflict, the castle is under attack, but I assure you," he continued, raising his voice over the sudden hubbub, "that the defending forces are sufficient to hold the walls for the next seven hours."

A splintering crash sounded from the large wooden doors near the front of the hall, and the tip of a bronze horn on the head of an unseen battering ram was withdrawn for another onslaught. The Grenouthian crew redeployed their cloud of floating cameras to capture the action at the doors, while not neglecting the wedding party, plus several wide-angle audience reaction shots.

"As a matter of fact," Jeeves continued, unperturbed, "I was able to hire a number of the attackers to provide a little pre-dinner entertainment as a gift to the bride."

Dorothy grabbed the Stryx's pincer and practically yanked it out of his body.

"Talk fast," she growled.

"Don't worry," Jeeves told her. "The raiders are only here for the dress."

"MY WEDDING DRESS?"

"They won't get it, of course," he reassured her. "It's all for the commercial."

"What commercial?" Dorothy hissed, twisting the pincer.

"The only way I'm ever going to make back my investment in that dress is if we get the marketing right," Jeeves said. "LARPing is just starting to peak as a tunnel network craze and we're in the perfect position to ride the wave. Do you have any idea how much producing this commercial is costing me?"

"A lot less than hiring professional actors and over five hundred extras to play wedding guests!" Dorothy glanced over at the splintering doors, and then back at the rows of benches where everybody seemed to be taking the attack in stride. "You owe me."

"I'd like to think we're even," Jeeves shot back, and then addressed the wedding party at a carefully calibrated volume that wouldn't carry to the guests. "I've got to get out of the frame now, but the goal is to get a number of thirty-second spots out of the footage. I swapped out all of your swords for noodle weapons while you were changing, but remember, it's not a LARP, so don't stop fighting even if you get killed. Above all, protect the dress!"

"Protect the dress!" Judith shouted, brandishing the noodle copy of her rapier. "This is going to be the greatest wedding ever."

One of the giant iron brackets holding the wooden bar across both doors pulled loose from the stonework and a party of raiders swarmed into the hall. Samuel, Judith, Thomas, Chance and Stick charged forward to meet the attack, and with an artistic flourish, Dorothy's brother disarmed the first swordsman he met and flicked the blade back toward the wedding party. Vivian snatched it out of the air and rushed to join them.

"Get that dress!" a giant Drazen bellowed, posing like a hero and pointing towards Dorothy with his two-handed axe.

"That could have been my line," Bork groused to his wife without taking his eyes off of the action.

"If you had accepted the part you would have been stuck waiting outside until after the wedding ceremony," Shinka reminded him, and patted his forearm. "You'll get it next time."

Jeeves pinged Dorothy over her implant. "Stop laughing and try to look angry, or frightened. Anything would be an improvement. And it would be a big help if you would keep turning to different cameras and repeating the tag line."

"What tag line?"

"Shaina liked 'Fashions worth fighting for,' but Brinda thought that 'Fashions worth dying for,' has more dramatic impact. Feel free to improvise, the Grenouthians can fix anything in post-production. And move a little to the left so that you're centered under the banner."

Donna nudged Kelly and pointed at the Frunge attorney Dorothy had drafted for the wedding party. He was obviously more intent on protecting Flazint than the intellectual property of SBJ Fashions. "Cute couple," she said.

Chastity leaned around her mother and mouthed, "Front page story," at the ambassador, who realized she was witnessing the closing of the loop that had allowed Becky to prophesize the wedding date.

"Did Dorothy know about this ahead of time?" Kelly asked Joe. "I guess I can understand if you all kept it from me because I would have put my foot down."

"I'm pretty sure she was just as surprised as we are, but I doubt she was planning for Bob and Judith to get married at her wedding either."

"You noticed that too? I think Bob must have talked Judith into it as a form of therapy, like trying it out to see it's not that bad. If you think they got hitched for real I'll have to get them a present."

"If they really got married, we just paid for their wedding," Joe pointed out. "But you should ping Lynx and make sure she gets enough pictures of the other happy couple."

"If she doesn't use up all of her film on the battle," Kelly responded, pointing to where their friend had positioned herself just behind the Grenouthian director. The alpha-bunny was waving his paws in the air and complaining loudly about working with amateurs.

Dring leaned forward from where he stood behind the McAllisters, having forgone a seat to accommodate his tail.

"I've attended hundreds of thousands of weddings in my life and I have to admit that they all run together in my memory. Something tells me I won't forget this one."

"But what will you remember it for?" Kelly asked plaintively.

"Celebrating with friends, of course, and the teaching of the prophetess. May the happy couples lead sequentially consistent lives and end their threads concurrently."

"Amen," the station librarian contributed.

LARP Night on Union Station is getting a sequel because I'm addicted to my own characters. You can sign up for notification of the next EarthCent release on my website, IFITBREAKS.COM.

About the Author

E. M. Foner lives in Northampton, MA with an imaginary German Shepherd who's been trained to bite bankers. The author welcomes reader comments at e_foner@yahoo.com.

Other books by the author:

Meghan's Dragon

Turing Test

EarthCent Ambassador Series:

Date Night on Union Station

Alien Night on Union Station

High Priest on Union Station

Spy Night on Union Station

Carnival on Union Station

Wanderers on Union Station

Vacation on Union Station

Guest Night on Union Station

Word Night on Union Station

Party Night on Union Station

Review Night on Union Station

Family Night on Union Station

Book Night on Union Station

LARP Night on Union Station

CPSIA information can be obtained
at www.ICGtesting.com
Printed in the USA
BVHW071350170920
588935BV00007B/806